MOON SHADOW

BY

MICHAEL MOON

This book is dedicated to

'My Elizabeth'

PART I

Contact

Moonshadow

The First Contact

Bruton, Somerset - September 1943

My memory of where things began is crystal clear in my mind. Of course, I did not know then that it was the beginning of anything.

The little station at Cole was deserted. There was no one around even to collect tickets. My mother took my hand, and walking out of the station yard we followed the rather drunken finger post that said 'Bruton ½ mile.' A few hundred yards along the lane we found a rustic wooden bench on a grassy bank, and we ate our picnic lunch of honey sandwiches and lemonade while enjoying a view of the outskirts of the ancient town below. I had become 'somewhat difficult' as the headmistress of my local school in Fleet described me, and with bombs dropping close by it was decided that the best solution all round was for me to go away as a boarder to my father's old school, in the comparative safety of sleepy Somerset.

I was not quite sure what it all meant, but from the way it was sold to me, it sounded quite an adventure. Lots of new friends, all boys, playing rugby and cricket, tuck boxes, weekly pocket money, regular visits by my mother and sometimes my father, if he had leave, to take me out for treats.

Perhaps, they said, if the bombing stopped, I could go home

for the holidays. I was quite keen to get on with it.

In the event, it was all of these things and more, but they forgot to mention Latin lessons, prep, choir practice, cod liver oil, and occasional canings. But on this day, I was full of anticipation and excitement.

My other life began that day as well; very shadowy and not within the cognitive compass of my seven year old brain. Nevertheless, instinct and my subconscious sent me a clear message.

We followed written directions to the preparatory school where I was to board. After fifteen minutes of walking we came to a straight bit of road, flanked on both sides by some of the school buildings. On the right was a massive, old stone wall some twenty feet high and about sixty or more yards long.

"I wonder if there are more school buildings behind the wall?" Mother enquired, waving toward the wall.

"No," I replied confidently. "That's the Abbey."

My mother looked at me in surprise. "How do you know that?"

"I don't know," I said truthfully, "but it is."

We arrived at the front door of the junior school, Plox House. In response to our knocking, the door was opened by the headmaster himself, a scholarly looking man of medium build with a slight stoop and a mass of untidy black hair. The introductions over, my mother said, "I am curious, Headmaster. What is that building over the road with the high wall?"

"Well," he said. "It is not actually a building but the remains of an old Augustinian Abbey that was founded here as a priory about 1100. Just the lower part of that wall remains, although other bits of the old priory and abbey buildings are incorporated into many of the houses in the town. One of our main playing fields is on the other side of the wall and is called Abbey Field. No doubt Richard will be playing rugby and cricket there before long." My mother looked at me curiously but said no more. I was vaguely aware though that something in my world had shifted and I was on familiar ground.

Moonshadow

The Second Contact

Abbey Field and Churchyard, Bruton - 1944

I was watching a cricket match on Abbey Field, sitting on the heavy roller that was parked against the churchyard wall. I was daydreaming when I heard shouting from some of the fielders and realised that a ball had been well hooked and was flying straight toward me. Before I could move, it struck the handle of the roller, fizzed over my head and over the wall into the churchyard.

Eager to please, I scrambled over the wall from the top of the roller and jumped down to find and retrieve the ball. Quickly locating it at the base of a grass hillock supporting an old tomb, I threw it back across the wall to the sweating fielder who had arrived in pursuit. Having earned his thanks, I was about to re-climb the wall when something caught my eye. An inscription on the side of the ancient looking tomb was covered in ivy. A single word was clean and clear; it read 'MOHUN.'

It meant nothing to me, but I remember that I felt strangely affected. The sights and sounds around me faded away, and I was drawn to examine the tomb more closely.

It was the largest monument in the churchyard: A small hillock or mound about five feet at its apex, with a crumbling, ivy clad, square stone structure perched on the top.

Now, when I looked again at the inscription, I could not

believe my eyes. It was totally covered in trailing ivy and totally illegible, no trace of any name. I looked around me. Had I imagined it?

I reached out tentatively and tugged the ivy away with my hand. The inscription underneath read,

'HERE LIE THE REMAINS OF THE de MOHUN
FAMILY, REMOVED FROM THE CRYPT BY
ORDER OF SIR HUMPHREY BERKELEY'

I sat for several minutes looking at the inscription and was sure that I had been led to uncover it by some strange force; but at that point, I had no idea why.

The incident remained at the front of my mind, and when some weeks later my father made one of his rare visits see me, I related the story to him. I thought he would dismiss it out of hand as a childish imagining, but to my surprise he seemed interested, and asked me to show him what I had seen.

That afternoon we went to the churchyard together and examined the tomb. The inscription was now clear. Someone had finished the job that I had started and stripped all the ivy from the tomb.

My father recounted that, as a boy, he had learned that the family name of Moon was derived from an ancient Norman family of de Mohun, who had come over to England with William the Conqueror. The name had been spelt in many different ways; Mohun, Moyon, and Moion among them, but had apparently been pronounced as Moon from a very early time.

"When I was here as a schoolboy," he said, "I did not know that there was any connection between the de Mohuns or Moons and Bruton, but obviously there was."

He went on to say that the link did not really interest him. He took the view that the future was much more important than the past, because we could influence one but not the other. He did acknowledge that my experience with the tomb was strange, although just coincidence, and he put the appearance and disappearance of the name down to a trick of the light.

I knew better. I was determined to try and find out more but, as time passed, other things like sport and girls seemed more urgent.

My memory of the whole episode retreated to the back of my mind until many years later.

Moonshadow

The Third Contact

Moyon, Normandy - 1980

It was some thirty seven years since I had experienced my initial subconscious and fleeting connection with the ancient ancestors in Bruton. My father's rather vague statement 'that there was a possible link between our name and the Norman de Mohuns had lodged in the recesses of my mind, but my schooldays, National Service, marriage, three children and a career had ensured that I had neither time nor inclination to pursue my ancestry.

However, at this point, I had just changed my job. Life was a little easier with a bit more time and money available and a holiday provided the trigger for me to pick up the idea and dig a bit deeper. My wife Elizabeth and I, and two of our three children, were about to embark on a family holiday in France. We were going to motor from north to south in stages, to finish up on a camp site in St Jean de Luz on the edge of the Pyrenees.

I decided that we would start the journey in Normandy with a small excursion to start off our family research. All that we knew about the de Mohun family, at this point, was that they had come over from Normandy with William the Conqueror in 1066. They occupied Dunster Castle in North Somerset, there was perhaps some connection with Bruton, and the original de Mohun had possibly come from somewhere close to the town of St Lo.

The idea was to travel over on the ferry from Weymouth to Cherbourg. We could spend a day in St Lo and see if we could find out anything about the history of the family.

I should say that none of the rest of my family—apart perhaps from my mother, who loved history—had any interest whatsoever in pursuing this vague family connection.

"While you are there, you had better check out the family Chateau." My mother said it half jokingly, perhaps a little hopeful that the supposed de Mohun connection might uncover some intriguing French relatives.

Arriving in St Lo at about lunchtime, we checked into our small hotel. The same afternoon, I visited the Town Hall to try to locate any Mohun family records. I got the typical Gallic shrug in answer to my enquiries. It seems that during the invasion in 1944 the Germans and the Allied Forces had between them pretty well flattened St Lo, and that all the historical records were lost. Nothing remained, and looking at some photographs of St Lo as it was after the war, I had to believe it was true.

The reconstructed St Lo did not boast much in the way of tourist attractions, so the following day we decided to forget the ancestors and move on to our next destination, Rennes in Brittany. Whether it was by accident or as I now believe by someone else's design, we got lost while getting out of St Lo and found ourselves on a minor country road, leading we knew not where.

We nearly turned back to St Lo, but it was a lovely day, the countryside was pretty, and I knew we were driving south in roughly the right direction. We decided to press on and see where we got to. A couple of kilometres later, at a small crossroad, Elizabeth suddenly shouted and pointed to a wooden finger post.

"It says Moyon. Isn't that what you're looking for?"

"Well, I'm not sure," I said. "I think there was some confusion about Mohun being spelt Moyon or Moion. We had better go and see what's there." I felt my heart skip a beat.

We drove about two kilometres down a narrow lane, and came to a tiny rural hamlet with a large stone farmhouse with outbuildings, a duck pond and a small chapel. I made the assumption, which later proved to be erroneous, that we had arrived at the village of Moyon. We parked the car and I got out, walked to the farmhouse door and knocked. After what seemed a long wait, a young woman appeared. Dark haired and rosy cheeked, she looked slightly nervous, with a cluster of children ranging in age between two to ten peering at me from behind her skirt.

"*Bonjour madame, je m'appele Moon ou Mohun ou Moyon,*" I started in my schoolboy French. I bumbled on in franglais, trying to explain that we were looking for information about the Mohuns who had been with '*Guillaume le Vincour dans dix cents soixante six quand il fait l'invasion de l'Angleterre.*'

When I stumbled to a halt, she smiled but looked rather nonplussed. "*Je ne comprends pas monsieur, un moment.*"

She called back into the house and a man I assumed to be her husband appeared. Dark haired, good looking, dressed in dungarees, every inch a Norman farmer. I repeated my little story, emphasising *Mohun and Moyon, ancestres and 1066* and throwing in hopefully, "*Le Chateau?*"

Suddenly his face lit up with comprehension. He spoke rapidly with his wife and children, and everyone seemed extremely excited. They piled out of the door, talking and gesticulating. The farmer went into the yard at the side of the house and roared out again in a dilapidated *deux chevaux;* the rest of his family piled in except for a couple of the older ones who jumped on bicycles. He motioned for me to get back into my old Jaguar.

"*Suivant, Suivant,*" he shouted and set off down the lane.

We followed in convoy. Within a few hundred meters, the *deux chevaux* followed by the bicycles swung off the road into a field. We all bumped across the grass through a rutted gateway where I feared for my car springs, and across a second field, arriving in a cloud of dust in front of a substantial earthwork, surrounded by rose bay willow herb and an insignificant wire fence. A rather dilapidated notice board hung off one of the fence posts.

We all climbed out of the cars and the farmer proudly

pointed to the area in front of us. *"C'etait le Chateau Moyon,"* he shouted.

My mother's flippant remark had turned into an amazing reality. We were standing at the entrance to somewhere that had perhaps been the home of my ancestors some 900 years before.

On close inspection, the notice board revealed that the site was a protected monument and that it was indeed the original home of *Guillaume de Moyon (William de Mohun).*

I was filled with emotion. I knew that somehow this moment had been predestined. A wrong road, a chance decision to keep on it and not turn back, calling at the first house we saw, and now being led directly to the ruins of an ancestral home of which we had no previous knowledge.

I was sure at that moment, without any of the experiences and evidence that was to follow, that I was indeed descended from the ancient de Mohun family, and for some unknown reason was being pulled slowly but inevitably towards the past.

Once more I resolved to dig deeper into Moon history but was again frustrated. Work suddenly became demanding, entailing considerable overseas travel. The resolve weakened, and family history went to the bottom of the 'things to do' file.

Until, that is, my shadow became impatient.

Moonshadow

Contacts: Three Telephone Calls and Lift Off

Denver, Colorado; Melbourne, Australia; London and Bodinnick, England - June, 1982

I was in room 1327 at a vast Holiday Inn, in downtown Denver, Colorado. It was my first visit there.

It was nine in the morning when the phone rang. I was expecting the call.

"Hi, this is Richard Moon," I said. "Is this Lawrence?" There was a long pause. "Hello," I repeated. "Is that you, Lawrence?"

"Yeah, this is Lawrence." A voice, throaty and marginally hostile answered, with what sounded like a West Country burr.

"But you bain't Richard Moon," he continued. The phone went dead. He had hung up!

Seconds later it rang again. Same routine; "Hello, this is Richard Moon, is this Lawrence?" Then, to be sure, "Lawrence Bird?"

It was the same voice that responded. "No, I bain't no Lawrence Bird, I be Lawrence Moon. I'm calling my brother Richard, and you bain't he." Again there were overtones of aggression and annoyance.

"No," I said, "you're right. I'm not your brother, but I am Richard Moon. I checked in last night from the UK. I'm expecting a Lawrence Bird to call me here, and we're supposed

to be meeting this morning. He is driving up from Texas and ..."
I tailed off. I sensed he didn't need my life story.

The voice shifted from aggression to puzzlement.
"Goddamn strange," said Lawrence. "This be room 1327 bain't
it?" I confirmed that it was. "I don't know whom you be," he
said, "but you take heed."

Abruptly he was gone, before I could ask any of the
questions that I wanted to ask.

Minutes later Lawrence Bird called. Our meeting later that
morning was interesting, but in the end, unproductive. At the
checkout that evening, I asked, "Do you have another Richard
Moon staying here? I took a call this morning for a Richard
Moon who wasn't me. I'm curious; it's not such a common
name."

"Hold on," said Alan, the cashier. He had a name tag on his
jacket lapel. "I'll just check the guest list." He peered at the
screen in front of him. "No," he said after a few moments,
"nobody but you, except ..." He tapped the keys a couple of
times. "Well, that's spooky. There was another Richard Moon.
He checked out yesterday from room 1327!"

We both marvelled at the coincidence. I mean, out of
hundreds of Holiday Inn rooms in Denver, to have two Richard
Moons staying in the same room on consecutive nights? "Pretty
weird," said Alan.

"Do you have an address for him?" I asked.

"I'm not really permitted to give that to you," he said, "but
just maybe ..." He scrutinised the screen again. Then he looked
at me hard. "It's the same address as yours. Are you kidding
me?"

"No, no I'm not. Somebody must have made a mistake with
the reservations. Maybe there was nobody in the room the night
before last, you just had me booked in twice."

He looked at me with some suspicion. "I thought you had a
phone call for another Richard Moon?"

"Yes," I said, suddenly feeling cold, "yes, I did."

By now a queue was building at the desk and Alan was
getting impatient. He receipted my bill, pushed it into an
envelope and gave it to me. "Have a good day now; hope you
find the other guy, come back soon."

Later, during the flight to Sydney, I checked my hotel receipt and realised that they had made a mistake. Although the bill was certainly mine, the address was not my home address. It was for a place I had no knowledge of, called 'Hall' in Bodinnick, near Fowey in Cornwall.

I made the decision, now I had an address, to look the other Richard Moon up next time I went down to the West Country.

It was an odd incident and made for a good dinner party story for a couple of weeks. It soon vanished from my thoughts as the usual pressures of work and family filled my days.

It was, after all, probably just a coincidence and some muddle in administration over the reservation.

But then ...

Some six weeks later, I was in Melbourne, staying at the Flinders Hotel while working on an assignment. I returned to the hotel on the last evening of my visit, to complete my report before flying back to Sydney the next day.

In my room, the red message light on the phone was flashing. I checked with the operator, and she gave me a number to ring in Tasmania. I was intrigued because I didn't, as far as I knew, actually know anyone in Tasmania. I called the number.

"G'day," said a voice, male and very Aussie.

"Hello," I said, "I'm Richard Moon and I'm returning your call; you left a message for me at the Flinders Hotel in Melbourne. What can I do for you?"

There was a long pause.

"Don't quite know what's going on," he said. "We had a message two days ago, left on our answer phone. It was from someone called Richard Moon, American I think. We had never heard of him before. He said he needed to talk to us and could we call him at the Flinders Hotel today, so we did. He wasn't there. We left the message, but he didn't sound like you, unless you change your accent from time to time; you're a Pom?"

"Yes," I said, "I am, but I certainly didn't call you before today. It's a bit weird. Something similar happened to me recently when I was in the States."

I gave him a brief version of the Denver incident. We both

agreed that something strange was going on.

"I don't actually know your name," I said.

"Oh, it's Charles, Charles Daunay. My ancestors were Poms too, from a place near Fowey in Cornwall, but a very long time back."

I swallowed hard and experienced the return of that cold feeling. "That's amazing," I said. "The other Richard Moon in Denver also had a Fowey address. This is all a bit odd; Charles, if this other Richard Moon calls you again, perhaps you could let me know."

I gave him my Sydney number. He kindly invited me to look them up if I was ever in Tasmania in the future, and that was that. Of course, I checked with reception, but no other Richard Moon was staying in the hotel, nor had anyone of that name stayed there during the past month.

Another coincidence?

A month later, almost to the day, I was back in the UK, in London for the night with my wife, Elizabeth. We were staying at the Cavendish in St James and had enjoyed a good evening, with a show and then dinner at one of our favourite restaurants.

We got back to the hotel around 1 a.m., feeling decidedly mellow and relaxed. In the room, the message light on the phone was flashing. We were immediately concerned because no one, other than our children and their aunt, who was looking after our house for the weekend, knew where we were. I immediately thought that one of our children was ill.

The telephone system was automatic and just gave the number that had called, along with the time of the call at 11.40 p.m. It was not our home number.

"It must be the hospital," said Elizabeth, immediately jumping to the worst-case scenario.

"Don't panic," I said. "If it was that serious there would have been more calls by now, and anyway, it isn't our area code."

I called the number. It rang twice and then a female voice, hysterical and almost incoherent with crying, answered. "Richard, I am so sorry," she sobbed. "You must be on your guard. Charles lives and seeks revenge. He knows you are coming and lies in wait for you. Tell Elizabeth I love her, and Richard, I wish ..."

There was a pause for breath.

"Hey," I said, "I'm really sorry, but before you go any further, I think one of us must have the wrong number."

"Oh God," she said despairingly. "Oh God, no."

"I'm ringing from the Cavendish Hotel in London," I said. "There was a message on my phone when we got in to call your number."

"I'm so sorry." I could hardly hear her voice. "There must be a mistake. This is Alicia. I must talk to Richard, Richard Moon."

The coldness I felt this time was palpable and overwhelming. I drew a breath. "Well, I am *a* Richard Moon, but not the one you want. Is there anything I can do?" By this time, Elizabeth was frantic with worry and curiosity, signalling her need to know what was going on. "Would you like to talk to my wife, who also happens to be an Elizabeth?" I asked.

"Oh no, oh God, no, I'm so sorry." Then, abruptly she said,

"Adieu Richard," and was gone.

I rang the hotel reception. There was no other Richard Moon staying in the hotel. I checked the phone number, and 01726 was the code for the Fowey area. I rang the full number again and got the message that I half expected; "I'm sorry but the number has not been recognised."

Coincidence was no longer an option. Without question, I had to go to Fowey and find my shadow, the other Richard Moon.

It was nearly six weeks before I could find the time to take a few days of holiday. My consultancy business was thriving and I was supervising a number of assignments in different parts of the world. Busy as I was, I could not get the telephone calls out of my mind. I tried to rationalise them as just very strange coincidences but it didn't work. I became more and more convinced that something really important lay behind them.

It was a cold, wet October morning when Elizabeth and I left Cheshire, with the rain coming sideways in the blustery west wind. We drove south west, using the country route through Shropshire and Herefordshire and across the Severn bridge before joining the M5 at Bristol. It was close to teatime as we crossed the Tamar into Cornwall, and we felt that our holiday had really started.

Intrigued and excited by all the strange telephone calls that had led us to take this unscheduled break, we had no premonition of the extraordinary events to come.

We stayed the night with friends near Bodmin and set off the next morning for the short drive to Fowey and Bodinnick.

We crossed the Fowey River on the ferry. It was a bright sunny morning, and the mix of tankers, fishing boats, private yachts and dinghies provided a ribbon of bright colour, offsetting the dark water of the estuary and the dense green foliage on the shoreline.

We drove off the ferry and up the steep, narrow hill out of Bodinnick. We didn't really know what we were looking for but hoped that we would know it if we saw it. I had written down a list of all the snippets of information gained from the three telephone calls which might be relevant; people, locations, numbers, etc. It was only a short list, but until I wrote it down, I had not realised that the room number in Denver and the telephone number in Fowey were the same.

Richard Moon
Lawrence Moon
Charles Daunay
Alicia
Elizabeth
Bodinnick
Fowey
Hall
Room 1327
Tel No 01726 (Fowey area) 1327

As we crested the hill, we stopped to examine the signpost on the junction. It did not seem to give us much help, just pointed straight on to Lanteglos and to the right for Bodinnick. I was about to drive on toward Lanteglos when Elizabeth pointed to a partly obscured board in the hedge. *Hall Farm B&B.*

"Hall," she said, "there's a clue for you." She still thought the whole thing was a bit of a joke and was still mildly suspicious about the hysterical woman calling the Cavendish Hotel.

"No harm in having a look," I said, and we turned down the track. I drove about three hundred yards, and instead of turning right, back to Bodinnick, I went straight on down a farm track into an open, spacious farm yard. There were solid looking stone barns and outbuildings to the front and left of us, and as we looked to the right we saw a picturesque, cream coloured, two storey farmhouse with a cottage garden, wicket gate and green lawns basking in the sunshine.

"Oh, it's beautiful," said Elizabeth. "Hey, if they have a vacancy, why don't we stay here for a couple of days while we do some exploring?"

As soon as we had entered the yard, I knew that I was supposed to be here. It was one of those extraordinary moments of *déjà vu,* and I knew that I had been in this place before.

I parked the car in the yard and we walked up the stone flagged path toward the weathered front door, which opened before we reached it. I am not sure why, but I half expected to see someone like me. The man who greeted us was, however, shorter, browner, fitter, and physically at least, unlike me in almost every respect.

"Hello," I said, "I hope we are not disturbing you but are you Richard Moon?"

He looked puzzled but smiled. "No. I'm Nathan Howell. How can I help you?"

I had been so sure that I would meet my mystery namesake. I was both embarrassed and disappointed. "This is Hall, isn't it?"

"Yes it is," said Nathan. "If you want Bed and Breakfast we do have a room available."

I rather rudely ignored him. "Does a Richard Moon live here?" I asked.

He shook his head. "No, just my wife Margaret and our children. I'm sorry, I don't seem to be helping you."

Elizabeth chipped in. "Take no notice of my husband, we are on a rather weird and wild goose chase which we will explain later; but the answer to your earlier question is, yes please, we would love to stay for a couple of nights if that is alright."

"Yes of course," said Nathan, looking rather relieved. "Would you like to look at the room?"

The room was charming, as was Nathan's wife Margaret, and after we had unloaded our bags from the car and installed ourselves we were invited to join them for tea and cake on the little terrace in the garden. I gave a potted version of the events that had led us to visit their home. They were as baffled as we were and I could see that they sided with Elizabeth in taking the whole thing with a pinch of salt.

It transpired that both of them were local and had lived at Hall for many years. It was a charming house in a lovely secluded position. I admired the stone construction and commented that it must be extremely old. Nathan smiled. "Actually, this house as you see it is not as old as it looks and has been modified many times. The bulk of it, and the walls that you can see from here, were constructed out of a quite grand Elizabethan Manor House that was burned down during the civil war. Prior to that, there was an older Medieval Manor that probably dated back to the 12th century." He pointed to the barns on the other side of the farm yard.

"If you look over there, behind the barn, can you see the tower?" I nodded. "Well, that is all that remains of a 14th century chapel that was part of the manor complex here when it was owned by the de Mohun family. It's a protected site now and ..." He stopped and looked at me. "Are you alright?" he asked.

Elizabeth took my hand. "You've gone very pale, Richard. Do you feel okay?"

I sat down and gathered my thoughts. "Oh, dear God," I said. "I never connected the phone calls and our family history. Mohun was spelled in many different ways although it was pronounced as Moon a long time ago, even as far back as the 13th century. At least, that is what I was told years ago by my father. I had no idea that the Mohun family were in this area. I knew that they came over from Normandy with William the Conqueror, and built a castle in Dunster in Somerset, and had connections with Bruton, where I went to school. Now I'm wondering whether a Mohun or Moon who lived here might have been called Richard."

"Wait a minute," said Margaret, "our local historian did a write-up on Hall for the county magazine a few years ago, I'm sure I've still got a copy." She went inside and a few minutes later, she emerged and handed me a photocopy of an article that had been published in *Cornish Life*. "I think you might find this interesting," she said.

The first lines took my breath away and caused the hairs on the back of my neck to stand on end. I read it again to be sure that I was not mistaken.

"I knew it," I said, "just listen to this."

'There is a story that, in 1327, Sir Richard de Mohun, coming into Fowey harbour with soldiers bound for Ireland, let fly his hawk at some game which came down in the garden at Hall, and that he thus first met the daughter of the owner, Elizabeth Fitzwilliam, whom he afterwards made his wife.'

I realised in an instant that all 'the happenings' in my life to this point had had a purpose; to contact me, lead me here and connect me with my ancestral family; in particular, with my namesake and shadow, Richard de Mohun.

My mind was suddenly in utter confusion. It was as though two separate forces were struggling to control it.

Everything melted away around me. First there was darkness; a totally black, noiseless, and all consuming darkness. Then, suddenly, I became aware of sunlight, the sound of the sea, and ropes creaking as I watched the story unfold.

PART II

The Story

Moonshadow

Chapter 1

Bodinnick and Hall - February 1327

The peregrine sliced through the clear air, wings shimmering in the bright sunlight. The dove was dead before it had even registered danger; death was celebrated in a halo of white feathers. The predator and victim dropped to earth behind the tree line, perhaps a furlong inland from the shore.

Richard shouted and clapped his hands with excitement, turning to the group of soldiers standing with him on the forecastle. "Well boys, that's how it's done. That is how we dealt with the goddamn French. Down from the heights with the speed of a hawk, total surprise," he said thumping his fist into his palm. "They never knew what hit them." There was laughter and excited comments among the group. The diversion was hugely welcome after the rigours of the last few days.

After leaving Bordeaux, the weather had made the journey across the Bay of Biscay and up the Cornish coast dangerous and uncomfortable. Today, as they sailed into the lee of Fowey harbour, the wind and rain died away revealing the anchorage and the Cornish countryside in a glorious sunny glow.

Walking up the muddy track from Bodinnick Steps, Richard used the high oaks as a guide mark as he set out to recover his peregrine. He knew that by now it would have gorged itself on the plump dove and would be ready to be hooded and carried back to its cage. He crested the hill, and was confronted with a high stone wall.

Following a track alongside it, he came to a small wooden gate topped with a carefully crafted stone arch. A carved shield with a vaguely familiar coat of arms was set into the stone. He pushed the gate open tentatively.

Inside there was a wide-open expanse of grassland, bounded on the right by the oak trees and on the left by the walls of a substantial manor house. The whole scene was redolent of peace and calm and modest wealth.

The peregrine was clearly visible, perched on top of its prey in the lee of the oaks. It let out a shrill cry when it saw him. He started across the grass, showing the leash and hood as he walked. Suddenly aware of another figure coming out of the trees and conscious that he was trespassing, he gestured towards the peregrine.

"Sorry to intrude," he said, "I just came to retrieve my bird."

"And well you might, sir," came the reply; an angry voice but with a tinge of humour and an attractive clarity of tone and diction. "Your bird killed one of my beautiful tumbling doves. How dare you hunt this land without leave from my father?"

The girl in front of him stood arms akimbo, head to one side, examining him with a steady gaze. She was tall, slim, and dressed in a pale grey day dress. Long, fair hair framed a soft featured and captivating face.

"Tell me, sir, who are you? Where are you from? Or did you just fall from the sky like your bird?"

"No, dear lady, I did not fall; I was blown here by the wind. I am Richard de Mohun of Dunster and Ugborough, in command of knights and soldiers from Ireland returning from service in Aquitaine. Our ship is in the harbour while we seek victuals and allow the soldiers and horses some shore time before they sail on to Waterford."

"And you sir, will you and your bird not sail with them and leave my doves in peace?" Her smile took the sting from her words.

"No, my lady. I leave the ship here and travel to Tavistock to visit my brother and then to my own manor in Ugborough. I released my bird from the ship to give it some much needed exercise. It saw your dove as easy prey. I apologise most humbly and would be glad to recompense you for your loss."

"Well sir, you have manners, at least. Your apology is accepted, but if you should fly your falcon again, test it against some less vulnerable prey."

As she spoke, Richard knelt down to hood and leash the bird. It perched on his wrist, quiet, satiated and replete.

"Elizabeth, Elizabeth, who is that with you?" A querulous voice called from the porch of the house. An elderly man, tall and lean, walking slowly with a stick, advanced toward them. His slight stoop did not hide his distinguished bearing.

"My father," said Elizabeth quietly. "I fear now that you will have to apologise all over again." She laughed. Then, as he drew close, she said, "Father, this is Richard de Mohun, a knight, back from fighting in Aquitaine. Sir, this is Sir John Fitzwilliam of Bodinnick. You had better tell him how you came to be trespassing here."

Her father smiled broadly and took Richard by the hand. "Put your bird on the post by the door, Richard. Leofric, my falconer, will take care of it." He gestured towards the house. "Come Elizabeth, fetch us some wine. Richard you are welcome, I know your family, of course. I fought alongside your father, Sir John, at Berwick. I know him as an honourable and brave man and I am very pleased to receive one of his sons here at Hall."

For an hour or more they talked in the solar of the great hall. The manor had recently been rebuilt and modernised with Cornish granite walls, and the additions of a separate kitchen, the solar, and a private bedroom for Sir John. The large central hearth, coupled with the stone walls, created a comfortable and warm environment.

Sir John revealed that his beloved wife Eleanor had died of a fever some four winters past, and that he and Elizabeth, his only child, ran his substantial estates.

"She is a great source of strength to me, and manages the household affairs more competently than anyone could expect of one so young. My main concern is ensuring that her future is secure. I am increasingly unwell and ... but enough of my concerns, tell me about your exploits in Aquitaine."

Their ensuing discussion was mainly of military matters, and the turbulence of the recent years with the changing fortunes of the reviled Despensers, the return of Mortimer and Isabella, the imprisonment of Edward II and the coronation of his young son.

An hour or so passed and it was clear that Sir John was growing tired. "Let us hope for better times to come. I crave your indulgence, Richard. I am somewhat weary and need to rest. We have visitors to lodge with us tonight and I need to be fresh for their arrival."

As he said this, he glanced at Elizabeth who sat quietly, embroidering and listening to their conversation. She grimaced and then brightened.

"Father, perhaps if Richard is not in a hurry to return to his ship, he could join us for our repast?"

Sir John frowned, clearly embarrassed. To his relief, Richard observed his discomfort and stepped in.

"I thank you for your kind thought, my lady, but I must return to the ship. I need to ensure that new supplies are on board, the horses are fed, and that my men do not overstep the mark while enjoying their shore leave. In fact, I have already stayed for longer than I intended." He rose, ready to leave.

"Sir John, thank you for your hospitality, and Lady Elizabeth, my apologies again for the loss of your dove. If I may, I will call again before I leave, to retrieve my bird and bring a small token of my regret."

"Indeed sir, you are welcome to visit Hall at any time," said Sir John. "Elizabeth, walk with Richard to the main gate and show him the path to Bodinnick."

"I am sorry that you cannot stay to dine with us this evening, but you extricated yourself very prettily," said Elizabeth with a smile, as they walked down the short drive to the impressive fortified gate.

Richard chuckled. "Who are the guests that you and your father regard from such different viewpoints?"

"You are observant, sir. Our guests are the Daunays; Sir Robert, his son Charles, and his daughter Alicia. My father and Sir Robert Daunay have been conspiring together for some time to match Charles and I. Tonight I fear that they will agree on the details and announce the match. It will bring the Daunay estates and our lands here together. As you have learned, my father is not in the best of health and he is very eager to see me settled and well provided for."

Richard's eyes narrowed at the mention of the Daunays and he was about to interject when he saw that she was struggling to maintain her composure.

"I take it that you are not entirely in agreement with the match."

"No sir, I am not." Her voice quavered. "I hardly know Charles Daunay; he has been away for the past three years. What I do know of him and his family, I do not care for. He is pampered and arrogant, drinks heavily, and people say he is wasting his fortunes away.

"His father, Sir Robert, is supposedly a godly and righteous man descended from Norman stock like us. But he is reputed to be increasingly irascible and treats his servants abominably. Father will not hear anything said against them, and I cannot disobey his wishes."

As they reached the gate composure deserted her, and she leant against Richard with tears streaming down her cheeks.

With a tenderness that belied his soldierly looks and manner, Richard cupped her face in his hands and smoothed away the tears with his thumbs. "Do not despair," he murmured, "maybe the touch of a good woman is all that Charles needs to bring him to his senses; but, if you are truly so unhappy, surely your father will listen to you, even if the conjoining of the two estates provides undoubted logic for the match."

"Oh fie, sir!" She pushed him away, stomping her foot. "No one can deny the logic, but what have logic and land to do with love? If my mother was still alive, she would understand and intercede with my father, but without her, I am without hope."

The tears flowed again. "I am sorry to have burdened you with my troubles, but I have no-one to confide in." She wiped her eyes and turned to him. "Your path to Bodinnick lies there, to the left. If you should come to Hall again, before you leave for Tavistock, please say nothing of our conversation to my father. He would not want me to reveal my unhappiness to others." Then, impulsively, she held his arm and kissed him gently on the cheek before turning and walking back toward the house.

Richard watched her go and touched his cheek where she had kissed him. He was unused to the softness and gentleness of women. His life since his early childhood at Dunster had revolved around the martial arts of the day. He was an accomplished swordsman, an exceptional horseman and a clever tactician. He had served his father and King Edward in battle, and shown courage and daring that had earned him recognition and praise in high places. While campaigning, he had caroused with his men and enjoyed carnal knowledge of whores and camp followers, but had not experienced tenderness or love since leaving the arms of his mother.

He was surprised then and somewhat disorientated by the mixed emotions of tenderness, compassion, desire, and opportunism that were mingling in his blood.

Returning to his ship by way of the steep path down to Bodinnick Quay and then rowing to the anchorage in Polruan, Richard busied himself with organising the loading of stores, and the sorting and transport of armour and arms in need of repair by the local blacksmith.

From time to time, the image of Elizabeth Fitzwilliam surfaced into his consciousness and eroded his concentration.

Toward the end of the day he went ashore at Fowey, to check on the progress of Alric the Blacksmith. He found him sitting outside the forge, slaking his thirst with a flagon of watered ale.

"Aye sir, all will be completed by tomorrow eve," Alric volunteered before the question was asked.

"Excellent," said Richard. Sitting down beside him, he asked the question that he really wanted to ask. "What do you know of the Daunays?"

Alric gave him a quick, sidelong glance and then spat on the ground. "Big landowners around here, they have manors at Sheviock and closer by at Boconnoc. Used to give me plenty of work and paid well. Now the work is all but gone and if any comes my way, I'm waiting for the money long past its due date.

"Word has it that the young master had been in London, drinking and getting into bad company. His father has had to forfeit lands to pay off his debts. Young Charles has been brought home now to keep him in check but he is a feckless wastrel and will be the ruin of the family."

"Yes, I fear so." Richard sighed. "And what of the Fitzwilliams, over at Bodinnick?"

"They be fine people, sir. Sir John is as true a Cornishman as any Norman could be, no offence to you, sir. He and his daughter are respected for their honesty and generosity by all around here. The estate is one of the best run in the whole of Cornwall."

Richard stood up. "Thank you, Alric. I will attend on the morrow to collect my helmet and pay your account."

Richard walked the few yards from the forge to the Livery stables close by the ferry.

His beloved Palfrey, 'Grisel Gris' seemed well rested from the sea crossing. She greeted him with a soft whinny of affection. The strong bond between them had been forged in battle and in play, and had enabled them both to survive many dangers. Richard instructed the young ostler to keep her and his little packhorse, 'Quenelle' fed, watered and exercised and to have both saddled and ready for moving off next morning.

Returning to the ship, he spent the next hour or so busying himself in preparation for his journey.

While ferrying his sparse belongings from the ship to the stables in Fowey, he reflected on what he had heard that day and what he already knew about the Daunays. Pondering his best course of action, he made a decision that would completely change the course of his life.

Chapter 2

Hall

As darkness fell, Richard retraced his steps back to Hall. It was clear from the horses in the stable yard that the visitors had arrived. He stayed concealed in the shadows of the gateway, trying to determine what to do next. Then fortuitously he saw a familiar figure emerging from the entrance to the falconry.

"Leofric," he whispered. "I need to speak with you. It is Richard de Mohun."

The falconer, a small stocky man with red hair and a trim beard, jumped.

"Sir, you startled me. Is something amiss? Or have you come early for your bird?"

Richard drew him into the shadows. "Falconer, I need your help. Be assured that what I ask of you is to the benefit of your Master Sir John and to Miss Elizabeth. I need you to get word to Sir John that I need to talk with him. I will be waiting for him here in the falconry, but no one must know that I am here. In particular, Sir John's guests, the Daunays, should not be aware of my presence. Can you do this for me?" He gripped the falconer's arms and looked straight into his eyes to impart the importance of the task.

"Sir, I will do my best, although approaching Sir John will not be easy while he is in the company of his guests."

"I understand," said Richard, "but this is a matter of extreme urgency and importance. I would not otherwise ask it of you. I will ensure that your resourcefulness and loyalty are well rewarded. Go now, for there is no time to lose."

The falconer slipped quietly into the house via the kitchen entrance. There was a flurry of activity in the main hall. Servants were preparing food, tending the huge log fire and setting out the great table.

The need for Leofric's resourcefulness was minimal and his task made easier by the fact that while Elizabeth and the Daunays were conversing in the solar, Sir John was in the main hall giving instructions to Godfrey the steward. Leofric waited, and as Sir John turned away to walk back to the solar, he picked up a ewer of ale from a side table and walked quickly across the hall.

Seeing him approach, Sir John looked puzzled. "Falconer, what brings you here? Has Godfrey enlisted you as an extra cup bearer for this evening?"

"Sir, I crave your pardon for this intrusion. I am here at the urgent request of Sir Richard de Mohun. He waits in the falconry and begs you to meet him there on a matter of great importance. He desired me to say that no one save you should know that he is there or that you are to meet."

Sir John was visibly taken aback, "Does he not know that I have guests and that we are about to dine?"

"Sir, he knows, and it seems that it is your guests that he wishes to remain ignorant of his presence here."

Sir John hesitated and seemed unsure of what to do. "If I may say, sir," interjected Leofric. "He seems an honest man and concerned for your wellbeing."

"Very well," said Sir John, somewhat tetchily. "Wait by the main door and I will accompany you to the falconry. Give me one moment to take leave of my guests."

Sir John climbed the short stairway to the solar. "Sir Robert, Charles and Ladies, my apologies but a small matter has arisen that needs my attention and I must absent myself for a few minutes." Sir Robert inclined his head and Sir John turned and descended the stairs. Elizabeth followed him.

"Father, is anything wrong? I saw you talking to the falconer and I wondered why he was here."

"No, my child, nothing serious, but I am needed for a few minutes. Go back now and keep our guests entertained."

He joined Leofric at the main door and they made their way together across the yard to the falconry. As they passed through the gateway, Richard stepped forward. His first words were for the falconer: "My thanks for bringing Sir John here. What I have to say is for his ears only, but can I ask you to wait outside the gate and protect our privacy?"

Leofric looked to Sir John who nodded his approval. As soon as he was out of earshot, Sir John turned to Richard angrily.

"Richard, what is this? You command my falconer and disturb me when I am entertaining important guests, and insist on secrecy. There had better be good reason."

"Sir John, I apologise most humbly for interrupting your meal and discussion with the Daunays. Before I left this afternoon, Elizabeth told me that the Daunays were your guests and that a match between herself and Charles Daunay was to be confirmed."

Sir John frowned. "That is true, but, much as I like and respect you Richard, I do not see that it is any business of yours."

"You are right, Sir John, it is not but please hear me out. Firstly, the Daunay's land at Sheviock borders upon my own manor at Ugborough. I received word lately from my bailiff that a large tranche of Daunay land at Boconnoc was being seized in lieu of debts.

"I also learned, from the same source, that some months ago, Charles Daunay killed one of the servants at Sheviock manor. The poor man died while trying to protect his daughter from Charles' drunken attentions. The family concerned was paid to buy their silence and then evicted from their home under threat of death if they spoke out, but ...." He tailed off as Sir John visibly paled.

"Richard, surely that is just rumour. I have known Sir Robert for many years and cannot believe such ill of him or his family."

Richard softened his voice. "Sir, I understand your doubt, and this information is at present unconfirmed. I was not certain if I should tell you at all. But asking about the Daunays over in Fowey today, it seems that the family does have some serious problems, with Charles Daunay at the centre of them.

"I fear, Sir John, if the rumours are indeed true, that any match between Charles and your daughter Elizabeth will be much to the Daunays advantage and your disadvantage. I decided that I should tell you now so that you can ascertain the truth, before you finalise the marriage terms."

Sir John slumped heavily onto a nearby bench. "Oh Richard, I hope you are mistaken. This marriage means much to me. It ensures that Elizabeth is well provided for. I know Elizabeth herself is not yet enamoured with Charles but that will no doubt change, given time, and she is anxious to please me. She understands the benefits of merging our two estates.

"If what you have heard about Charles Daunay is true then I cannot go forward with it, but I fear the consequences. Sir Robert is a powerful and determined man and will not take it well if I do not agree to the match."

He sat for a moment, and then with a heavy sigh, Sir John stood up and put his hand on Richard's shoulder.

"God bless you Richard for your concern. You were right to tell me what you have heard. I will find a way to defer matters until I have established if there is any truth in these rumours."

"Sir John, I am truly sorry to be the cause of your pain. If there is anything I can do, be assured that I am at your service. I will return tomorrow before I leave for Tavistock."

Richard turned and quickly merged into the shadows of the yard, departing through the gate.

Sir John dismissed his falconer and thanked him for his efforts. He walked slowly back to the house, trying desperately to think of a plausible reason for deferring the decision that the Daunays were expecting.

As he entered the hall again, Sir John checked with Godfrey that the food was ready and immediately called to Elizabeth and his guests to come to the table. It gave him some time to think as they seated themselves and filled their platters, and to compose an answer to the inevitable question.

It came from Elizabeth.

"Well father, what did the falconer need you for that was so important?"

"Nothing to worry about," he responded. "He was concerned about one of my new goshawks and wanted advice. I am sorry to have left you all but he seemed rather agitated. I felt obliged to take a look for myself. I had asked him to tell me if anything was amiss. I paid a lot of money for those birds."

Trying to deflect any further discussion about his absence, Sir John launched into a long description of his recent hawking exploits. The ensuing conversation was lively and diverse, encompassing farming, hunting, a recent jousting tourney, and the war in France. Toward the end of the meal, Elizabeth recounted the story of Richard de Mohun's unexpected visit that morning. At the mention of his name, Sir Robert and Charles looked at each other and seemed noticeably uncomfortable. Alicia put her hand to her mouth with a small cry.

"We know of Richard de Mohun as a neighbour across the Tamar from Sheviock," said Sir Robert.

"We have had some minor difficulties with his bailiff over boundaries, but we do not know him well."

"Alicia met him last year while out riding," said Charles. "She was quite taken with him; maybe a match to be made there. The Mohuns would be quite a catch."

Alicia blushed and giggled. She was quite a beauty; small and petite with long dark hair and pale clear skin. Her large brown eyes, often rather sad looking, sparkled now.

"Be silent Charles. I met him but the once and we barely spoke. He is handsome I think, but very rough and unpolished."

"The man is an uncouth soldier as are most of the Mohuns," spat Charles, with some feeling.

Elizabeth retorted quickly. "Oh, I did not find him so. He was very civil and charming, wasn't he, Father?"

Sir John nodded and attempted to change the subject again but Sir Robert questioned Elizabeth.

"Not more charming than your husband to be, I trust? Did he talk about us?"

"Not much," said Elizabeth. "Only to say that the joining of our estates made for sound logic."

"Nothing more," insisted Sir Robert.

"No, nothing more than that," Elizabeth said, but remembering the emotion that she had shown earlier, she felt both excited and uncomfortable.

Sir Robert Daunay was an imposing figure; tall with jet black hair silvering at the edges, and aquiline features with a strong, beaked nose. His deep, dark eyes seemed to penetrate her innermost thoughts. Elizabeth shivered inwardly but held his gaze. Sir Robert seemed satisfied and turned away.

As conversation resumed, Elizabeth covertly eyed her prospective husband across the table. Charles was, in many ways, the antithesis of his father. Although tall and well proportioned, he had unkempt, fair hair grown long, sallow skin and restless blue eyes. A deep scar from the corner of his right eye to below his mouth had drawn his top lip into a permanent sneer. Sensing her inspection, he glanced at Elizabeth and grinning, held up and salaciously licked his index finger. His question, when it came, was the one that Sir John had been dreading.

"Well Father, and Sir John, when are Elizabeth and I to be wed? I am growing impatient with a cold bed." He glanced again at Elizabeth and grinned. She shuddered and looked down at her platter.

"Hold your tongue, sir," said Sir Robert. "That is no way to talk at the table of our host and in front of your intended bride."

Charles' grin froze and he muttered an apology. The look he gave his father, however, was venomous in its intensity.

"Forgive my son. His time in London did nothing to improve his manners. Nevertheless, Sir John, I think you and I should get down to the final details of the match. I have had my scribe draw up a list of the remaining points that need to be settled. They are trifling and it will not take us long to agree." He pushed a one page document across to Sir John.

"If Elizabeth and Alicia would retire perhaps we can conclude matters."

Sir John took the piece of parchment and then passed it back without reading it. He took a deep breath. "Sir Robert, I am sorry to disappoint you but I find I need to take a little more time. I have to deal with some other urgent affairs relating to my estates before I consent to this match."

There was a gasp of surprise from Elizabeth. Sir Robert and Charles were clearly dumbstruck.

When Sir Robert did speak, he was visibly holding in his anger. "Sir John, I was given to understand that you had all but given your consent to this match and that tonight we were to celebrate its conclusion. Indeed, since we arrived here, you have given no indication of any change of heart until now. I must demand a full explanation and urge you to stand by your original intent."

Charles interjected, his voice rising with emotion. "It was agreed. You cannot go back on your word now."

Sir John raised his hands. "I have not gone back on my word. I had not and have not given my consent. That can only be given when all matters are agreed and signed. You are right. It was my intent to conclude matters tonight but I have now decided, for reasons known only to me that I need more time."

Sir Robert stood up and leaned across the table. "I do not understand what has so suddenly caused this change of mind." He paused. "What happened when you left us before we dined? Up to that point everything was as expected."

His voice rose from restrained anger to a frustrated bellow. "I do not believe your story of a sick bird. Something else happened and I demand to know what it was."

Sir John went very pale but he raised his voice in reply.

"You forget yourself, sir. This is my house and you have no right to make demands of me. I understand your anger and frustration, and I too hope that we will move forward to complete the match in due course; but it will not be done this day."

Charles intervened again. "You cannot do this, we need to sign now. We—"

Sir Robert cut him off. "Enough, Charles," he said, and pausing to collect himself, went on. "Sir John, we are disappointed and displeased but if you need more time then so be it. Just tell us how long you need before you are ready."

"Let us say one month," said Sir John, "and then, you have

my word, we will bring the matter to a conclusion. Now I am fatigued so please forgive me if I retire. We can talk again on the morrow before you depart."

Chapter 3

Hall

Elizabeth awoke with a start. It was just after dawn and the sea fret had dropped a curtain of fine gauze over the manor. She had slept fitfully. The Manor was overcrowded with the visitors and the close quarters of the sleeping arrangements in the solar made for a noisy and uncomfortable night. There was a lot of movement before dawn and she was half aware that Alicia, who had shared her bed space, arose early but she finally relaxed into a deep sleep.

As she looked around, she realised that she was alone in the solar. She pondered the events of the previous evening and her immediate feeling was one of enormous relief, although she had been as perplexed as the Daunays at her father's sudden decision to delay the finalisation of the match.

She put on her gown, and looking down into the Hall, she could see no sign of the visitors. She started down the stairs to the hall to find her father, but just as she reached the bottom step she heard a scream.

Seconds later, her maid, Ada, came running into the main hall.

"The birds have killed him!" Ada screamed. "They are eating him! The blood, all the blood ..." Elizabeth and Godfrey reached her at the same time as she collapsed on the floor, sobbing.

"Who has been killed?" said Elizabeth. "Where is my father?" Fear filled her as she waited for a reply. "Stop crying girl, tell us what happened," Elizabeth demanded, but Ada was shaking from shock, unable to speak.

Elizabeth rushed out into the courtyard, followed closely by Godfrey, but could see nothing untoward until they reached the main gate, where two small bundles of blood and feathers could be seen outside the falconry.

"Your father's goshawks," said Godfrey. They ran through the gate to the falconry and recoiled in horror. A body lay on the ground just off the path. It was unrecognisable because of the mass of gorging game birds; peregrines, goshawks and harriers were feasting on the corpse, tearing strips of flesh from the blood soaked head and face of their prey.

"God have mercy," whispered Elizabeth. "Is it father?"

"No, my lady," said Godfrey. "It is Leofric. I can see from his boots and hose."

Relief and revulsion flooded through Elizabeth as she sank to her knees. "How could this happen? How did the birds get free and why would they attack poor Leofric?"

Godfrey gently grasped her hands and pulled her to her feet.

"Come away now, my lady, let us find your father. We will recapture the birds when they are sated and try to discover what has happened."

A crowd of other servants had now joined them and were staring aghast at the awful scene. Godfrey emerged from the falconry holding Elizabeth, who was on the point of collapse.

Sir John came hurrying towards them. He waved his stick. "Elizabeth, what has happened? What is all the noise about?" He caught sight of the two dead birds. "My goshawks," he breathed. "Who has done this?"

Seeing the crowd of servants, he pushed through them into the falconry. He took in the grim scene and immediately took charge of things. Ordering all the servants save three back to the house, he instructed Godfrey to take Elizabeth inside and fetch some shroud cloth from the wardrobe. Then he supervised the recapture of the birds.

Most of them had eaten their fill and were content to be re-tethered and hooded to keep them calm, and put back on their various perches. Two or three needed to be forcibly removed and placated with food from the falconer's store, but in a few minutes all was done and the body was fully visible.

It was now apparent that the falconer's throat had been cut with brutal force; his head nearly severed from his body. The tethers of all the birds had simply been cut through, allowing them to reach the blood and the open wound.

Sir John was hardened to the grim sights of battlefield carnage, but even he was shaken by the mutilation of poor Leofric's face and head.

"Who could have done this," he said, but even as he said it, he thought that he probably knew the answer to his question.

Godfrey returned, and Leofric's body was wrapped in shroud cloth, laid on a board, and removed to the grain barn to await burial.

The hall was abuzz with horrified excitement as servants cleaned and tidied in the wake of the visitors. Elizabeth and her father sat together in the solar, both in a state of shock.

Elizabeth's initial bewilderment turned to anger after Sir John told her the details of Richard de Mohun's visit the previous evening. He also told her of the unexpectedly early departure of the Daunays that morning.

"Godfrey woke me early and told me that Charles left the house well before dawn, saying that he was going to tell their groom to saddle the horses to be ready for an early departure to Boconnoc. When he returned he apparently awoke his father, sister and the other servants, and Godfrey said they were all about to depart.

"I went down in my night robe to see them but they had already gone, leaving like thieves with no courtesy or thanks."

"Did they kill poor Leofric?" asked Elizabeth. "I can scarce believe it."

"I do not know what to think," said Sir John. "I cannot believe that Sir Robert would countenance such a crime despite his anger at my decision, but given all that I have now heard, the possibility that Charles ..." He sighed.

"I am sure that they did not believe my story about the goshawks, and Charles was desperate to conclude matters. Maybe he tried to get the truth from poor Leofric. He paid a heavy price for his service and loyalty. May God rest his soul."

"So what now, father; how do we find out what really happened? Will you follow them to Boconnoc?"

Before he could reply, Ada, now recovered from her shock, ran up the stairs into the solar.

"He's here Miss Elizabeth, the man from yesterday, the one that killed your dove. Do you think he killed the falconer, too?"

"Do not be so silly, Ada," said Elizabeth. "He is our friend."

She and her father went over to the window and saw Richard riding across the yard toward the stables. He looked altogether different from the rather rough, soldier knight of the previous day.

He was mounted on his beautiful white palfrey, dressed in a black tunic emblazoned with the gold crenulated cross of the Mohuns. With his black hose, cap and cloak, he cut a very distinguished figure. When he dismounted, Elizabeth was struck by his easy athleticism and sureness of movement. Even when giving instructions to the groom, his air of quiet authority was plain to see and yet, his handling of his palfrey and little packhorse demonstrated an underlying gentleness.

As they watched, he removed his cap, ran his fingers through his close cropped dark hair, unhitched a small cage from the back of the laden packhorse and walked towards the front door.

Elizabeth realised with some surprise that her heart was beating faster, and that she wanted to be the first to greet him. Running down the stairs followed slowly by Sir John, she reached the door, somewhat breathless, just as Richard arrived.

He bowed to her and proffered an exquisite little golden cage that contained a diminutive nightingale. "A small token of recompense for the loss of your dove," he said, smiling. "Not as beautiful, but it will sing for you every day and in its cage it will be safe from any marauding hawks."

"Thank you sir," said Elizabeth. "Its song may help to cheer this sad house a little today. We have much to tell you." Sir John joined them in the doorway.

"Welcome, Richard. I am glad to see you. We have shocking news to discuss and decisions to make which, after yesterday evening, concern us all."

Richard had become increasingly concerned as he sensed the troubled atmosphere. "What has happened? Have the Daunays left? Did you delay your decision?"

"You had better come with me," said Sir John, and he led Richard back across the yard to the stables where Leofric's shrouded body lay.

As they walked, Sir John outlined the morning's drama. Richard was clearly shaken, and when he saw Leofric's body became angry and remorseful. "I should never have involved him," he said. "I did not want the Daunays to know that I was warning you, in case there was no foundation for my concerns. They are my neighbours … if I had not seen him here yesterday evening, he would still be alive."

"Do not blame yourself," said Sir John. "No one could have foreseen this evil act. I am just as culpable because my story about the goshawks, to explain my absence before dinner, was weak and unconvincing and led to them being suspicious."

"The problem we have," said Richard, "is that without witnesses, we cannot be certain that it was the Daunays. I agree with you that Charles has to be the most likely suspect but the evidence is only circumstantial. We do not even know if Leofric told them of my visit and our meeting."

"Your name was mentioned during our conversation at dinner," said Sir John. "They were clearly worried that you had been here, but from that conversation alone they could not have connected you with my decision to delay the marriage settlement."

They walked slowly back to the manor house. Sir John looked very pale and drawn, and staggered slightly as they climbed the stairs to the solar to rejoin Elizabeth.

"You must rest father," she said. Sir John nodded.

"A bit too much excitement for me," he said. "I do feel very weary. I will just rest here for a while and try to decide what to do next."

"I too need to think," said Richard. "I have some ideas but I would like to walk in the fresh air while I decide what to do. Perhaps, Lady Elizabeth, you would accompany me and test my reasoning."

Chapter 4

Hall and Boconnoc

The two of them walked through the gardens and Elizabeth led them onto the path above the narrow creek that ran from the estuary up to the mill at Pont.

Richard was deep in thought and they walked in silence for about half a mile. Elizabeth was content with the silence; it was somehow intimate and companionable. Suddenly, Richard stopped. He sat down on a grassy bank and motioned Elizabeth to sit beside him.

For a few moments, they gazed at the view across the creek and down to the mouth of the estuary. The variety of lush greens and browns of the surrounding fields and woods, and the sea colours ranging from cobalt to turquoise, created a magical vista but the events of the day somehow overlaid and dulled the image.

Then Richard spoke. "I have decided on two actions," he said. "Firstly, I will ride to Boconnoc to see the Daunays and try to determine the truth of their involvement, if any, in Leofric's murder."

Elizabeth looked at him anxiously. "You should not go alone, Richard. If they are responsible, then there is no knowing what harm they might do to you, and if they know from Leofric that you were responsible for my father's change of heart, they will be seeking revenge."

Richard smiled. "Don't worry; I will take care to avoid confrontation. I will call on them as a neighbour to their Sheviock manor. I have a small land dispute to discuss with them which gives me a legitimate reason to call and it also happens to be on my route to Tavistock. I do not think that they will attempt to do me any harm while on their property. They will be very cautious about making enemies of the Mohuns. My Father is too well known and respected for them to take the risk. If it does come to a fight, I am certain that I could prevail."

He spoke with such an air of authority and confidence that Elizabeth decided not to pursue her concern.

"So what is your second action?" she asked. To her surprise and pleasure, Richard reached out and took her hand, and gently kissed it.

"If you would agree, Elizabeth, when I return from Boconnoc, I will ask your father if he would accept me as a suitor for your hand in marriage."

Elizabeth snatched her hand away in shock; then regretting her reaction, reached out to him.

"Sir, you do not know me. I only met you yesterday and until my father makes his decision, I am still betrothed to Charles Daunay; I do not know you sir and ..." She ran out of words and breath.

Richard stroked her hand. "I think that the events of yesterday and today may have ensured that Charles Daunay, is no longer likely to have your fathers approval, guilty or not. That at least should please you." Elizabeth nodded and gripped his hand.

"At the same time," Richard went on, "he wants to see you well settled. The match with the Daunays seemed to be a good solution. But my family is well respected and known to him. My manor at Ugborough is not too distant and the joining of our lands and property would be advantageous to us both and would at least equal the Daunay match." He stopped as Elizabeth withdrew her hand and looked at him steadily.

"So your reason for wanting to marry me is back to 'logic and land!' What of love and my feelings?"

Richard reached out and gently touched her face.

"Elizabeth, I am a soldier. I am not schooled in the arts of love and romance but your beauty and your spirit affected me from the moment that we met. I admit that the 'logic' and circumstances have given me the opportunity and the courage to act. But I am sure that our love will blossom ..."

Elizabeth pressed his hand to her cheek. "You are so formal sir, but underneath I believe you are kind and considerate, and you know how to use words to your advantage." She leaned towards him. "Kiss me," she whispered. He hesitated, but somewhat awkwardly he complied. It was a brief and fleeting embrace but it was the spark that kindled Elizabeth's fire.

She stood up and pulled him to his feet. Kissing him again quickly, she tugged his hand. "Come on," she said, laughing, "let's go and see father."

"No, Elizabeth; I must first visit the Daunays at Boconnoc. For your father to agree to our marriage, he will need to know for certain that Charles Daunay was responsible for Leofric's death. He is a man of honour and will want to be sure that he is justified in deciding against the Daunay alliance. Besides, a few more hours will give you time to consider your own wishes. I know my proposal has been sudden and unexpected, and whilst your father may agree to it, I do not want to ask him for your hand unless you too desire it."

Elizabeth was overcome by his sensitivity to her feelings. Tears came to her eyes. "I do not need more time," she said, "and I wish you would not go to Boconnoc, but I understand. Just come back safe and soon."

Within the hour, Richard was on his way to Boconnoc. Sir John was sleeping after the exertions and excitement of the morning and they decided not to wake him. Elizabeth wrapped some cold venison that he could eat while riding, kissed him again, and tearfully waved to him as he rode through the main gate.

After a brisk ride from Hall, following the path that echoed the twists and turns of the Lerryn River, Richard came to the edge of the Boconnoc estate. He approached the Manor House and farm in full view, riding up the gently sloping floor of the valley towards the group of stone and wooden buildings nestling below the ridge line. The buildings were set in an open grassy area, surrounded by oak and beech woods.

From a distance, Boconnoc looked substantial and picturesque but as he drew closer he could see that the buildings were run down and neglected. Some of the farm buildings on the left were in a state of collapse with rotting thatch and broken beams.

The Manor House was a single story, part wood and part stone, with no windows other than narrow slits. Untended vines and ivy all but obscured the walls. Whilst he knew that Sheviock was the main Daunay residence, he was surprised at the poor condition of the buildings. It seemed to bear out the rumours of the declining financial circumstances of the family. There was no sign of life other than three or four horses grazing nearby.

Whilst he gazed around him, and before he could dismount, the main door was flung open and Sir Robert Daunay came down the steps.

He looked immaculate and imposing but tired and drawn. Smiling thinly he spoke, with no sense of welcome in his tone.

"Sir Richard de Mohun, what brings you, unannounced, to Boconnoc?"

"Sir Robert, I bid you good day and offer my apologies for calling on you uninvited and unannounced. I am travelling to Tavistock and called this morning at Hall by Bodinnick. Sir John Fitzwilliam, hearing that I would pass close to Boconnoc, asked if I would enquire as to your wellbeing. A servant at Hall was brutally killed early this morning and Sir John was concerned for your safety and that of your son and daughter. They believe that a local outlaw may be responsible." He dismounted. Sir Robert held out his hand.

"Welcome then to Boconnoc, but I fear we shall be poor hosts as we are only visiting to assess the requirements for much needed repairs here. My daughter Alicia and I are travelling on to Sheviock in an hour or so. You may reassure Sir John that we are all safe and unharmed and that we saw nothing of any note when we departed from Hall."

At that moment, Alicia appeared in the doorway. Her dark eyes widened as she saw Richard. She came down the steps to join her father, but before she could speak, Sir Robert recounted the reason for Richard's arrival at Boconnoc, finishing with, "I have told him that we are well and saw nothing untoward when we left Hall."

Alicia echoed her father. "That's right, we saw nothing." But her face belied her words; she could not look at Richard and was struggling to compose herself. Sir Robert quickly interjected.

"Sir Richard, I am sorry that we cannot entertain you but we have much to do before we depart. Unless there are other matters to discuss, we should wish you God speed to Tavistock."

Richard turned as if to remount but then turned again. "There is the small matter of the dispute my bailiff had with your son Charles over a boundary line at Cornwood near my Manor at Ugborough. While I am here, perhaps I could talk to Charles to see if we can settle the matter." Sir Robert visibly tensed and Alicia gave an involuntary gasp.

"Is that difficult?" asked Richard.

"Yes, it is," said Sir Robert. "Charles is on his way to London on a matter of urgent family business; you will have to talk with him when he returns to Sheviock, which will not be for some weeks. Now, sir, I bid you farewell."

Grasping Alicia by the arm, he hurried her up the steps and through the door, which slammed behind them.

Richard remounted Grisel Gris and slowly rode away, instinctively aware that he was under close scrutiny from the house. The brief conversation and particularly Alicia's demeanour had convinced him that the Daunays were lying. They knew what had happened at Hall that morning but there was still no evidence. If Charles had indeed left for London then there was little hope of learning the truth for some time to come, if ever.

To give credence to his story of being en route to Tavistock, he followed the track that headed northeast, away from the house toward the Liskeard and Tavistock road. Once well into the woods and out of sight he turned off to the left, intending to take a wide sweep to the north and double back on a southerly route to Lleryn and Bodinnick.

A little later, as he crested a hill well to the north of the house, he could see wood smoke drifting along the valley floor. He reigned in and stayed very still under the cover of the trees for several minutes. There was no sign of a dwelling other than a small hovel about half a mile away on the opposite hillside. Nothing moved and there was no sign of life other than birdsong and a busy squirrel in the beeches just behind him.

He slackened the reigns and nudged Grisel Gris forward, letting her pick her own way softly and delicately down the slope, heading for the source of the smoke. Coppice trees and scrub provided adequate cover. At about a hundred paces from the fire, Richard dismounted and drew his sword before advancing cautiously on foot.

The fire was smouldering in a small clearing with no sign of anyone in the vicinity. As he got closer to the fire, Richard could see fragments of cloth among the ashes. One piece was quite large and he hooked it out with the tip of his sword. It was the remains of the sleeve of a yellow jerkin which at first glance he thought was badly scorched. On closer examination, however, he could see that the marks were heavy, black-red bloodstains. Then, as Richard turned the fragment over, a feather fluttered from it and fell to the ground. Richard knew, without doubt, that it was from the wing of a Goshawk.

Proof enough, he thought.

He carefully folded the sleeve and together with the feather, took it back to where Grisel Gris was standing and put them in his saddle bag.

He set off again, slowly climbing the steep slope towards the tumbledown hovel on the ridge above him. Suddenly, Grisel Gris pricked her ears. Richard stopped and listened, and seconds later he could hear hoofbeats, still some way off, but coming towards him from the direction of the manor. He dismounted and led Grisel Gris into the cover of a small thicket. He stroked her nostrils softly and motioned her to stay still and quiet.

He moved quickly on foot to a position higher up the slope where he could see both the hovel and the track that led to it, which the rider was obviously following. Lying down and well hidden, he waited.

As the rider came into sight, he immediately recognised

Alicia. Her dark hair and boyish figure were unmistakable. Her eyes were fixed on the hovel and as she got closer she called out, "Charles, it's only me. Father said I should bring you some food." There was silence then a muffled curse. The door of the hovel opened and Charles Daunay, rubbing sleep from his eyes, emerged.

"About goddamn time," he said ungraciously. "I'm starving. How long does father say I have to stay here?"

"It is as well that you are here," said Alicia. "We had a visitor an hour ago; Richard de Mohun, asking if we had seen anything this morning at Hall. He had called there this morning and knew about the killing of their falconer. Sir John had asked him to call. They think the falconer was attacked by an outlaw and were concerned for our safety."

Charles laughed. "So what happened? Did father kill the interfering bastard?"

"Father lied for you, Charles," Alicia said angrily, "so de Mohun has gone. Father is so angry at your stupidity. He says you must stay here for another two days and then follow us to Sheviock. Why did you kill that poor man, Charles? What good did it do us?"

"Served the goddamned fool right," muttered Charles. "He should have answered my questions and he might have lived. Give me the food and get you gone; I will see you at Sheviock."

As Alicia disappeared from view, Richard lay still, trying to decide on a course of action. Should he confront Charles Daunay now and mete out his own justice? The element of surprise would be in his favour and the law would be on his side. Or, should he return to Hall with his news and allow Sir John to decide what to do?

In the event, the decision was taken out of his hands.

Grisel Gris, growing impatient at her confinement in the thicket, whickered softly in complaint. There was an immediate snort of response from a horse that had been out of Richard's sight on the far side of the shack. Charles came out of the door, sword drawn and wild eyed. "Alicia," he shouted, "is that you?" Gazing around him and seeing no-one, he unhitched and mounted his own horse and eschewing a saddle, rode furiously down the track towards the house.

Richard watched him go. He was frustrated, but at the same time, relieved that the decision had been made for him. Nevertheless, he felt in his bones that he might one day regret that matters had not been settled on this day.

Richard rode through the arch into Hall well after dark, weary from the events of the long day. After ensuring that Grisel Gris was stabled and had feed and water, he washed in the stable yard trough before making his way to the house. Sir John and Elizabeth were clearly relieved to see him safe.

Elizabeth impetuously put her hands on his shoulders and kissed him warmly. They sat in the solar as he was plied with a flagon of strong ale and a huge platter of assorted meats and cornbread. As he supped, he recounted his meeting with the Daunays and his discoveries at Boconnoc. Sir John and Elizabeth listened in fascinated silence except when he produced the bloodstained sleeve and the goshawk feather. Elizabeth confirmed that the sleeve was the same colour as the tunic worn by Charles Daunay. She wept and held on to her father.

"Sir John," said Richard in conclusion, "I'm afraid there is no doubt. Charles Daunay tried, unsuccessfully, to learn the reason for your decision last night from your falconer. When Leofric, God rest his soul, refused to tell him, Charles killed him. Sir Robert and Alicia, although not directly implicated, both know what he did and are protecting him."

Sir John was overcome. "And you will swear to this? Because I intend to see to it that Charles Daunay will hang."

Richard nodded. "Yes, I will swear. But remember, Sir John, these people are powerful and cunning. It will not prove easy to lay hands on Charles Daunay and even if that is done, Sir Robert has strong influence both at court and with The Bishop of Exeter."

"We shall see," said Sir John. "I too am not without influence and neither is your father. But now Richard, I understand from Elizabeth that we have another important matter to discuss." He chuckled. "Although the day started with bloody murder, she seems to be in remarkably good spirits. Elizabeth, it is time for you to withdraw. Richard and I have business to discuss."

Elizabeth smiled and blushed but stood up and kissed both her father and Richard, then went down the stairs to the main hall.

"Sir," said Richard, "I apologise for discussing my intentions with Elizabeth before first seeking your approval."

"Never mind all that," said Sir John. "I approve and agree to the match, but with three conditions." Richard nodded.

"First, I want the marriage to be conducted quickly, and I mean within a matter of days."

"But—" began Richard; Sir John held up his hand.

"Hear me out," he said firmly. "I believe that I am dying, Richard and it is my greatest wish that I should witness my Elizabeth safely married before I go to meet my maker. I offer my lands and property, in their entirety, as Elizabeth's dowry but I seek assurance that they will be retained and that Hall will continue to prosper for the benefit of my daughter and the generations to come.

"Finally, I have long desired a chapel to be built here at Hall for the family to use. I would like you to promise that you will, by the grace of God, build such a chapel as a lasting memorial to my name. So, Richard, do you accept the conditions?"

"Of course, Sir John, most willingly and I thank you humbly for your consent, but is Elizabeth happy that the marriage shall take place so quickly?"

"If her mood today is anything to go by," said Sir John, laughing, "there is no doubt that she will be happy with the idea, but you should go and ask her yourself. And Richard," his tone grew serious.

"There is no need to tell her that I am dying. That can wait until after you are married. She means the world to me and I am entrusting her to your care with the fervent hope that you will treat her well and keep her safe from harm."

"Sir John, you have my word on that," said Richard and the two men embraced.

Elizabeth was indeed very happy that her father had agreed to the marriage but somewhat puzzled that he wanted the wedding to take place so quickly.

"I think," said Richard, who had been prepared for the question, "that he wants to be sure that affairs are settled and that you are happy. He knows that if I first ride to Tavistock or Ugborough and the Daunays return, he might be in a difficult position and he doesn't know what they might do. If we are married, it is a fait accompli."

Elizabeth nodded. "Yes I can see that, but what about you Richard; are you ready for things to happen so quickly?"

"Indeed I am," he said. "I see no reason to delay. I would like to have spoken to my father but I am certain he will approve and will understand our need to avoid delay."

Elizabeth laughed and came into his arms. "So then, my soldier knight, when shall we marry? Today? Tomorrow? And where? And who shall be our witnesses? We must have time to make ready!"

"Hold on," said Richard, "there are some things to be done. I think first of all we have to bury poor Leofric."

Elizabeth clapped her hand to her mouth. "Oh of course, God forgive me, how could I forget?"

"And," said Richard, "if it is possible, I would like to get word to my brother, Lawrence, in Tavistock, to see if he might journey here to be my witness alongside your father.

"We will need to tell the household of our plans and prepare for a celebration. Five days should be enough for all that to be done so let us set the day at that. Our wedding day, God willing, shall be Tuesday, 1st of March."

Moonshadow

Chapter 5

Hall

Leofric was buried at the little church of St Wyllow in Churchtown. A simple service was conducted by the priest Edwin Carrow, youngest son of the Carrows of Polruan, and was attended by Elizabeth and Richard, and most of the servants from Hall. Leofric had no living relatives that anyone was aware of. His closest companions had been his birds.

Sir John, Richard and Elizabeth all agreed that it was better to keep their knowledge of the Daunay involvement in his death to themselves, until they could take some positive action. They felt that as long as the Daunays believed themselves to be free of suspicion they would be less likely to be on their guard.

Among the servants, there was still a great deal of talk and speculation about the manner of his death. But the news of the wedding had now come to the fore as the main topic for discussion.

On the day before the wedding, Godfrey, calm and dignified, oversaw the hectic but well organised preparations.

The kitchen staff was busy preparing a feast for the occasion; butchering and spicing venison, wild boar, goose, partridge, quail, and pigeon, collecting apples from the store and early cabbage from the kitchen garden. The smell of baking bread, flavoured with dark ale, pervaded the air.

The brew house master in Bodinnick was busy conveying his entire stock of ale and cider to the Manor.

The obligatory notice of the intended marriage had been posted on the gate to the Manor, and garlands and the wedding bower were being assembled from a massive collection of wild flowers and greenery garnered by the servant's children from the surrounding woods and fields.

Even the wedding night arrangements were in hand, with Sir John insisting that Elizabeth and Richard should have his private bedroom while he slept in the solar. Bed linen was being washed and dried, scented with herbs, and folded, ready for use.

Elizabeth and Ada were reworking the simple but elegant, mid-blue linen wedding dress that had belonged to her mother.

Frederic, the senior stable lad, had been despatched to Tavistock with a message from Richard, summoning one of his younger brothers, Lawrence, to the wedding. Although younger, Lawrence had married early and already had two young children. Lawrence looked after the family estates in and around Tavistock, including the mill and the weekly market.

Sir John and Richard were engaged in drawing up the dowry documents. They had enlisted the aid of Edwin Carrow, the priest from Polruan, to act as both scribe and witness.

Although Richard clearly had the most to gain in terms of land, Sir John was delighted to know that his daughter was to be part of the well regarded and wealthy de Mohun family, with its long and proud history of service and sacrifice. The arms of Mohun and Fitzwilliam would sit well together on the shield that was being carved for the occasion.

The morning of March the first dawned with the promise of spring, matching the mood of the day; sunshine, light winds and the bluest of Cornish skies.

Lawrence arrived mid morning, having stayed the previous night in Pelynt. He found Richard in the courtyard, tending to Grisel Gris and little Quenelle, and they embraced warmly. They had always been close through their childhood.

"You sly old dog," said Lawrence when they had exchanged greetings. "You kept this secret enough. We expected you to be with us last week. We were beginning to worry about you and then your messenger arrived and told us the news; but why the hurry, Richard? You should have talked to father, you know. I have heard him speak of the Fitzwilliams and I know he thinks well of Sir John, but he won't be pleased at you marrying without his approval."

Richard took Lawrence for a stroll round the Manor garden and recounted the events of the past week. Lawrence listened and took it all in, only asking questions to be clear on certain points. Like his brother, he was logical and decisive.

"I think you have made the right decision. I am pleased for you. If Elizabeth is half as beautiful as you have described her to me, then you are doubly blessed because her dowry and inheritance are beyond your expectations. I'm sure that father will understand and approve.

"All the same, Richard, I am worried about the Daunays and their reactions to all that has happened. You know, as do I, that they are powerful and well connected; both down here and in London. They may choose to lie low, but they may also choose to deny everything, brazen it out and go on the attack. You need to be vigilant, Richard."

"Yes," I know," said Richard. "But for now brother, I am going to be married this morning and I need you to be my witness, sign the dowry papers and join me in the celebrations. Thank you for coming, Lawrence. It means a lot to me that you are here. Now, come and meet Sir John and let us make ready."

Elizabeth observed them from her father's bedroom which she was now using to get dressed and ready for the day. Her heart beat faster as she thought how distinguished and manly her bridegroom looked. It seemed like a fairy tale that instead of submitting with fear and disgust to the advances of Charles Daunay, she was soon to be in the arms of this handsome man who she had never set eyes upon until a few days ago.

Ada and Ellen were making up the nuptial bed with a lot of giggling and ribald comments.

"Miss Elizabeth," said Ellen, a buxom and cheerful young maid who was married to Frederic the head stable boy, "don't 'ee let your man get in the cider at the feast. My Frederic did when we were wed and we spent all night trying to get 'is little soldier to stand up straight, but every time he came to advance 'e fell down!" Ada collapsed into giggles and Elizabeth laughed out loud.

"Thank you Ellen, I will keep a close eye on him."

"An eye on who, Miss?" asked Ellen. "Your man or 'is little soldier?" She and Ada fell on the bed and screeched with laughter.

"I think that will do," said Elizabeth, scarcely containing herself. "It is time to get ready. Ada, I need you to brush my hair and Ellen, you can go and tell my father that I will be ready one hour from now."

In truth, Elizabeth was still a virgin. She was, however, not sexually naïve or ignorant. Living in the country and simply observing nature had educated her in the generalities of sexual behaviour and reproduction. Being naturally curious, as well as living in close proximity with the many occupants of the Manor, had given her a very good understanding of carnal activities and pleasures. She was therefore nervous of, but eagerly anticipating, the exploration of the marriage bed.

It had been some thirty years since the last wedding at Hall, when Sir John himself had married Lady Eleanor. As noon approached, the courtyard began filling with people. Most of the Hall Manor servants and farm workers, and what seemed to be the entire population of Bodinnick, plus a few from Polruan—perhaps a hundred in all—were in a great state of excitement. Someone was tip-tapping a makeshift drum and the son of the local miller from Carne was playing his reed pipe. A pathway of strewn reeds led from the gated entrance across the courtyard to the main door of the house, where the heavy oak doors were closed.

Rough cut boards were laid out on trestles outside the kitchen entrance, in readiness for the food and drink being offered to the local guests while inside, the great table was already decorated and groaning under the wedding fare.

Richard, resplendent in his crimson and black, Lawrence, and Priest Edwin Carrow were waiting together in the garden at the back of the house, as were Ada and Ellen, holding the pretty floral bower made up with early spring gatherings of ivy, brightened with celandines and wild early daffodils.

Then Sir John appeared at the small door that led into the garden, with Elizabeth on his arm.

Richard was thunderstruck. She was more beautiful than he could have imagined. She was dressed in a simple, long blue linen dress, falling softly around her slender figure. Her waist length fair hair was coiled on top of her head, covered with a cap of lace and exposing her shapely and unadorned neck. In her right hand she held a small symbolic spray of ivy and fir. Her naturalness and honesty of spirit shone through.

Lawrence looked at Richard and grinned. "All this," he said, gesturing to the manor and the garden around them, "and an angel as well. God is being good to you, brother."

Richard hardly heard him. He was spellbound by his bride as she came towards him and took his hand.

"Are you ready, sir?" She smiled. "You still have time to change your mind." She turned to Lawrence. "And you sir, I presume, are his brother Lawrence?"

Lawrence bowed.

"Welcome to our wedding, Lawrence. I hope that, despite the haste, you approve of the match. I know that Richard set great store by your attendance and willingness to witness our union."

Lawrence laughed. "My Lady Elizabeth, were I not already married, and happily so, I would disapprove most strongly and try to marry you, myself."

Elizabeth touched his arm in acknowledgement and then the whole group moved across the grass to the little garden door that Richard had entered just a few days before. Then they walked round on the outside of the manor wall until they came to the main gate. Ada and Ellen raised the floral bower above the heads of Richard and Elizabeth.

With Sir John leading the way, and Lawrence and Edwin the priest following behind, they entered the courtyard and walked in procession along the reed strewn path toward the main door of the house. The crowd of people in the yard pressed forward to see them and the buzz of excitement and admiration rose to a crescendo. Some of the women were openly weeping, overcome by the beauty of the bride and the whole colourful spectacle. When the small procession reached the main door and stopped, Sir John turned and raised his hands for silence.

"Thank you all for coming to witness and celebrate the marriage of my lovely and dear daughter Elizabeth to Sir Richard de Mohun; Knight, and son of John de Mohun, Lord of Dunster. I am happy to say that after the marriage, Elizabeth and Richard will live here at a Hall and continue to maintain and develop our estates."

A cheer went up from the crowd at this news for many had anticipated that Elizabeth would move away to manage her husband's home and that Hall, with no other heir, might decline and decay.

Sir John acknowledged the cheering with a smile and went on. "Lady Elizabeth and Sir Richard will now exchange their vows in the sight of God and before witnesses."

Elizabeth and Richard stepped forward from under the bower turning to face one another. They joined hands and in turn, Richard first, delivered their vows.

Sir John stepped forward and took from his pocket a simple, red-gold ring. He gave it first to Richard. "This belonged to my beloved Lady Eleanor and I have kept it for this day."

Richard took it and placed it on Elizabeth's finger and then spontaneously kissed her.

The watching crowd cheered again—egged on by the dancing drummer—and Richard and Elizabeth, smiling and radiant, waved to them. Then they turned again towards the main door and Edwin Carrow moved to stand in front of them.

He raised a small wooden cross and proclaimed God's blessing on the union. Sir John then ceremoniously opened the big oak doors and the couple, hand in hand, walked into the great hall as man and wife.

"So Richard, it is done," said Elizabeth softly. "Your falcon has a lot to answer for but perhaps my dove sacrificed itself for me."

The feasting went on throughout the afternoon, both in the courtyard and in the great hall. As the day wore on, prodigious quantities of food and drink were consumed and the sound of merriment, music, and noise in the courtyard rose to new heights. But as dusk fell, there were more supine bodies than those standing and most of the noises were either murmurings of over indulgence or amorous intent. Inside the great hall, after Lawrence and Edwin had added their signatures to the marriage and dowry agreements, the smaller group with a number of the more prominent local families also feasted and drank well. At one point, Sir John asked the drummer and the piper to come inside and set their feet tapping with some country music and rounds.

Soon though, the exertions and the excitement of the day took their toll on Sir John. He became very pale and Elizabeth helped him up the steps of the solar and into his big chair.

"Well, my child, I am content to see you wed and to a fine man who will support and care for you. I am glad too that I did not force you into a match that you did not welcome. I am sad that it took the sacrifice of poor Leofric to make me see reason, but I will be able to thank him face to face soon enough. Now, go; eat and drink and dance and sing, and enjoy your marriage bed. Kiss me and let me sleep; I am very weary."

Elizabeth was concerned for her father as she left him to sleep. As she came down the steps into the hall, with the fire now lit to take the chill off the evening, the candles were flickering and Richard was talking animatedly to his brother. Despite the merrymaking and the cheerful chatter, she felt a wave of sadness sweep over her, and within it, a darker premonition of disaster.

When Richard looked up and saw her, he instantly went to her side. "What ails thee?" he asked softly. "You look troubled. Is it your father?"

"Yes," murmured Elizabeth. "In part, but I think it is the realisation that everything is changing and life will never be the same again." She sighed. "But I am glad you are here to be a part of my future." They sat down again at the great table and Richard beckoned Ellen to re-fill their cups.

As Ellen bent to pour the wine, she whispered in Elizabeth's ear. "Ee 'ain't had no cider miss, I think 'is little soldier' will stand up and fight." Elizabeth choked on the sip of wine she was swallowing and was patted on the back by Richard. At once her dark thoughts were banished and she was back in a joyful mood.

Before long, shouts could be heard from some of the more resilient guests in the courtyard.

"Time thee were abed" and "Do 'ee need some help" were some of the more polite remarks.

Lawrence took his brother's arm. "They are right my brother, I think you have another duty to perform." He grinned. "I think you should go to it, and brother, treat her gently. There is plenty of time."

Richard smiled and nodded. Elizabeth, aware of what was expected, whispered to Richard. "Stay here, husband while I ready myself. When Ada and Ellen return then you shall know that I await you." She signalled for Ada to follow her and walked steadily up the stairs.

On the way, she stopped to see that her father was comfortable. He was sleeping soundly and she kissed him lightly on his forehead.

In the bedroom, Ada helped her to undress and put on a white linen nightdress. Then, while Elizabeth sat on a stool beside the big oak framed bed, Ada gently uncoiled her mistress's hair and brushed it till it shone like burnished gold as it fell around her shoulders.

"My lady, you look so beautiful," said Ada, softly." Are you afeared? Ellen says the first time it hurts. It's like being pierced with a sword."

"Ellen seems very well and lively for someone who has been run through with a sword," said Elizabeth.

"Do not be concerned, Ada. I am not frightened. I know what to expect, and pleasure and pain are close bedfellows. Now, extinguish all the candles other than the two beside the bed, then go downstairs and tell my husband that I await him."

When Richard entered the room and closed the door behind him, Elizabeth was sitting up in the middle of the bed with her nightdress unlaced and her small but budding breasts clearly outlined. The room smelt strongly of herbs and floral essence.

Richard was at once entranced and aroused. He had not known what to expect and could only draw upon his previous experience with camp followers and whores, which he knew was not the stuff of romance; just the slaking of battle fear and lust. Without speaking, he quickly undressed, standing with his back to Elizabeth, embarrassed to display his fierce arousal.

He heard her stir, and then with a nervous giggle she said, "Do we not have to do this face to face, or have I been misled?"

He turned to her and gasped. She had taken off her gown and was kneeling up on the edge of the bed to face him, composed but flushed and staring in some wonder at his engorged manhood. Then with perfect timing, she removed the potential for embarrassment.

"Oh sir, you should remove your sword before you enter your wife's bed," she jested. They both laughed aloud and she took him into her arms.

The night was one of passion, pain, and pleasure. By morning they were lovers as well as man and wife.

Chapter 6

Tavistock, Dunster and Ugborough

In the days following the wedding, the guests gradually dispersed. Lawrence returned to Tavistock, enjoining Richard to visit him soon and urging him to go see their father at Dunster.

Richard and Elizabeth indulged their new found passion and lost themselves in exploring each other's minds and bodies.

Elizabeth was able to show Richard the full extent of the Hall estate, including the farms and the coastline above Pont creek. Together they visited and were warmly welcomed by their tenants in Boddinick village.

The only cloud on the horizon was the health of Sir John. Once the wedding was over it was clear that he was in decline. It seemed that having held himself together to see his daughter settled, he now gave in to his illness.

Richard told Elizabeth of her father's reason for wanting the wedding to be conducted at such speed. It was not the blow that he had expected it to be.

"I know he is dying," she said. "I have known it for some time; it was the reason that I did not refuse outright to marry Charles Daunay. I knew that father would die unhappy if I did." She kissed Richard. "Then you came along, my chivalrous knight, and now I am happy, and my father will die happy."

Indeed, although frail and growing weaker by the day, Sir

John was in good spirits. He even walked with them one morning, leaning heavily on Richard for support, to a small field about a hundred paces from the southern wall of the house.

"This," he said, "is the place for the chapel that you are going to build in my memory, and in the centre of the chapel will be my resting place. So mark out the site quickly, for I shall be at rest before you begin to build."

Two days later, he took to his bed for the last time. Edwin Carrow was sent for to administer last rites, and with Elizabeth and Richard at his bedside, he slipped away peacefully.

Three weeks later, the burial over, the chapel site agreed and marked, and the household once again on even keel, Richard decided that it was the right time to take Elizabeth away to visit both the family home at Dunster and his own Manor at Ugborough. He knew that by now his father, John de Mohun, Lord of Dunster, would have been advised of the marriage and would be expecting them to visit. Richard had asked Lawrence to send word of the marriage when he returned to Tavistock.

Lord John was the major landowner in Somerset and a powerful Baron who had consolidated the various Mohun estates. A soldier through and through, he had distinguished himself in battle in both Gascony and Scotland.

En route to Dunster, Richard and Elizabeth were warmly welcomed by Lawrence and his wife Joan in their modest manor in Tavistock.

Fortuitously, another brother, Baldwin, was also in Tavistock, visiting the priory to recruit two novice monks. One to serve at Newenham Abbey, founded by his great grandfather, Reginald de Mohun, and the other to assist Baldwin with his parish at Luppitt in Devon.

An unlikely looking priest, Baldwin was a huge man with obvious Norman lineage; dark complexioned with jet black hair, craggy features and a smile as wide as Chesil Beach.

"Married then, my little brother? And to the prettiest girl in Cornwall," he roared, engulfing them both in an exuberant embrace. "And you couldn't even wait to get your own brother to conduct the marriage?"

Richard laughed and explained the circumstances of the

speedy wedding.

"I forgive you then," said Baldwin, "but I expect you to attend mass in Luppitt soon, just to set the family seal on things."

They all dined together that evening. As convivial a gathering as can be imagined, three of the eight Mohun brothers strengthening their bonds and welcoming Elizabeth as part of the family.

The next morning, Richard and Elizabeth took their leave of Lawrence and Joan and set off on the long journey from Tavistock to Dunster. They lodged that night in the priory at Bow and the next day rode on to Bickleigh, where they were welcomed by the de Bickleigh family. Hugh de Bickleigh had been an armourer to Lord de Mohun of Dunster and had served with Richard in Aquitaine.

On the third day, as they rode out of Tiverton on the road alongside the river Exe, Richard was in good spirits.

"We are in Mohun country now," he said and indeed everyone on the road seemed to know him. Many of his soldiers and family retainers came from the small holdings and farms along the route. They and their families acknowledged his passing with smiles and salutes.

At one point, just outside Winsford, they met another knight, Giles de Boudroucai, and his retinue, coming from Dunster. Both parties stopped to exchange greetings.

"Your father is expecting you," said Giles, smiling. "He is trying to sound angry that you married without consulting him but it is easy to see that he is proud and pleased, and anxious to see you both."

They came into Dunster late in the afternoon; past the nunnery, through the outer gates and then up the steep hill and through the stone arch and gatehouse into the ancient courtyard.

Two young squires were waiting and rushed to attend them, jostling to be the one to help Elizabeth dismount.

"Calm down you two," said Richard. "She is mine, so mind your manners and watch where you put your hands." Elizabeth laughed, if a little nervously. She was clearly somewhat in awe of the surroundings.

Dunster Castle was a massive building in comparison with

anything she had seen in Cornwall. It was a solid fortress on a rock. The view from the ramparts, even at the ground floor level, was magnificent, with forested hills to the rear and the sea in front and to both sides. Waves crashed against the rocky shore far below.

Gervais, one of the squires, spoke quietly to Richard.

"Your father will see you and your Lady at dinner in the great hall," he said. "I am to show you to your rooms in the west tower."

"Thank you, Gervais, lead on," said Richard.

Inside, the castle seemed less impressive. The passageways were dark and damp and the rooms they had been allocated, although spacious enough, were sparsely furnished, and despite a recently lit brazier, rather cold and musty.

Richard, sensing Elizabeth's disappointment, put his arm around her. "Do not worry, my love. These are my old rooms, when I was first a squire here. I doubt they have had much use since then. They will soon warm up and the bed will be warmer than it ever was when I was here alone!" Elizabeth laughed and embraced him.

"Gervais," said Richard, "have another brazier lit in the anteroom and tell my father that we look forward to dinner. Please come and escort us when it is time."

They had time enough to use the privy chamber and the cold water sluice in the corner turret, and change into the clothes that they had worn for their wedding. Elizabeth missed having Ada to help her but enjoyed the novel intimacy of having Richard in attendance.

Gervais led them through the Castle to the top of the steps leading down to the great hall. The top half of the stairway was hidden from the hall but when they arrived at the top of the final flight, Elizabeth gasped. The hall was spectacular. Battle flags and flickering tallow torches lined the walls, and a great log fire blazed in the huge hearth at the right hand end of the room.

Down the centre was an enormous oak trestle table, laid with silver and pewter plates and goblets gleaming in the flickering torchlight. Some twenty or more people were assembled around the table. They stood and applauded as

Richard and Elizabeth descended the stairs. A murmur of approval grew in volume as Elizabeth's grace and beauty became apparent to all.

At the head of the table sat Lord John de Mohun and his wife, Lady Aida. Lord John motioned Richard and Elizabeth to join them, Richard on the side nearest his father and Elizabeth next to Lady Aida. As the hubbub died down, Lord John hammered on the table with an empty goblet and gained immediate silence.

"I command you all to drink to my son Richard and his new bride, Elizabeth, daughter of my old friend Sir John Fitzwilliam. I can see now why my son failed to ask for my approval to the marriage." He paused for effect. "With such beauty before me, I might have refused and married her myself," Lady Aida looked at him reprovingly but joined in the laughter.

Lord John clapped his hands and the feast began to arrive. It outshone the wedding feast at Hall and it was obvious that Lord John had chosen to show his full approval of the marriage.

During the meal, Richard was able to tell his father the full story of the events that had transpired during his visit to Hall. Lord John was amazed and concerned in turn. "You must tread carefully with the Daunays," he said. "Sir Robert is favoured at court. He has always been loyal to Queen Isabella. As for Charles, he got away with his behaviour in London because of Edward's proclivity for good looking young men. He will not be in favour now but even so, you must be doubly certain of your ground before making accusations against the family."

He leaned across the table to speak to Elizabeth.

"You are most welcome here my dear lady. I grieve to learn of your father's death. We bore arms together many times and I knew him to be a kind and courageous man."

"I thank you, my Lord," said Elizabeth, "he said the same of you and was very happy, as am I, that I married a Mohun."

Lady Aida had been regaling Elizabeth with stories of Richard's life as a child at Dunster. It was clear that, of her eight sons, Richard had a special place.

"He was always so determined to succeed in everything he undertook, but was happy to take advice and learn from others. Apart from being groomed and trained to fight, he was thoughtful and resourceful and always well prepared. I am sure that you have already experienced the kind and gentle side of his nature." She smiled and Elizabeth, blushing, nodded her agreement.

As the evening and the feasting drew to a close, Lord John took Richard aside into one of the small ante rooms.

"I have been told that Mortimer and Queen Isabella require all the 'Lords Ordainer' barons to attend a Parliament with the young King in London, to swear their allegiance and debate matters of State. Your brother John should by right accompany me but he is still in France, so I would like you to attend in his place. You should warn Elizabeth that you are likely to be summoned soon and may be gone for some time. What are your plans now? You are welcome to stay here and ride with me when the call comes. Your mother will be very happy to comfort and keep company with Elizabeth."

"Thank you father," said Richard, "but I plan to take Elizabeth first to Ugborough, to check on affairs there, and we had intended to return soon to Hall, to take stock of the inheritance and commence the building of the new chapel. With no intended disrespect to you or my mother, I am certain that if I am to be called for service, Elizabeth would want to be at Hall among familiar surroundings."

Lord John looked somewhat disappointed. "Your mother will be sad to see you go so soon, as will I; but given the circumstances, we understand. Will you stay another day at least and hunt with me tomorrow? We have arranged some good sport for you and it will give Lady Aida and Elizabeth a little time to become better acquainted."

"Of course," said Richard." I can think of nothing more pleasurable than a day of hunting on familiar ground."

The following day was bright and clear, ideal for the hunt. Richard, mounted on Grisel Gris, his father, the two squires and three foresters, hunted all day in the Brendon forest, carrying home a giant but ageing stag that had nearly outrun them and two boars that they had put up during the chase. Father and son enjoyed each other's company and their shared love of horsemanship.

That evening, pleasantly tired but still exhilarated from the hunt, Richard enjoyed good food and wine with Elizabeth and his parents, all at ease in front of the blazing fire in the great hall. Looking across at his beautiful young wife, who was in animated conversation with his father and flushed from the heat of the fire, he was filled with desire for her. She caught his eye and seemed to sense his mood.

Making their excuses of the early start next day, they bade good night to Sir John and Lady Aida and made their way back to their bedroom, progressing from a decorous stroll while in view to an unseemly rush through the dark passages.

Their lovemaking that night was passionate and uninhibited. Familiar now with each other's bodies and still fuelled with their new found emotions, they were able to reach new heights of sensation and pleasure.

Quite spent, they lay in each other's arms. Soon Elizabeth drifted into a deep and untroubled sleep while the miracle of life was already stirring within her.

Richard dreamily reflected on a perfect day and on the extraordinary good fortune that had befallen him since retrieving his bird in the garden at Hall.

Early the next morning, Richard and Elizabeth set off on their journey to Ugborough, accompanied by Gervais who had been assigned to them by Sir John. They had taken their leave of Sir John and Lady Aida after early Mass and breakfast, and Sir John had again warned Richard not to take any precipitous action against the Daunays.

"I will be seeing you again soon in London," he said. "We will see how the land lies, then."

The journey was relatively uneventful. They retraced their steps as far as Tiverton, again lodging with the de Bickleigh family, then on to Exeter where they attended a mass at The Cathedral. On the third night, they decided to stay at Buckfastleigh rather than travel after dark. They were warmly welcomed by Abbott Peter, who was known to the Mohuns through their generous foundation of Tor Abbey and support of Buckfastleigh.

On the morning of the fourth day, they rode off the ridge that bounded the moor and down the steep hill into Ugborough.

The hamlet was comprised of the Saxon church, with its recent addition of a Norman tower, the manor house itself, the farm, and half a dozen dwellings.

The manor house was modest but in a good state of repair and had benefited from the addition of a solar and a bedchamber. Richard had employed a local stonemason who had worked on the church tower to undertake the modernisation.

The couple were greeted by everyone in the manor who had gathered to welcome them.

Elizabeth, tired after the travelling of the last few days, had a short tour of the house, and having met the housekeeper and maid, she retired to the solar to rest.

Richard walked over to the farm buildings to meet with Ralph Purves, his bailiff. Despite the modest size of the hamlet, Ugborough Manor had extensive land holdings to the north and west, and Ralph was kept busy ensuring that the land was well used and productive. After getting up to date with the farm news, Richard asked about the boundary problem with the Daunays at Cornwood. Ralph spat on the ground.

"It seems that some of the Daunay land adjoining ours has been gifted to the Church at Cornwood as part of the living and Parson Wideslade is the one who has taken over three of our fields for grazing land. When I went to speak with him, he laughed at me and said I should take it up with Sir Robert, but much good it would do me. He said the parish records proved it was their land."

"Well," said Richard, "our records show them to be ours, so either he is lying or someone has made a mistake. I will be taking Lady Elizabeth out tomorrow to ride the bounds so we will call at Cornwood and speak to Parson Wideslade."

The following morning, Richard, Elizabeth and Ralph set off early in the day to ride round the bounds of the estate. It was a pleasant and picturesque ride along the edge of the moor, skirting the village of Ivybridge then uphill onto Hanger Down, descending again into Storridge woods and emerging finally beside the disputed fields on the edge of Cornwood.

As they approached the weir at Moor Cross, they could see the cloaked and hooded figure of someone standing and facing the water, while a fully saddled palfrey stood on the opposite bank, quietly grazing. The roar of the weir drowned out the noise of their approach but the horse heard them and pricked up its ears. The figure turned quickly. It was Alicia Daunay. She stared at them wide eyed, frightened and tearful.

"Alicia?" said Elizabeth. "What has happened?" Looking more closely, she realised that Alicia's cloak and dress were soaking wet and muddy. "Oh you poor thing, did he throw you?"

"Yes," Alicia said. "He was frightened by a tree branch that was being swept down in front of him. He reared suddenly and I fell off. Now I am wet and cold and bruised, and he won't come back to me; and of all the people I know, you are the last that I would wish to see me in this state." She started to weep openly and turned away from them.

"Ralph, give your cloak to Lady Alicia," ordered Richard, "and take her across to her mount."

Alicia took off her dripping cloak and gratefully donned the one that Ralph held out to her. He helped her up onto his saddle and urged his horse forward through the fast flowing stream, followed by Richard and Elizabeth. Safely on the other side, Alicia was soon remounted.

"Thank you," she said, smiling slightly for the first time. "I am obliged." Then she looked directly at Richard. "It's true then, you are married to her?" she asked, gesturing towards Elizabeth.

"Yes," said Richard. "Praise God, I am."

"My father and my brother are so angry with you," said Alicia. "They say you discredited them and tricked your way into her affections. If they see you here on their land they will seek to do you harm."

"The land is mine," said Richard softly. "I am here today to see Wideslade and to dispute his claim to the grazing rights he says were awarded by your father. As for their views of my marriage to Elizabeth, they know full well that they have no one to blame but themselves. The actions of your brother annulled any possibility of pursuing a match between him and Elizabeth, as you well know. When your brother dares again to show his face, he will have to defend his bloody actions before the courts and before God!"

Alicia paled and stammered. "I don't know what you mean.

What do you think he has done that is so terrible?"

Before he could answer, Elizabeth interjected. "Be calm, Richard; nothing is to be gained by distressing Alicia further. She is soaking wet and cold, and should go quickly to get into warm clothing and recover."

Alicia glanced gratefully at Elizabeth. "Thank you," she whispered. Then, visibly collecting herself, she said, "Thank you all for your assistance in reuniting me with my horse. I have fresh clothing at Cornwood House and I will return there now. I'm afraid though that your journey to see Parson Wideslade has been in vain. He is at Sheviock to meet with my father. I return there tonight and I will tell them you desire to discuss the grazing rights." She rode off up the track to Cornwood without a backward glance.

Elizabeth touched Richard on the arm. "I'm sorry I interrupted you, Richard but I was worried that you might say too much in the heat of the moment and ..."

Richard took her hand. "You were right to stop me. I would have said too much. It seems though that our journey has been in vain."

As they rode back into the manor courtyard, Richard's heart sank. A sweat streaked and dusty horse was tethered in the yard drinking from the water trough, its saddlecloth bearing his father's coat of arms. As they dismounted, Gervais came out of the doorway with a man that Richard recognised as Thomas Breve from Dunster.

Gervais looked excited. "We are to go to London," he gabbled. "Queen Isabella and Mortimer have called for the Barons to attend the young King. Your father is already on the way and wants you to join him. Will I be with you?"

Elizabeth gave a little cry and grabbed Richard's arm. "So soon? I so hoped we could return together to Hall."

Richard addressed the messenger. "When are we required?"

"Immediately, sire. I was delayed in reaching you here and many of the knights and barons are already assembled."

"I will ride in the morning," said Richard. "Gervais, attend to Thomas's needs and send word to my men at arms that they should assemble here tomorrow morning at daybreak, ready to march." Putting his arm round a tearful Elizabeth, he led her into the house.

"Dry your tears," he said. "We have a lot to do and talk about before tomorrow morning."

Elizabeth soon recovered. She had been through this many times before with her father and was able, at least for now, to concentrate on the practicalities.

There was indeed a lot to be done: Armour and weapons to be assembled and cleaned; horses and pack horses to be inspected, shod and harnessed; victuals for the journey to be readied and packed. Everyone in the household worked late into the night.

Elizabeth and Richard retired to their bed for a brief time before dawn. They made love tenderly, sad in the knowledge that it could be sometime before they could enjoy being in each other's arms again. Elizabeth was determined to journey back to Hall the day after Richard left. He understood her wish to do that and was happy that she would be back on familiar ground to manage the Manor at Hall with able and trusted retainers. His own Bailiff, Ralph Purves, was entrusted with accompanying Elizabeth on the journey and ensuring her safe arrival.

Daybreak came all too soon. Filled with a mixture of pride, love and sadness, Elizabeth watched the small band ride away, with Richard on Grisel Gris at its head.

Chapter 7

Sheviock

As Alicia walked into the main hall at Sheviock Manor, the three men huddled round the table started guiltily and turned to look at her.

Her father rose from the end of the table, taking her hand and bidding her welcome.

"You know all present here Alicia; Canon Henry Bloyou from Exeter Cathedral, and Richard Wideslade, Rector of Cornwood. We are discussing a most serious issue which concerns you as a witness to events that these gentlemen are investigating."

Alicia looked puzzled and anxious but greeted the two churchmen politely and recounted the meeting with Richard and Elizabeth at Cornwood. Her father laughed.

"He will soon have more pressing issues than grazing rights to occupy him. With the help of our friends here, his marriage to Elizabeth Fitzwilliam will be declared illegal and a decree of divorce issued."

Alicia gasped. "But how and why? They are clearly happy together and to all accounts, their marriage was properly conducted."

Canon Bloyou spoke. "My dear, there are a number of good reasons why this marriage cannot be held lawful. First, as these papers show, Elizabeth Fitzwilliam was already betrothed to your brother Charles, and a marriage contract was signed."

"But ..." Alicia started to object but Canon Bloyou held up his hand.

"Hear me out, Alicia. I have here the original draft terms of marriage drawn up and signed by Sir John Fitzwilliam, God rest his soul, and your father. I also have a further document drawn up by your father entitled, 'Outstanding details of the marriage agreement.' This document is also signed by both parties and we are assured by your father and brother that, following some difficult negotiations, Sir John finally gave his assent to the marriage."

Alicia looked at her father in astonishment. He could not meet her direct gaze but said, very formally, "I am certain my daughter will add her testament to that of myself and my son." And then, suddenly fixing her with a fierce stare, added, "Isn't that so, Alicia." She nodded her head in mute response.

In the uncomfortable silence that followed, Richard Wideslade interjected. "The Bishop is satisfied that the grounds for the annulment are sound. He has signed the decree. It is unfortunate that a key witness, who was present when Sir John finally agreed to the marriage, is dead under mysterious circumstances. But that is a separate issue."

Alicia blanched and looked again at her father. "Do you mean the falconer," she said, her voice cracking.

"Yes indeed," said Canon Bloyou. "We understand he was present in the yard of Hall Manor early in the morning when the final document was signed and added his mark." He lifted the document and showed Alicia the roughly executed cross underneath the signatures.

"Now, Alicia," said Sir Robert. "Thank you for your testimony. Leave us now to conclude our discussions. We will talk again later and you can tell me about your visit to Cornwood."

"But father," she started to say, but the look that Sir Robert gave her stifled her response and she fled tearfully from the room.

"Now gentlemen, let us conclude our business. The signed documents and testimonies around the marriage agreement are in order and you have my daughter's statement so I assume that we can proceed?"

The two churchmen nodded. Both were dressed in black, and with similar, rather bird-like features—long noses and sleek dark hair—they resembled a couple of crows. Canon Bloyou clearly fed well, and his corpulence contrasted with the slighter but taller frame of Henry Wideslade.

"So, how soon can the decree be issued?" continued Sir Robert.

Canon Bloyou answered. "Given the Bishop's agreement, and the positive findings of our investigation, the decree will be issued immediately."

"Excellent." Sir Robert rubbed his hands. "And now gentlemen, the speed and diligence of your services should be rewarded. We agreed, I believe, that Canon Bloyou should become the beneficiary for life of all the land and revenues of my Cornwood manor, and that you, Parson Wideslade, shall be moved from Cornwood to the rich living of the parish at St Ives and have for life the dwelling and small parcel of Daunay land that adjoins the church there.

"As for Bishop Berkeley, please convey my felicitations and assure him that the gift of the manor at Aylebeare is given free of encumbrance, on the sole condition that prayers for the salvation of my soul are said on the first Sunday of each month following my death.

"All the necessary documents have been drawn up, witnessed by my bailiff and my son Charles, and can now be exchanged." He pushed a small stack of papers across the table. "Needless to say, my friends, these transactions are to be kept private between us."

The two crows nodded and smiled in unison.

"As I have told you, there may be the need for one or the other of you to deliver one more service for me to conclude this whole matter, but I will send for you when I am ready. Thank you again gentlemen and good day to you."

Alicia wandered across the courtyard into the stables. She needed time and space to collect herself; her mind was in a whirl. She was appalled that her father, for whom she had always had great respect, seemed to be indulging in fraud and trickery involving the two churchmen; both of whom, she knew, were dependent on his patronage for their living.

She could vividly recollect the events at Hall when they had quit the Manor so early in the morning.

It was true that her father and Charles had been in the yard saddling the horses, while she had still been getting herself ready inside, but she had seen no sign of Sir John. And why would Charles have so savagely slain the falconer if he had just witnessed the agreement to the marriage? And why had she only just been told about it? It didn't ring true or make any sense.

She realised that she now was a party to the deception. She had, through fear and confusion, implied that she had seen the signing of the agreement.

Her thoughts were interrupted by the sound of her father's voice calling her name from the yard outside. She went out to him and he took her hand.

"Come with me, Alicia; we need to talk." They walked out of the manor gate and across the lane to the churchyard. He led her to the stone seat that overlooked the family mausoleum. They sat and he gestured towards it.

"There is a long and proud history buried there, dear Alicia, and we owe it to our ancestors to ensure that the family of Daunay survives and prospers." He paused.

"At this moment, it falls on me to avert the possible dishonour and demise of our good name and fortune." Alicia felt her eyes widen in shock. "Sadly," he went on, "the combination of the rash and profligate behaviour of your brother Charles, and the growing tax demands from the crown, have reduced the financial viability of our estate to a dangerously low situation.

"I had hoped and prayed that the marriage of Elizabeth Fitzwilliam and your brother would more than restore our fortunes and at the same time, help Charles to mature and take ownership of his responsibilities. Alas, that night at Hall and the events of the following morning dashed my hopes and may forfeit Charles' his life. The chances of recovering the situation have been laid waste by Elizabeth's marriage to de Mohun."

He turned to face Alicia and took both her hands in his.

"We are on the edge of ruin, my dear. To avoid it, and to

save your brothers miserable skin, I must now stoop to deceit and subterfuge that I can barely contemplate." His voice shook with suppressed emotion, and he gripped her hands so tightly that she cried out and pulled away.

"Is that why you have been untruthful about the marriage agreement and are getting those two priests to declare Elizabeth's marriage illegal?"

"Yes, Alicia. I am sorry that I could not give you any warning but I'm afraid that, for the sake of the family and yourself, you have to be involved. I have conceived a plan that may save us all and restore our fortunes. The annulment of the marriage between Elizabeth and Richard de Mohun is but the first step and I need your support and your help with the next, more difficult and dangerous actions that we have to take."

"Oh Father, surely lies and deceit cannot make things better; you should not need to stoop so low for the sake of my profligate and unruly brother."

"If it were just Charles' folly that had to be dealt with I would agree with you dear Alicia, but it is not. We are all implicated by his evil actions, including you; and beyond that, I cannot stand by and see the Daunay family ruined, which it surely will be unless I act. I really have no choice." Sir Robert put his head in his hands in a gesture of despair.

Alicia had never before seen her father this way. He was usually so strong and confident. She was filled with sadness and compassion to see him brought so low. She touched his bowed head.

"Of course I will help and support you, my dear father," she said softly. "What is it that we have to do?"

He motioned her to sit close to him and in low and urgent tones he told her his plan, and the part she had to play in ensuring its success. Alicia was both appalled at the duplicity involved and at the same time, excited by the danger and the potential implications for her future life and happiness.

Chapter 8

Ugborough and Sheviock

In the early dawn light, Elizabeth took one last tour of the Manor and bade farewell to the servants. There was some consternation because Eric, the newly employed stable lad, and one of the brood mares were missing. He should have been saddling up the horses but was nowhere to be found. It was assumed that he had run away after getting the rough edge of Ralph's tongue, and a cuff round the head the previous day for failing to clean out properly. Ralph was very angry.

"If he's run back to Cornwood he can damn well stay there," he muttered. "I only took him on out of pity. He said both his mother and father had died and he had been turned out of his home and needed work."

The task of saddling up their two horses, Saxon and Magi, and the pack pony was quickly organised. Then, with Ralph leading the way, Elizabeth set off on the road home to Hall.

She was still feeling lonely and sad after Richard's departure for London and although excited at the thought of returning home to Hall, that too was overshadowed by the knowledge that her father would not be there to greet her.

Nevertheless, her spirits picked up as they left Ivybridge behind and with the rising sun on their backs, headed for Plymouth and the ferry.

Ralph was not the most communicative of people. As with many smaller men, he liked the power vested in him and as bailiff he was used to giving orders and cracking the whip over the farm labourers and servants. She knew that he was not too pleased to be acting as her chaperone and he was still fuming about the missing stable lad. He did, however, seem to be taking his duties seriously. He gruffly pointed out the boundary of de Mohun lands as they passed Lea Mill.

"Stay behind me now, my lady," he said, looking around him. "For a short while now we will be passing through Daunay lands and Sir Richard said we need to take extra care and avoid any trouble."

Elizabeth smiled but looked around her somewhat nervously, doing as he had asked and riding close behind him. After another couple of miles in silence, Ralph indicated they were in the clear and she rode up alongside him.

"Thank you for your protection, Ralph. It is comforting to have you with me although I expect you would rather be about your work at Ugborough. My husband told me that you were the only man he would trust to deliver me safe to my home."

Ralph visibly responded to the flattery, sitting taller and puffing out his chest. "Thank you, my lady. I shall not betray his trust."

A few minutes later, a lone horseman came into view riding toward them.

As he came nearer Ralph said, "It's Wideslade, the parson from Cornwood. Have a care, my lady; he is a sly fox and a gossip, and Daunay dependent. No doubt he will want to pry."

To their surprise, however, Wideslade simply rode by, eyes averted, totally ignoring their existence.

"Good day, Parson Wideslade," Ralph shouted at his retreating back. Without looking round, Wideslade raised a limp hand in acknowledgement and continued to ride away.

"Not quite the gossip you described," said Elizabeth, laughing.

"Very strange," said Ralph, "he must have some very weighty matter on his mind; I've never known him to pass by the chance of finding out whose who and what's what, in case he can learn something to his advantage."

The road they were travelling was well used, leading as it did to the growing and thriving port of Plymouth. They would pass the priory at Plympton, skirt round the silted and muddy mouth of the river Plym, and head for the ferry boat that plied between Devil's Point and Cremyll on the far side of the Tamar. Richard had suggested this route to enable them to travel along the coast road, skirting to the south of Sheviock and thus minimise the chances of meeting with any of the Daunay family.

They made good time, and just before noon they were on the water's edge at Devil's Point, partaking of refreshment while waiting for the ferry boat to return from Cremyll.

The sea was calm albeit with a strong, tidal flow through the small gap separating The Sound from the Tamar River. Elizabeth was glad to see and taste the salty air again and her spirits continued to rise as she got nearer to her home.

At Sheviock there was tension and suppressed excitement. Eric, the stable lad from Ugborough, had ridden exhausted into the Daunay compound an hour since, with the news that Lady Elizabeth and her bailiff were on the way to Hall and would be travelling by way of the Cremyll ferry and the coast road.

"I come by the boat myself and if they made good time they could be on the next trip over, so they will be into Cremyll very soon now, I reckon." Eric was given food and drink and promptly fell asleep.

Sir Robert indulged in a little self congratulation at having had the foresight to put his spy into the Mohun household. This was the chance that he had been waiting for, even though it was a little sooner than he had expected.

He issued his instructions and within the hour, everything was organised. Alicia, escorted by Armand and a small band of armed riders, had galloped off towards Pelynt. All he had to do now was wait.

"Not too far to go now, my lady." Ralph spoke over his shoulder as they crested the hill that they had climbed from Downderry on the coast.

"I think we will just about reach Hall before night fall, but even if we are delayed, the moon is near full and should light our path well enough."

At the old stone cross on the junction of the paths, he turned left onto the track through Hessenford woods, towards Pelynt.

Elizabeth paused for a few moments at the top of the hill to look back at the coastal view. When she turned to follow Ralph into the woods, she was suddenly confused. There was no sign of Ralph on the trail in front of her; he and his horse, Saxon, and the pack pony had vanished.

The thick woodland had reduced the afternoon light and it was somewhat gloomy but not dark; visibility was still good enough for her to see some two hundred paces in front of her, and there was nothing but a straight and empty track.

She reigned in and stood silent, listening. Nothing moved. She called out rather tremulously. "Ralph?" Still no sound. She shouted then, her voice seeming to echo back from the surrounding trees, then silence again. She spurred Magi on but he skittered, pricked his ears and refused to go forward.

Frightened now, Elizabeth turned to ride back out of the wood. Then she saw, to her dismay, that the path was barred by three figures on horseback. The figure in the centre threw back the hood of its cloak and she realised, with some relief, that it was Alicia Daunay.

"Alicia! What are you doing here?" Elizabeth rode a couple of paces toward her. "What is going on? Where is Ralph?"

"Don't worry, Elizabeth, you are safe. We have come to look after you. You shall come with us to Sheviock now, where my father will talk to you and explain everything." Alicia spoke softly and at the same time, rode forward and touched Elizabeth gently on the arm, trying to reassure her. Elizabeth pulled away from her angrily.

"What do you mean, I am safe now? I was in no danger. Where is Ralph? I have no desire to talk with your father. I am going home to Hall."

She turned her horse again and went forward a couple of paces before three more horsemen emerged from the dense woodland. To her horror, they were leading Ralph, who was bound and gagged and slung face down across his saddle. Blood was dripping from a deep cut on the side of his face. At first she thought that he was dead but he twisted his head and looked at her with eyes that spoke eloquently of his anger and frustration.

"What have you done to him?" shouted Elizabeth. "Set him free, immediately. Alicia, what are you doing with this band of thieves? Tell them to let him loose and allow us to continue our journey."

As she spoke she dismounted and went toward Ralph, but before she could take more than a couple of steps, she was stopped in her tracks by one of the men, who leapt from his horse and grabbed her by the arms, roughly turning her round to face Alicia.

Alicia was ashen faced and trembling but spoke firmly enough. "Elizabeth, I am sorry, but for your own good you must come with us back to Sheviock. There are things you need to know and my father has ordered these men to ensure your attendance. Rest assured you will be well treated and your bailiff will receive attention to his wounds; although his pride is more damaged than his body."

Elizabeth looked wildly around her. She realised with a sense of hopelessness that there was no way out of this. There was nowhere to run even if she tried. She struggled to be free of the man who was holding her.

Alicia said, "Let her go, Armand." He let go her arms and stepped back. Elizabeth recognised him as one of the Daunay servants who had been at Hall.

"Come, Elizabeth," Alicia pleaded. "The sooner we get back to Sheviock and you speak with my father the better it will be, and you will realise that this is all for your own good. Get back on your horse and ride with us."

Elizabeth glared at Alicia but she had recovered some of her composure, realising that Alicia was herself under some strain and was not comfortable with the situation. She decided that she had no option but to comply for now but would keep herself prepared for flight if the chance arose.

"I will come," she said, "but know well that I come against my wishes, and regard this attack on me and my bailiff as cowardly and unworthy of you and your family. I come only on the condition that you loose the bonds on Ralph and allow him to ride with me."

Alicia glanced at Armand who nodded his head and she

ordered that Ralph be untied.

Within a few minutes, both Elizabeth and Ralph were remounted. Ralph was still looking the worse for wear with the cut on his face oozing blood, but he had regained some dignity and smiled lopsidedly at Elizabeth.

"My thanks, my lady; let us see what these wretches want."

The group set off in the direction of Sheviock, with Elizabeth and Ralph closely guarded by Daunay men and Alicia leading the way.

In less than forty minutes they rode past the church and into the courtyard of Sheviock Manor. Large wooden gates were closed behind them and the small group of horsemen dispersed around the perimeter of the yard. Alicia dismounted and signalled to Elizabeth to do the same.

"Come," she said, "you must be tired and hungry after your long ride. My father will talk with you while you eat and rest."

Elizabeth sat firm. "Your father shall come to me and say what he means by ordering this unlawful act of abduction, and then we shall proceed on our way to Hall."

She spoke with strength of purpose that she did not feel. She knew that it was unlikely that they would be allowed to leave after being caught in an obviously well prepared trap but she was determined not to show her fear.

"For now, please honour your promise and have Ralph attended to and his wound cleaned and treated with salve."

"Do as she says." A voice she knew and dreaded rang out behind her. Sir Robert Daunay emerged from the manor. At his command, the man she knew as Armand, who had manhandled her so roughly, came forward and motioned Ralph to dismount.

Ralph looked at Elizabeth. "My place is with you, my lady; my wound can wait."

"No, Ralph. If you are to serve me well, go with them. Have them tend your wound then rest here tonight. I will hear what Sir Robert has to say and then, if you are recovered, we will leave in the morning for Hall."

"But, my lady …"

Sir Robert raised his voice. "Do as Lady Elizabeth bids you and you shall come to no harm."

Elizabeth nodded to Ralph and reluctantly he dismounted. Staggering and disorientated, he was supported by Armand and disappeared into the manor.

Sir Robert came up to Elizabeth and took hold of her bridle.

"My lady, I am truly sorry for the manner of your arrival here but I had no choice. Your safety is foremost in my mind." He held out his hand to her.

"Please, come with me and I will explain the circumstances that have brought you here."

Elizabeth hesitated but the events of the day caught up with her and she was suddenly engulfed by weariness. She allowed Sir Robert to help her to dismount and they went together into the manor, followed by Alicia.

Inside the great hall of the manor, Alicia took her hand. "Come with me, Elizabeth; you need to rest and compose yourself and then we will take some refreshment while my father talks to you." Elizabeth tried to protest but allowed herself to be led to Alicia's bed chamber.

Once there, Alicia helped her out of her cloak and shoes and rather proudly showed her the recently installed turret privy and sluice.

"I will leave you for a while, so that you have some privacy and time to collect yourself. I will be close by, so call if you want for anything."

As soon as she left, Elizabeth slumped into a chair and gave way to her repressed emotions of helplessness and fear. Shaking and shivering, she cried silently for several minutes, praying for courage, the opportunity to escape, and a way to get word of her plight to Richard. Wearily she climbed the steps to the bed and within minutes, she was asleep.

Alicia let her rest for a couple of hours, then woke her and together with her maid, helped Elizabeth to wash and tend her hair and change into a fresh dress that had been recovered from a pannier on her packhorse.

In the solar, Sir Robert sat at a large table with a number of documents in front of him. Some platters of cold meats and cornbread, together with flagons of ale, were laid ready. As Alicia and Elizabeth entered, he motioned Elizabeth to sit opposite him and Alicia to sit next to her.

"Elizabeth my dear, I trust you feel better now you have rested? Please, eat your fill, you must be famished."

Elizabeth waved the food away. "The only hunger I have is to be free and back in my own home at Hall. If you have something you wish to say to me, apart from an apology and an explanation of your conduct, then say it and let us have done with it."

Sir Robert frowned, fixed her with his piercing gaze and cleared his throat.

"Elizabeth, what I have to tell you will come as a great shock and will be hard for you to bear; but I ask you please to hear me out and suspend your disbelief until I have told you all. Firstly, you must understand that your marriage to Richard de Mohun has been adjudged illegal and has been dissolved by order of Bishop Berkeley of Exeter. I have a signed copy of the document here." He pushed a parchment roll towards her across the table.

The blood drained from Elizabeth's face. She looked at him uncomprehendingly, unable to speak.

Alicia put an arm round her. "I am so sorry; this must be a dreadful shock."

Elizabeth pushed her arm away and stood up. "What do you hope to gain by this?" She threw the parchment roll back at Sir Robert. "This is trickery. I demand you let me go this instant!"

Sir Robert looked at her and said softly, but with underlying menace, "Sit down, Elizabeth. You are going nowhere, there is more that you need to hear. You were not free to wed de Mohun because you were already affianced to my son. I have here signed and witnessed documents that set out the marriage terms."

"That is nonsense," said Elizabeth, close to tears. "You know full well that my father refused to sign that document, and you, Alicia, you were there."

"That is true," said Sir Robert. "In the evening, because of some poisonous slander fed to him by Richard de Mohun, your father decided to delay the agreement; but overnight he thought better of it and early the next morning, as we were readying our horses, he signed the document and had his falconer witness the document with his mark. Here, see for yourself." He again pushed the roll of documents across the table to Elizabeth. "The agreement is attached to the marriage dissolution."

This time, with trembling hands, Elizabeth undid the ribbon, smoothed out the parchments and studied them. As she did so, Sir Robert and Alicia exchanged glances. Elizabeth paled as she read the dissolution and studied the signatures and seals. She looked up and with great control, looked Sir Robert straight in the eyes.

"These are false documents. That is not my father's signature and as you well know, you murdered the poor falconer that morning and fled. If it were true that my father changed his mind, he would have told me. I do not know how you persuaded the Bishop to sign this, or what you hope to gain, but it is a lie and I will see that you are brought to justice."

"Elizabeth, I understand your distress and anger. I did tell you that what I had to say would come as a shock. I'm afraid that you have to understand that you have been cruelly deceived and used. Not by us, but by the rogue de Mohun.

"Let me enlighten you. First you say that your father would have told you that he signed our agreement; but he told us, and Alicia will confirm this, that he did not want you to know about the arrangement until he had time to explain the reasoning for his final decision to you. Before he could do so, his falconer was murdered and the foul deed was blamed on us.

"Then it seems that Mohun, after visiting us briefly at Boconnoc, managed to convince you both that my son Charles was indeed the assassin, then moved in indecent haste to secure your hand and fortune."

"But this is a travesty of the truth," Elizabeth said in protest. "You—"

Sir Robert put up a hand to stifle her response.

"Think back, Elizabeth. Just for a moment, think about what happened. Richard de Mohun arrived at Hall unannounced, supposedly by chance, on the very day that we were visiting your father to conclude the marriage agreement.

"He goes out of his way to stop your father from giving his final approval by trumping up some story against us. Then, finding out that it has been of no avail, he slaughters your falconer and throws suspicion on us.

"He rides to Boconnoc on some pretext of warning us of a killer outlaw and returns to tell you that my son is the murderer. He very quickly worms his way into your father's confidence and your affections. Then, within a matter of days, having sensed your father's imminent demise, which maybe he hastened, he rushes through your marriage and ensures the de Mohun claim on your estates.

"You have been most cruelly used Lady Elizabeth, and now you are in mortal danger."

"Shame on you, Sir Robert; you have twisted the truth to suit your own ends. Your monstrous lies can be exposed for what they are as soon as my husband returns. You must know that we have the evidence of your son's guilt."

Elizabeth's voice shook with the combined emotions of anger and fear. "And you, Alicia; are you not ashamed to lend credulity to this wretched—"

"What evidence?" Sir Robert demanded. "You have no evidence."

"Indeed we have. My husband carries it with him, ready to bring Charles to justice as soon as he catches up with him. Now, enough of this, I am in no danger. I demand that you release me and let me return to Hall."

Sir Robert sat back and gave a twisted smile. "If you so wish, you shall leave in the morning. It is now dark, so use the time wisely. Eat, drink and sleep and reflect upon my words. Maybe you will realise that my version of events is the true version and your perceptions are coloured by your infatuation.

"You must realise that the only part of you that de Mohun desires is your fortune and that you are an expendable impediment to his ambition. We had no reason to detain you other than to save your life.

"The marriage agreement between you and Charles is now worthless. You are tainted goods and Charles can find a thousand better matches. If it was not for Alicia's concern for you, we would have left you to your fate." With that, Sir Robert nodded to Alicia, left the solar and went down the stairs to the great hall.

Alicia took Elizabeth's hand. "Come Elizabeth; you would do well to heed my father. We have your interests at heart and would not want you to come to harm. You should take some refreshment and then rest for your journey to Hall tomorrow."

Elizabeth had been shaken by Sir Robert's words. She had assumed that the reason for her capture, and the elaborate trickery of the marriage dissolution and the forged agreement, was to pursue the Daunay ambition of gaining her hand in marriage to Charles. The fact that Sir Robert had eschewed that ambition had left her confused.

The fact that she was being allowed to go home to Hall was a huge relief. Nevertheless, she felt she needed to be on her guard.

"Thank you, Alicia; but first I want to see Ralph, to be certain that he has been well attended to and to be sure that he can accompany me tomorrow morning."

They went down to the servants' kitchen and Elizabeth was relieved to see Ralph sitting on a stool by the open fire. His wound had been cleaned and although ugly and covered with a greasy salve, did not look too debilitating. He stood up as soon as he saw Elizabeth.

"Have they treated you well, Ralph? We are to be released in the morning. Are you recovered enough to ride with me?"

"Indeed, my lady. I have been treated well enough, excepting that we should not be here at all. I am sorry that I could not protect you more."

"We will ride at daybreak, then. Rest well Ralph, and do not worry; you did all you could."

"Now, Alicia, I should like some refreshment before I retire."

They returned to the solar and Elizabeth, with some of her spirits restored, ate and drank a little of the repast that had been set out. When she retired to Alicia's bedroom, she lay half awake for a long time, pondering the events of the past weeks and trying to make sense of everything. Was there any credence to Sir Robert's actions and explanations?

In her heart she knew they were false but she recognised that to anyone removed from the actual events, they could appear to be credible. The speed at which everything had happened, the fact that Richard had been the instigator of the doubts about the Daunays and the deliverer of the evidence of

Charles' guilt in the murder of the falconer ...

Elizabeth was suddenly jolted wide awake. The evidence, the bloodstained sleeve and the feather, it wasn't real evidence; it could have come from anywhere. The blood could belong to anyone. There was only Richard's word that it had come from Boconnoc! But now she had told Sir Robert that Richard was carrying the evidence, and it had provoked a strong reaction. If they were guilty, they would be desperate to destroy it. It was Richard that was in danger!

She realised that somehow, she needed to get word to Richard, let him know what had happened to her and warn him to be on his guard.

She knew then that they would not let her go back home to Hall. If the Daunay's were guilty, she would be detained until any evidence was destroyed or discredited .She was still wrestling with these thoughts when sleep overcame her.

In the Great Hall, Sir Robert was giving final instructions to Alicia and Armand.

"Alicia, you will ensure that they leave at daybreak and make certain that they are observed to be leaving by at least some of the servants.

"Armand, you and two of your men at arms will leave well before dawn, conceal yourselves on the edge of Sheviock woods and wait. When they reach you, do not attempt parlay or entertain thoughts of chivalry. Kill the bailiff and secure Lady Elizabeth. Make sure that she is blindfold, gagged and securely tied. Bury the bailiff's body in the wood and then take Lady Elizabeth downstream to the river. John Tavy will be waiting at the jetty with his boat, and all of you will go with him to help guard Lady Elizabeth until I arrive."

Armand raised a hand. "Where is it that we should take her?"

"Better for now that you do not know," said Sir Robert. "John Tavy will instruct you.

"When you reach your destination, Lady Elizabeth is to be kept under lock and key and if she escapes, have no doubt you will pay with your life. Go now and prepare yourselves. Remember; no one is to know of this, save those directly involved."

When Armand had left, Alicia gripped her father's arm. "Father, are you certain that this is the only way? I am fearful of the consequences for us all if this plan should fail. I know it is against your instincts and nature to act in this way."

"You are right, Alicia, but we have no choice. I am acting to save the honour and prosperity of our family. I wish it was not so, but it is. Remember, you have an important role to play when we move to the next step. We must learn quickly what specific evidence Richard Mohun claims to have and where it is hidden. You have to gain that information from Elizabeth.

"When you get to Elyot later today, be ready to absorb her anger and then try to gain her trust. You will need to be subtle. She must think that you are a friend and that you will help her.

"Henry Denyss and the priest Wideslade have been summoned to Elyot and should be with us tonight. We will conduct the marriage immediately when all are present.

"Tomorrow I ride to London. The bride will go with you to Arworthal, Denyss will go back to his sick bed and our fortunes will, once again, be secure.

"Then we await Mohun's response."

Chapter 9

Sheviock, St Germans

The cockerel in the farmyard heralded the new day. Elizabeth shivered in the cool, morning breeze blowing in from the sea while Ralph checked the pack horse load. Satisfied, he gave a nod and they moved off toward the gateway.

Apart from a couple of the kitchen servants, Alicia alone had come to see them leave. She looked pale and anxious. "Go safely and God be with you Elizabeth; dwell on that which my father told you, do not be blinded by love."

" You too, Alicia," Elizabeth retorted sharply. "A daughter's duty to her father should not be tested so. I had respect for your father if not for your brother, but now I have only contempt. I am sorry, but as long as you aid your father's lies we cannot be the friends that we might have been."

She and Ralph rode out onto the lane and turned toward Pelynt. As soon as they had ridden round the first bend in the road and were well out of sight of the manor and Alicia's gaze, Elizabeth reigned in and turned to Ralph.

"I fear that we may not reach Hall in safety. I do not believe after all that has happened that they will let us go so easily." She spoke rapidly but succinctly and told him of all that had transpired during the previous evening; the marriage dissolution, her inadvertent revelation of possible evidence against Charles, and the danger that Richard might now face. Ralph's face betrayed his shock and concern.

"Ralph," Elizabeth continued, "I know you will protest but I must command you to leave me here now and ride with caution but all possible speed to London. Seek out Sir Richard and tell him of all that has happened in his absence."

"But, my lady, I cannot leave you. I am charged by Sir Richard with your life and safety. If I leave you now and some harm befalls you, then it is I that he will blame. I will lose my livelihood at least and maybe my life."

"I understand your charge over me but I am certain that when Sir Richard hears of all the circumstances, he will absolve you of any blame," Elizabeth assured him. "This is a command from me, not a request." Taking her wedding ring from her finger, she gave it to Ralph.

"Take this to him, to prove my need of him and my trust in you. You have no time to lose. I do not know what is planned for us but I feel that my liberty and your life are in jeopardy."

"Then ride with me, my lady; let us both escape together and return to Ugborough, or even to Dunster."

Elizabeth shook her head. "If I ride with you we will be more conspicuous and I will slow you down. Alone you stand a chance. You need guile and luck but if anyone can succeed in this, I believe it is you. Go, please; find my husband and bring him to my rescue."

Her emotion and flattery finally won through. Ralph tucked the ring into a pocket of his jerkin and nodded.

"My lady, I will do as you bid me. With God's grace you will arrive safe at Hall and my journey will not have been necessary."

"God bless and protect you, Ralph. You must decide your own plan but if you could reach Tavistock, Sir Richard's brother, Lawrence, can offer shelter and support. Now go, and God speed!"

Ralph turned down the farm track toward the tree line and the river, and quickly disappeared from view.

Elizabeth felt very alone and, for a moment, was tempted to follow him; but she resolutely spurred her horse forward, pulling the little pack pony with her.

Armand and his two men at arms sat on their horses, motionless and well concealed in the shadows of the wood. Armand, with his flaxen hair and blue eyes, looked at first glance, younger than his twenty seven years. His mouth, though, was thin lipped and when he smiled it exposed badly decayed and broken teeth, betraying that first impression.

His two men at arms, Gregor and Harald, were the sons of the Daunay armourer and only recently recruited for service. They were inexperienced and untried, and Armand knew that killing Ralph would be down to him; a thought that caused him to smile. The task of securing Lady Elizabeth he would delegate.

The sound of hooves on the track alerted them and he held up his hand in warning. A look of puzzlement crossed his face as he observed the figure of Lady Elizabeth coming into view, apparently riding alone and leading her pack horse. He gestured to Gregor and Harald to stay still and wait.

Ralph, he thought, must be some way behind but then, as Lady Elizabeth passed their hiding place, there was still no sign of her escort. Armand made the decision and all three spurred their horses out onto the track some twenty yards behind her.

They were on her before she could react to the noise of their pursuit. She did not even see them before the coarse hempen sack was over her head and she was roughly hauled to the ground. No words were spoken as her hands and legs were bound with strong twine and the neck of the sack was secured around her waist, rendering her blind and helpless. She screamed in panic but knew that no one was going to come to her aid. She knew too that all her fears and premonitions had been justified.

"Where is the damned bailiff?" A voice she recognised as that of Armand bellowed close to her ear. She didn't answer. Armand turned to the men at arms.

"I will ride to the manor to see what has happened. You two take her and go to the quay. I will meet you there. Tell the boatman to wait until I arrive. Keep a sharp lookout for the bailiff. If you see him, kill him before he kills you."

Gregor and Harald exchanged glances and looked nervously around them but without a word, Elizabeth was quickly and unceremoniously dumped face downwards across the back of her horse and led away through the wood. She could hear the sound of the stream alongside the path.

Armand was back at Sheviock in minutes and quickly learned from a distraught Alicia that Elizabeth and Ralph had ridden away from the Manor together and had given no sign that they suspected a trap.

Sir Robert was angry but philosophical. "We will stick to our plan, but we need to be doubly vigilant in case the bailiff is going to attempt some daring rescue, though it is more likely that he will try to return to Ugborough and raise the alarm.

"Armand, get back to the quay immediately and get Lady Elizabeth on the boat. During the journey, try to find out where Ralph is headed. Use whatever means you can but she is not to be harmed. Send Harald to ride now to Cremyll, to find out if he has already crossed on the ferry, then return to the priory at St Germans to tell us.

"Send Gregor to Boconnoc, to inform my son Charles that he is to return to Sheviock immediately. Gregor should accompany him back there and they should both await my return and prepare to go in pursuit of The Mohun bailiff. Do you understand?" Armand nodded, saluted, and rode off at a gallop towards the river.

Ralph, after reluctantly leaving Elizabeth, had ridden down the farm track, then turned into the woods, instinctively seeking cover. Within minutes he was facing the broad Lynher river. He was unfamiliar with the detail of the terrain but knew that it was going to be difficult to find his way out of the Daunay estate without being detected.

Going back to the Cremyll ferry was his first thought, but he was sure that if they knew he had separated from Lady Elizabeth they would be expecting him to do that and would be waiting for him there. He sat quietly, trying to think about his options. Going north would mean going round or across the river. Behind him to the south was the sea; to the east was Sheviock, to be avoided at all costs, and riding west would take him away from his destination and into the woods where they had been ambushed yesterday.

He liked the idea of making for Tavistock, as Lady

Elizabeth had suggested, to seek out Lawrence de Mohun. He would need fresh horses and even if he failed to reach London safely, he would be able to acquaint Lawrence with all that had happened. Tavistock, though, was to the north, so somehow he had to cross the river.

As he came to this conclusion, he heard someone riding at a full gallop on the farm track. Surely he had not been seen already? He quickly dismounted and led his horse into a thicket of alders and reeds by the river bank. Peering out through the leaves, he recognised Armand riding hell for leather. To Ralph's relief, Armand passed his hiding place without a glance but he tensed again as he heard the noise of the hooves slowing to a trot and then to a stop. After a few moments, he heard voices and what sounded like urgent commands. Then, just as he was about to cautiously move forward, two riders galloped by, this time headed for Sheviock.

Ralph tethered his horse to a low branch and crept forward towards the point where he could still hear voices. He came to the edge of a large clearing and wriggled forward on his stomach until he had a clear view. Directly in front of him, about twenty paces away, he could see a small wooden jetty alongside the junction of a wide stream that came down from the wood and joined the Lynher River.

Armand was standing on the jetty, talking to a boatman on a sturdy raft rigged with a single square sail and tied up to the quay. Then, with a shock, he saw Lady Elizabeth's horse grazing on the far edge of the clearing; he recognised its distinctive white forelock. The little pack horse was also visible, tethered to a fallen tree. There was no sign of Lady Elizabeth.

He contemplated rushing Armand but realised that it would probably be a futile gesture and might finish his chances of getting help for Lady Elizabeth, if she was still alive.

As he watched, the boatman manoeuvred the raft around the end of the quay into the shore, and roped the vessel to a large tree trunk. Armand collected the pack horse and led it back to the water's edge.

He rode onto the raft and secured his own horse together with the pack horse in a crude stall in the centre of the vessel. Finally, he returned to the shore and picked up a bundle which had been lying in bushes on the edge of the wood, out of Ralph's sight. As he carried it toward the raft, Ralph could see tresses of golden hair trailing down from Armand's arms and realised that the bundle was Elizabeth. She was dumped onto the deck in a sitting position with her back to the mast, and was secured there with a cord around her already bound and trussed body.

Again Ralph had to restrain his instinct to run forward and try to release her. Armand called to the boatman.

"Let's get this journey done, this raft leaks like a bucket with a hole in it. I will be thankful to get to Port Priory safe and dry."

The boatman muttered something that Ralph did not catch, unhitched the rope from the tree and used a long pole to push back from the shore. Sliding a single broad oar over a rigger at the rear of the raft, he used it to both propel and steer. The sail filled with a light breeze and the unwieldy looking vessel moved off up river at a surprisingly fast pace.

Ralph edged back into the cover of the trees and stood up. At least he now knew where Elizabeth was being taken to. He knew of the church and the monastery at St Germans, sometimes called Port Priory.

He had to make a decision quickly. Should he try to follow Elizabeth and attempt her rescue, or do as she had ordered and go to London?

The likelihood of single handedly freeing Lady Elizabeth and then escaping with her seemed remote, so he stuck with the idea of crossing the river somehow and riding north toward Tavistock. He had noticed that the Lynher River in front of him was near the peak of high tide. If he could catch it on the turn, it might just be possible to swim across at the narrowest point. He could just make out what looked like a farm building on the far bank and a track leading down to the water's edge.

His first action was to collect Elizabeth's palfrey, Magi. At least he would have a spare mount if something went wrong. Magi came willingly enough and he then retrieved Saxon from the thicket and led them to the water's edge. He had worked with Saxon for some six years on the estate at Ugborough and the horse was used to wading through streams and sometimes flooded meadows, but he had never asked it to swim before.

For several minutes he watched the flow of the river very carefully and then, as it perceptibly slackened, he took off his tunic and his boots and put them in his saddle bag. Then, making sure that Lady Elizabeth's ring was secure, he mounted and gently urged Saxon forward into the shallow but muddy edge of the river, leading Magi behind him.

As he went forward, Saxon slipped a little in the mud and tried to pull back, but Ralph spoke to him softly and caressed his neck while firmly spurring him forward. In only a couple more paces, both horses had lost contact with the river bed and with ears pricked and soft whinnies of fright, they were afloat and swimming. Ralph leaned forward, virtually lying on Saxon's back and talked him forward.

As they progressed further out into the river, the tide was still running very gently upstream toward St Germans but slackening all the time.

Ralph dreaded it turning too soon. If he miscalculated, the ebb current would sweep them past the promontory on the opposite bank and out into the estuary. The horses, nostrils flaring and eyes rolling, were swimming for their lives and making good progress. Soon Ralph could sense that they were out of the main current and swimming in virtually still water toward the shoreline, almost dead on line toward the track that had been his target.

As the horses struggled through the thick mud to reach firm ground again, Ralph offered up a prayer of thanks for his safe crossing.

Leaving Saxon and Magi to graze and recover in a small grassy area, concealed from the river by an ancient earthwork, Ralph walked barefoot up the track toward the farm building. As he drew near he could see, with some relief, that it was a derelict and tumbledown byre with no sign of habitation. He returned to the horses, unhitched his saddle and saddlebag, stripped off all his clothes and set everything out on the ground to dry in the strong noonday sun.

Sitting naked, he rested and took stock. He was over the first barrier of the river and now needed to head north to Tavistock as fast as possible. He estimated that if he was lucky and found good tracks, he should strike the Liskeard to

Tavistock road in about fifteen miles. Allowing another six or seven miles into Tavistock itself, he could possibly be there before nightfall.

Chapter 10

St Germans Abbey and Church

Elizabeth sat shaking with anger, fear, and cold on a stone bench, in a monks cell in the Monastery at St Germans. The stout oak door was firmly locked and a tiny window high up on the wall was barred, letting in only a sliver of dull light.

At least her bonds had been loosed, and she had rubbed her chafed arms, wrists, and ankles to get her blood flowing again after the painful hours she had endured since being captured. Her screams and curses when her gag had been removed by Armand had provoked no reaction.

Closing the door, he simply grinned and said, "Save your breath and remember you are in a house of God."

She knew where she was. Armand had removed the sack from her head when she was on the boat and she had recognised the priory at St Germans as they had landed. She remembered the monastery building adjoining the huge Norman Cathedral. Her father had brought her here to pray after her mother died. They had attended a mass conducted by the Bishop of Exeter.

She consoled herself with the thought that she had made the right decision in ordering Ralph to try to get to London and find Richard. She had also been right to think that the Daunays could not allow her to go free.

Armand had alternately threatened and cajoled her in a

futile attempt to get her to tell him where Ralph had gone, but she had refused to speak and he soon gave up trying, replacing her gag.

An hour later she heard voices outside her cell. The door was unbolted and Alicia came in, followed by Armand who was carrying a small wicker basket with water, wine and bread. Alicia motioned for him to put the basket down and leave.

"Are you sure, Lady Alicia?" he said.

"Yes Armand, I will be alright. Just bolt the door, wait outside and I will call when I am ready to leave."

Armand nodded and went out, closing the door behind him.

Elizabeth remained seated and glared at Alicia. "Are you not afraid that I will attack you?" she said. "Because that is what I would like to do."

"Apart from assuaging your anger, what good would it do you," said Alicia softly. "I have come to see how I can help you get out of here and home to Hall. Before we talk, you must drink and eat. You must be famished."

She reached into the basket and took out the wine flagon, poured some into a drinking cup, added some water and passed it to Elizabeth, who drank greedily and held out the cup for more. When she had drained it for the second time, she put it down and stood up to face Alicia.

"I do not believe that you can or indeed want to help me. I do not know what you and your father want from me, or your purpose in fabricating the lies about my betrothal to Charles. Why are you trying to implicate my husband in the horrible murder of Leofric, our falconer? I can only assume that it is to divert attention away from your brother's evil crime. I have no trust in anything you say."

Alicia could not hold her gaze and moved away to sit down on the stone bench. "I am afraid that the shock of all this has clouded your good judgement," she murmured. "You must know that what my father said rings true. Why would you possibly think that Charles killed your falconer?"

"I do not think it; I know it, *I know it.*" Elizabeth was suddenly flushed and staggered slightly. "We have proof," she said, her voice catching. "We have proof, we have ..."

She started to cry, and her breathing became shallow and rapid. She lurched towards Alicia and sank down onto the bench.

Alicia shook her and spoke urgently. "What proof? Tell me, Elizabeth. If you really have proof, I will go against my father and help to bring my brother to justice. You must tell me." Elizabeth tried to struggle to her feet again but couldn't. She opened her mouth but no words came out. Alicia, alarmed and frustrated, shouted at her.

"Come on Elizabeth; what proof and where is it?" But Elizabeth's eyes had closed and she appeared to be in a deep sleep. Alicia banged on the door of the cell and shouted for Armand. When he entered Alicia berated him.

"I said a drop of henbane, just enough to dull her wits. How much did you use? She drank two draughts of the wine but she should not have collapsed like this. If you have killed her, God help you."

Armand looked shocked but he checked Elizabeth's breathing and lay her down on the rush strewn floor.

"She will be alright," he said. "I only used a small amount of tincture. She will sleep heavily for a while but will recover soon enough." He ran out but returned a minute later with a rough blanket retrieved from a nearby cell and covered Elizabeth with it. "I suggest we leave her now, Lady Alicia. In half an hour we will take her up to the church and await your Father."

Sir Robert looked with some distaste at the man facing him across the table in the prior's office. Tall, but emaciated and gaunt, his previously thick head of hair reduced to a few straggling grey tufts, Henry Denyss was clearly in the later stages of the wasting disease that seemed to claim so many lives. His wife Joan and his son Cedric had died of the same disease the previous year. Once an industrious and respected merchant of provisions and cloth in Liskeard, he was now too ill to trade and slowly dying in poverty on his modest estate, adjoining the Sheviock land at Polbathic. His clouded blue eyes struggled to focus on the paper put in front of him by Sir Robert.

"So, Sir Robert; if I do as you wish, you will administer my estate, such as it is, and see that I am laid to rest next to my beloved wife and son? You will endow the church here at St

Germans with a gift in my name sufficient for a memorial stone, and ensure that prayers are said for my soul on the first Sunday of each month for the next five years?"

Sir Robert nodded. "All that, I will swear on oath, witnessed by my priest who attends me here."

"And for this service, I am to agree to enter into a marriage of convenience with Elizabeth Fitzwilliam. She will consent to marry and care for me until I die because she is disgraced and has no hope for the future, save your generosity?"

"Yes, Henry; that is the bargain."

"To conclude our bargain, I am to sign these papers that you have put in front of me, passing all my estates to you?" He paused.

"Sir Robert, I do not know what it is you expect to gain from this, although I have an idea. But, you have shown me kindness and patronage in happier times so I will agree. I have no one to manage my affairs or tend to me in the little time left before I depart this life, so let us proceed without delay."

Sir Robert visibly relaxed. He opened the door and summoned Parson Wideslade into the room.

"We have concluded our business and need you now to witness our signatures to the agreement." Wideslade nodded and all three added their signatures to the documents on the table. Sir Robert collected the papers together and placed them carefully in the drawer in the table.

"We should proceed now to the church where Lady Elizabeth awaits us."

With Henry Denyss leaning heavily on his stick and supported by the priest, they made their way slowly up the path.

Lady Elizabeth was already waiting, flanked on either side by Alicia and Armand. Barely conscious, she stared glassy eyed at the group entering the chapel. Henry Denyss turned to Sir Robert.

"You are sure she is a willing party to this marriage?" He queried.

"Do not concern yourself," said Sir Robert sharply. "She is distraught and full of remorse about her illegal marriage and subsequent divorce, but knows that this is her best hope of survival and salvation." He beckoned to the priest.

"Come, Wideslade," ordered Richard, "let us proceed quickly and get this matter settled."

Wideslade moved to the centre of the aisle and motioned for Henry and Elizabeth to be aided to stand in front of him.

"Do you take this woman, Lady Elizabeth Fitzwilliam, to be your wife?" he asked. Henry Denyss affirmed with a nod and a barely audible response.

"And do you, Lady Elizabeth Fitzwilliam, take this man, Henry Denyss to be your husband?" Elizabeth gazed at him blankly but shook her head.

"She is too overcome to speak," said Alicia, "but has instructed me to speak for her, and her answer is yes."

Wideslade hesitated for a second but Sir Robert quickly interjected.

"Here is the ring." He thrust a plain gold ring into Wideslade's hand. He, in turn, gave it to Henry, who slipped it onto Elizabeth's ringless wedding finger. She looked at it uncomprehendingly but made no move to discard it.

"I now pronounce you man and wife," intoned Wideslade. He was about to embark on concluding prayers but Sir Robert stepped forward.

"Thank you, Wideslade, your task is done. You will sign the marriage document now, then you may return to Cornwood. If you wish to stay the night at Sheviock you will be welcome."

"Henry, one of my men will ride back with you to Polbathic. Thank you for your services and may God bless you and have mercy on your soul. Be assured that our agreement will be honoured to the full." Henry Denyss nodded and shuffled out of the chapel.

"Alicia," said Sir Robert. "Did you learn what happened to her bailiff or what so called proof they have?"

Alicia shook her head. "No father, she has said nothing."

Sir Robert grimaced. "Alright, take her to her room and prepare her for tomorrow's journey. Armand, return now to Sheviock. Tell Charles to await my return and prepare to ride with me tomorrow for Exeter and London. We will need horses, armour, weapons. and two men at arms."

Moonshadow

Chapter 11

Tavistock and the road to London

As the onset of evening took shape with a brilliant, golden sunset lighting up the red earthed landscape, Ralph was close to the outskirts of Tavistock. Riding down the hill, he could see wood smoke above the trees, drifting across the Abbey tower.

Saddle-sore and weary, he was relieved to have made the journey in daylight and with no sign of pursuit.

His own horse was close to exhaustion. He had deliberately preserved Magi for the onward journey to London and hoped that Lawrence de Mohun would be able provide a second fresh mount.

He rode into the market square in front of the Abbey and was given directions to Lawrence's house by the blacksmith who was shoeing horses outside the Abbey gate.

"Take the road alongside the river. First house you come to be Mohun's. That horse of your'n do need shoeing," he added.

"That he does," said Ralph, "but he needs food and water first."

Lawrence was astounded by Ralph's account of what had happened. He was all for setting off for St Germans, there and then. Ralph and Lawrence's wife, Joan, dissuaded him.

"Before we do anything, Sir Richard must be told and I

have to get to London as soon as possible," said Ralph.

"Elizabeth may still be at St Germans or may have been moved to Sheviock or somewhere else. We need to know exactly what is going on, plan what to do, and have strength and surprise on our side if we are to take on The Daunays."

Lawrence acknowledged Ralph's good sense.

"If you go to London, you will be able to summon both Richard and Sir John with their men at arms. On your way, you should stop at Luppitt and tell my brother, Baldwin and our cousin William at Mohun's Ottery what has happened. They should prepare to join us when Sir John and Richard return.

"I will ride with my eldest son, Adam, to St Germans, to find out if Elizabeth is still held there. If she is, I will remain and keep watch and send word with Adam.

"If she has gone from St Germans, we will try to learn where she has been taken and get word to you here to await our return. Now Ralph, food and rest for you. We will attend the horses and have everything ready for you to depart at first light tomorrow. All praise to you for your courage. Pray to God that Elizabeth is alive and unharmed."

After a welcomed rest, Ralph started out in the pre dawn and reached Luppit in the early evening. He had skirted the moor and rested briefly at hostelries in Oakhampton and Exeter to feed and water the horses. He had left Saxon in Tavistock to recover, and was riding Magi and one of Lawrence's young palfreys in turn to try and preserve their stamina.

Baldwin was in the church at Luppit when Ralph arrived and as soon as Ralph had told him of the situation, he took Ralph's bridle and walked with him down the lane to Mohun's Ottery, the house belonging to his cousin, William. While he was fed, he retold his story and answered their inevitable questions.

William was a notorious soldier and bore the scars of battle, including a scar from a sword blow that ran in a straight line across his broad brow, making him look as if he was permanently frowning.

He and Baldwin agreed that they would travel to Tavistock as soon as they were able and await the arrival of Richard and

Sir John. They urged Ralph to rest and ensured that his horses were fed and watered. They also cautioned Ralph.

"The bastards will be watching for you, Ralph," said Baldwin. "They will want to stop you reaching London."

"I know," said Ralph. "I expected an ambush all day but so far so good. I did notice a man in Exeter looking at me strangely when I was watering the horses and I took a back way out of the city as a precaution. I am not sure which might be the safest way to go tomorrow."

William tugged at his small trimmed beard. "While you sleep, I will think out a route for you and I will also have one of my men at arms accompany you on the journey; as an extra pair of eyes and ears and a deterrent to any thieves or outlaws."

As another day dawned, Ralph sat with William de Mohun and Geoffrey le Strade, a young armiger, and studied the rough map that William had drawn up.

"Better to avoid all the main routes," said William. "So I am suggesting that you strike north as soon as possible, avoiding Salisbury and Winchester. Use the sheep routes and the old Roman roads. Take the main route, Fosse Way, from here," he said, pointing, "and after about 30 miles, cut off east to Bruton. You are sure of good hospitality at the priory there; they owe their living to the de Mohuns.

"The next day," he continued, 'take their directions to the old Roman road that lies a few miles to the north east and cuts cross country to Old Sarum, north of Salisbury. Pick up the Portway track to Andover, and try to rest up outside the town.

"The following day, pick up the Portway again through St Mary Bourne and on up to Silchester, then take the Devil's Highway into London. With luck and a fair wind, you could be in London in four to five days."

Ralph grinned. "Sounds easy," he said, "but I think I will need more than my fair share of luck."

William slapped him on the back. "You will do it," he said. "You are a brave and resourceful man. Geoffrey here will guard your back. He is a force to be reckoned with if you meet any trouble. He will have two extra horses so you should be able to keep fresh mounts for most of the way."

"If we are to reach Bruton by nightfall, we should go," said Geoffrey. He was clearly of Viking ancestry, with golden hair and deep blue eyes. Tall and wide shouldered, he gave Ralph some much needed confidence in the likely success of his journey.

They made good progress. Compared with the main thoroughfares, the more ancient routes were quiet and unpopulated. After turning off The Fosse Way, Ralph and Geoffrey tracked cross country to Bruton. There, as Sir William had forecast, they were made very welcome by the prior and monks of The Augustinian Abbey.

Next day, refreshed and well fed, they set off northwards to try and link up with the Portway, to take them on to Andover. The terrain was difficult and the road hard to follow. They lost their way on two occasions and had to retrace their steps, adding unwanted miles to the journey. They were weary and hungry as they came over a hill and saw Andover below them.

Tiredness had dulled their wits and it was only as they were well into the busy main street that Geoffrey reigned back and cautioned Ralph.

"We should have avoided the town," he said. "There could be danger here."

"I know," murmured Ralph, "but turning back now would probably draw more attention than going forward."

"I agree," said Geoffrey, "but we will not stop at the inn up ahead; just keep going. You ride ahead now with the spare horses. I will watch you from behind to see if anyone takes notice of you. Don't worry; I will have you in my sight even if you cannot see me. We will join up again once we are well clear of the town."

Ralph signalled his understanding, took the leading reins of the spare horses, and with a wave of his hand, urged Magi forward.

Passing the inn, the horses smelt the water in the trough and whinnied loudly in displeasure at not being allowed to stop and drink. Ralph had to shout and urge them forward. The commotion caused a number of people in the street to look twice at Ralph as he rode by. One man stared hard and hastened into the inn.

After a couple of minutes, Geoffrey arrived at the inn and decided to let his horse drink while he could still see Ralph, now some way in front of him. As he waited, three men ran from the inn into the stable yard ,shouting for the ostler to bring out their horses. While they were milling about in the yard, Geoffrey remounted and moved quickly down the road, breaking into a gallop as he passed the last few houses. He veered into the trees that bordered the road, disappearing from view before the three men emerged from the inn yard.

The trees were relatively sparse so he was able to maintain a gallop, and soon came parallel to Ralph who was looking over his shoulder.

"Ralph," he called. "I think they are on to us, three men from the inn. I don't think they know that I am with you. Just keep riding forward but be prepared. I will surprise them as they get to this point.

"When you hear me shout, turn round and check the situation. If I am engaging all three and no one is approaching, you ride like hell away from here and hide when you are out of sight. I will catch up with you when I have finished here. If I do not come just go forward on your own.

"Good luck. Just keep riding as you are, slow and steady; I can see them coming now."

Ralph called out, "God be with you." His instinct was to turn and fight alongside Geoffrey but he knew that the overriding need was to get word of Elizabeth's abduction through to his master. He had only ridden another hundred paces or so when he heard Geoffrey yell at the top of his voice. He quickly turned and saw Geoffrey, broadsword raised above his head, charging into the group of three horsemen who had been totally surprised.

As he watched, the horse of one of his pursuers reared up and threw its rider before galloping toward him.

Reluctantly, but heedful of Geoffrey's instructions, Ralph turned and with the spare horses—and the riderless horse alongside him—galloped for his life, leaving the melee behind him.

After a couple of miles with no one seemingly in pursuit, he came to an opening in the now dense woodland. He rode into the wood and very soon came to a large grassy clearing, and to the delight of the horses, a stream and small pond. Leaving them to drink and graze, Ralph himself doubled back and hid in a spot close to the road.

Half an hour passed and Ralph was growing increasingly anxious. Then he saw a lone horseman approaching. As he came nearer he saw, with great relief, that it was Geoffrey, but it also became apparent that all was not well. His horse was lame and walking slowly, and Geoffrey was slumped in the saddle, one arm hanging limp and useless.

Ralph moved out of hiding and went to met him. "What happened? Are you hurt? Have they gone? Who were they?" He could not get the questions out fast enough.

Geoffrey gave a brief laugh that turned into a groan. "Wait Ralph, get me into the wood and off this horse and I will tell you all."

Ralph led him through the trees to the clearing. Getting Geoffrey off his horse was achieved with difficulty. He was obviously in great pain and close to collapse. Ralph propped him up against a tree giving him the flask recently filled with fresh water from the stream.

Geoffrey had difficulty in swallowing but seemed to revive a little. He spoke slowly and his breathing was laboured.

"Two of them are dead and one escaped. They were Daunay men. The one who got away had a Daunay crest on his jerkin."

"What did he look like?" Ralph asked.

"Dark hair, tall, ugly battle scar on his face."

Ralph nodded. "Charles Daunay, no doubt. And you, what happened to your arm?"

"One of them fell off his horse and I dispatched him quickly with one blow. The second man, not Daunay, I ran through, but his horse bolted while my sword was still embedded. I was caught off balance and fell. My horse got tangled in the harness and is lame." He paused and grimaced in pain. "I broke my arm; I heard it snap. Daunay, if it was he, took advantage and thrust into me while I was still on my knees. I barely felt it and as soon as I got to my feet, he turned tail and ran. The coward has no stomach for a fight."

He coughed convulsively and a spray of blood came from his mouth. "I fear the sword wound has done more damage than I thought," he whispered. His voice had grown weaker and his words had begun to slur. He opened his mouth to speak again but no words came; just blood and his last breath.

Ralph used Geoffrey's broadsword to dig a shallow grave. He laid Geoffrey to rest, covered the body with loose soil and leaves, said a prayer for his brave soul and plunged the sword into the ground as a makeshift cross. He knew that wolves might find and scavenge the body but he had no choice other than to leave him there. He knew that he was on his own now and that Geoffrey had died in an attempt to ensure that he completed his mission. He had to go on.

He went back to the clearing and the pond. The horses were grazing contentedly and Ralph, feeling drained and weak, sat for a while under the shade of the trees to gather his strength. In a matter of moments he was asleep.

He awoke again as the midday sun speared the shade of the overhanging branches and dazzled him as he opened his eyes. He stretched and yawned and then realised with horror that there were no horses in view. He leapt to his feet and wildly looked around him. To his immediate relief he saw that they were all gathered at the edge of the wood on the far side of the clearing, then his heart skipped a beat as he realised that they were being held there by a group of perhaps a dozen men.

He started to walk toward them but had only taken a couple of steps when he felt a sharp point jab him in the back. A voice said, "Hold hard or I'll run you through."

Ralph stopped and turned his head. A tall, emaciated, fair haired man stood behind him with Geoffrey's sword levelled at his back. His clothes were ragged and his face and hands grimy.

"Outlaws," thought Ralph, with a sinking heart. The man behind him confirmed his fears.

"Thanks for the gift of the horses; now we want your money. Don't say you have none just hand it over."

"And then you will kill me?" asked Ralph.

"I'll kill you if you don't," was the laconic reply.

Ralph sighed and brought out his cloth purse, containing most of the small amount of money that he had been given by Lawrence in Tavistock. He still had a silver crown sewn into his shoe and Elizabeth's ring concealed in the secret pocket of his jerkin. He wasn't going to give them up just yet.

He tossed the purse to his captor. "That's all I have," he said. "You are welcome. Will you give me back one of the horses and let me go?"

The outlaw examined the meagre contents of the purse and slipped it into his own pocket.

"Why not," he said, prodding Ralph in the back. "Let's go over and you can select your horse."

Ralph walked quickly towards the horses and the rest of the outlaws, hope rising with each step. He reached the group of desperate looking men and stopped. He realised that they were all grinning and had a flash of perception just as the hilt of the broadsword struck him with a sickening blow, and he collapsed into blackness.

When he came round, he was lying in a makeshift shelter of interleaved branches on a bed of dry leaves. His hands and feet were trussed with strong vines and he felt as if his skull was split in half.

His first thought was to check the ring, and relief washed over him when he felt it still nestling in the lining of his jerkin. He could hear voices and became aware that there was fire flickering in the vicinity of his shelter; but overriding all these sensations was the smell of roasting meat. He was ravenous.

He lay quietly, trying to think of a way out of his predicament, fearful that all the effort and the sacrifice of Geoffrey's life would come to naught and that he would have failed in his mission. Without meaning to he groaned, partly in pain and partly in frustration. The chatter outside ceased and his fair haired captor came into the shelter.

"Well, horse stealer, you are awake. I thought maybe I had hit you too hard but your skull must be thicker than your brains." He bent and untied Ralph's bonds.

"No tricks now or next time I will hit you with the blade," he said.

He assisted Ralph to his feet and led him outside to where the group of outlaws were sitting round a glowing pit fire with a gutted roe deer being turned on a rudimentary spit.

They made a space for him while watching him curiously.

"They call me Red," said his captor. "Now, tell us who you are. If we like your story you get to eat and drink with us. If we don't ..." He made a throat cutting gesture.

Ralph decided to blend fact with fiction. It seemed that they thought him a horse thief so he went along with that and made up the story that he had been turned off his land in Devon for avoiding his dues, had stolen a horse from the local manor belonging to Richard de Mohun, and had just ridden day by day, living off his wits and collecting horses as he went. He realised that they must have found Geoffrey's grave because they had his sword, so he claimed that Geoffrey had pursued him from Andover and he had killed him in a fight but decided to bury him, leaving the sword in case it incriminated him. Exhausted by his flight and fight he had rested in the clearing to give the horses grazing and water, and had fallen asleep.

When he had finished his story there was a short silence. Red sliced off a piece of venison from the roasting carcass and thrust it toward Ralph on the tip of his dagger. Another of the outlaws handed him a flagon of fermented apple juice and a buzz of conversation welled up among the group. Ralph needed no other encouragement and tore into the hot, succulent meat with grateful gusto. Red sat down beside him.

"Well 'horse thief' you are lucky. They seem to accept your story. I am not so sure myself, but we need your horses and we need a horseman to look after them, so you have a chance to stay with us and prove yourself useful. We live off the land and steal what we can. When we get caught we will hang but until then, you can eat well enough." He laughed. "What say you?"

Ralph forced himself to laugh with him. "I say yes," he said. "I would rather hang in company than hang alone. Shall I tend the horses now?"

"Oh no," said Red, still chuckling. "Not so fast. We need to keep you confined until we can be sure of you."

Ralph's heart sank as he was again bound hand and foot, and put back in his leafy shelter. Helpless and angry with himself for his carelessness, he resolved to be patient and to gain the confidence of his captors while seeking to escape as soon as the opportunity arose. Sleep soon overwhelmed him.

For two more days the group of outlaws remained in their makeshift camp, and Ralph, under close guard, tended the horses. He organised grazing and watering in the nearby clearing, he bathed and poulticed the swollen fetlock of Geoffrey's lame charger, and he very carefully checked the fitness and well being of Magi. On the third day, Red awoke him early.

"Come, horse thief," he said cheerfully. "It is time to prove yourself. We need more supplies. We have been spying out the land to the north of us. There is a small village by the river about eight miles distant; St Mary le Bourne. Not many souls but a manor is there with stables, pigs, chickens and a grain store. Ten of us will go in with your horses and a cart and take what we need. Your job will be to find us two or three more horses to bring back with us, then we will move on from here, south toward the coast."

Ralph's heartbeat quickened. Might this be the opportunity he was seeking? He remembered from William de Mohun's rough map that St Mary le Bourne lay across the ancient Portway and would put him back on his route for London.

His inner excitement was somewhat dampened when Red said, "Don't get any ideas horse thief; I will be with you."

Ralph managed to ensure that when they set off he was astride Magi. He explained to Red, with the earnestness of truth, "I need my own horse because he knows how to work with me and is a calming influence on the horses that I may steal."

The compact and pretty little manor was on the edge of the village, contained within low boundary walls. It was the home of the Hillier family, of mixed Norman and Saxon stock, who had prospered there for the last two hundred years. Fortuitously, Sir Peter Hillier and his bailiff had left for market in Andover at daybreak.

His wife, infant son, and the household servants did not attempt to resist when the outlaws stormed into the courtyard, shouting and wielding their weapons. They were quickly secured in a stone outbuilding while the house was ransacked for valuables, the contents of the grain store loaded into the cart along with slaughtered pigs and chickens.

Ralph, under the watchful eye of Red, expertly cut out two fine palfreys from the small number of ponies and farm horses in the paddock.

It was all over in a matter of minutes and the raiders were back on the road out of the village, whooping with exuberance and the realisation that all had gone to plan; there was little likelihood of immediate pursuit. As they came to the edge of the forest, he reigned in and dismounted from Magi. The main group of outlaws, together with the cartload of plunder, were disappearing into the trees.

Red rode up alongside him. "What are you doing?" He shouted. "Why have you stopped?"

Ralph was bending down, feeling one of Magi's forelegs. "My horse is lame," he said. "I will have to leave it here but I need to transfer my harness to one of these." He gestured to the two stolen palfreys.

"Here, will you give me a hand?" He held out the halter ropes and Red dismounted and took them. Ralph moved Magi a few steps away and then, in one convulsive moment, mounted, turned, and dug his heels into Magi's flanks. He was fifty yards down the road toward the village before Red comprehended what was happening. Ralph gambled that Red would not want to leave the safety of the group and the forest, or revisit the site of the raid. He was right. Red shook his fist and yelled obscenities after him but did not follow, and Ralph was on his way. He rode past the manor at full gallop, aware of commotion in the yard, but there was no sign of pursuit and the little village seemed deserted. Very quickly he was climbing the long ridge out of the valley on the old Portway, now a sheep track, and was back on route to Silchester and London.

Moonshadow

Chapter 12

London

Sir Robert lost no time in seeking an audience with Queen Isabella. His frantic journey to London, together with Armand and two men at arms, had been tiring but straightforward. He knew that time was of the essence and had already instructed Armand to seek fresh horses and prepare for the return journey.

Queen Isabella greeted him civilly enough but there was an underlying coolness in her manner. He had forgotten her striking good looks and her regal bearing. As a child bride she had seemed pretty but insignificant and out of place in the clannish and sycophantic court of her young husband. How times had changed.

The reason for her coolness soon became apparent. "I hope you are not here to plead for your son to be accepted here at court," she said. "He has been excluded, together with others of his persuasion. Unless he desires to be treated as a Despenser supporter, he will do well to keep out of our sight until he can demonstrate his contrition."

"Your Majesty, I have not come to plead for him. He has felt the full force of my anger for the disrepute he has brought to our family name. I am aware of his indiscretion and can only offer his youth and inexperience in mitigation. He has been under my influence of late and regrets his past actions. I had arranged a suitable marriage for him that would, I think, have ensured a change in his maturity and behaviour. It is, however, the circumstances relating to the proposed marriage that bring me here today."

Isabella inclined her head and raised her eyebrows in curiosity, waiting for him to go on.

"Your Majesty, I come to you because there is currently a serious dispute between my family and that of Sir John de Mohun. I am certain that they will seek audience with you also, and I want to be sure, given my son's reputation, that you understand the issue and can judge it without prejudice."

Isabelle raised her hand. "Before you proceed, take care. Sir John de Mohun is a man of honour and, like you, is well regarded and esteemed by all here."

"Indeed, Your Majesty, and the dispute we now have saddens me but here are the facts of the matter."

Sir Robert explained succinctly and clearly the story of the engagement of Elizabeth Fitzwilliam and Charles, the arrival of Richard de Mohun, the dithering on the agreement by Sir John Fitzwilliam, and then the sudden marriage of Elizabeth and Richard, despite the prior engagement.

The death of the falconer was touched on but glossed over as probably irrelevant. Finally, he produced the divorce and marriage documents signed by Bishop Berkeley of Exeter.

Queen Isabella studied the documents and handed them back to Sir Robert.

"It sounds a tangled tale," she said, "but right would seem to be on your side. However; I do not understand this marriage to another man so quickly after the annulment of the Mohun marriage. Could she not then have married your son?"

"Sadly, no, Your Majesty. She is seen as a tainted chattel and for her to marry my son after the divorce from Mohun would have provoked greater hostility between our families and caused accusations of fortune seeking as she is sole heiress to her father's estate.

"Elizabeth came to me, seeking some solution to her plight and herself suggested an immediate marriage to Denyss. She knew him as a family friend, needing a companion to care for him. She wanted to make herself secure from any other suitors.

"I agreed to help her as I felt in some small way responsible for her predicament. The marriage was arranged very quickly and she has withdrawn to her role of companion to Denyss who, I fear, is not long for this world. Elizabeth has confided in me that it is her intention to seek refuge in a nunnery when her husband dies."

Isabella pulled a face. "She sounds a fickle and weak girl and a nunnery is perhaps the right place for her. I think perhaps there is more to this than meets the eye, Sire; but your story is plausible, all the documents appear to be in order, and the signature of Bishop Berkeley lends some credence to them. We know you as an honourable man, Sir Robert. It will be interesting to see if the de Mohuns also petition me and what version of the story they present."

"Your Majesty, all that I have told you has happened with great speed. It is possible that Sir John and Richard de Mohun do not yet know what has transpired. They are, I believe, here in London awaiting your Majesty's call to service."

"Thank you, Sir Robert, for your enlightening tale. I trust that any disagreement between you and the Mohuns can be settled amicably, and make sure that you rein in that recalcitrant son of yours before he comes to serious harm."

Richard was tired of waiting. Along with fellow knights, he had been attending the Court daily for the past week while the barons individually and collectively sat with Isabella, Mortimer, and the boy king to pay homage, swear allegiance, and debate in parliament. He had seen but avoided Sir Robert Daunay, who had arrived some three days later than himself but there was no sign of Charles Daunay and enquiries as to his whereabouts drew a blank.

The large number of men at arms and soldiers billeted around the city were also growing restless and causing trouble; fighting, drinking and despoiling many of the taverns.

The lords and knights had arranged impromptu jousting competitions almost every day, to while away the time and practice their battle skills.

On the ninth day after his arrival, Richard—mounted on Grisel Gris—was at Greyfriar's Field, preparing to challenge yesterday's champion, Hugo de Ferrers, in the final joust of the day. He took the lance from his aide, Gervais, and settled it into the sling, pointing forward at an angle. He lowered his visor, and leaning well forward in the saddle, he spurred Grisel Gris forward into a gallop. Twenty yards before the two knights clashed, Richard saw something that caused him to immediately raise his lance and veer away from the jousting line, thus conceding the match.

Amid catcalls and jeers he threw down his lance, raised his visor and rode to the side of the field with a face like thunder.

"Ralph," he roared. "What are you doing here? Did you see Lady Elizabeth safely to Hall?"

Then he noticed that Ralph was riding Elizabeth's horse and that they both looked exhausted.

"Why are you riding Magi? What has happened to bring you here?" Halfway between anger and distress, his voice cracked.

Ralph reached into his jerkin pocket and produced Lady Elizabeth's ring and proffered it to Richard.

"Sir, the news I bring will be hard for you to bear but I am here at Lady Elizabeth's command. She safe guarded me her ring to prove to you her love and her desire that I should seek you out; to warn you that you are in danger, and bring you to her aid." As he spoke, Ralph swayed and as he tried to dismount, he toppled to the ground, unable to stand after being so long in the saddle.

Richard stood aghast then summoned some of the surrounding onlookers to carry Ralph into the shelter of the jousting tent and fetch fresh water. After taking a few sips Ralph sat up.

"There is no time to lose, sir. You must come with me, together with your father. Your brothers, Lawrence and Baldwin, and your cousin William await you in Tavistock."

"Hold, Ralph," said Richard gently. "Take more water and tell me, from the beginning, all that has passed since my departure from Ugborough. Leave nothing out."

Ralph told the story of the initial journey and kidnap. The Daunay revelation of the annulment as told to him by Lady Elizabeth. He mentioned her concern that she'd revealed there was evidence of Charles' involvement in the murder of the falconer. He praised her foresight of the second kidnap and then recounted the details of his journey after leaving her; to Tavistock and Mohun's Ottery and finally, after the incident in Andover and the death of Geoffrey le Strade, to London.

Several times, with growing incredulity and anger, Richard asked questions to clarify or confirm. When Ralph had finished, Richard was ablaze. He turned to Gervais.

"Go quickly and find my father. He will be resting at his lodgings in The Abbey. Bring him here as speedily as you can. Tell him it is a matter of extreme urgency."

Queen Isabella was in waspish mood. "Mohuns in force, is it?" she said with some contempt as Sir John and Richard were ushered into the audience chamber of the great hall of Westminster. "Cannot hold on to your women, I am told."

Richard flushed. "That is—," he began angrily. Sir John raised his hand to silence him.

"Your Majesty, it seems that you have already spoken with Sir Robert Daunay and have doubtless been informed of the abduction of my daughter in law, Elizabeth Fitzwilliam. I do not know what story he has told you, but the facts are ..." He halted, mid sentence, as Isabella raised her hand.

"The facts are, sire, that I have seen the annulment papers and the marriage documents signed by My Lord Bishop of Exeter and witnessed by his clergy. The matter seems clear enough. The Fitzwilliam girl is fickle and you, Mohun," she said, pointing to Richard, "tried your luck and failed. There is nothing I can do."

Richard's jaw dropped and he moved towards The Queen. Sir John gripped his arm, squeezing it painfully to warn him not to speak.

"I crave your indulgence, Your Majesty," he said, keeping a calm exterior albeit seething underneath. "We do dispute the legality of both the alleged annulment and any subsequent form of marriage. We have no knowledge of either event and believe serious crimes have been committed. I petition you most humbly to allow my son Richard and I to return home, and to seek my Lord Archbishop's opinion in Exeter as we fear he has been most grievously misled. Our men at arms can be left here if needed, but my son and I need to attend our affairs most urgently."

Isabella gestured dismissively. "You are free to leave with or without your armigers and men at arms. Go, attend your affairs, but be careful sire; despite the follies of his son Charles, Sir Robert Daunay is held high in our esteem. I have no reason to doubt his word." Then, in a softer tone, she said, "You too, Sir John, are held in high esteem so take care that your paternal pride does not drive you to rash actions."

"Thank you, Your Majesty," replied Sir John. "All we seek is truth and justice in the sight of God and within the jurisdiction of your law."

The Queen waved an arm in dismissal and Sir John and Richard withdrew.

As soon as they were outside the audience chamber, Richard exploded. "What annulment? What marriage? Have they dared to force her to marry Charles? I will kill him with my bare hands."

"Temper your anger," said Sir John. "Let us not speculate or conjecture. We will ride tonight for Exeter and then Tavistock. There we will hold council and try to determine exactly what has transpired, then act accordingly. Go gather your men and check if Ralph is fit to ride with us. We will meet here in the palace yard in one hour. I fear Daunay has a head start on us but maybe we can catch up with him; if we are careful enough, he may inadvertently lead us to Elizabeth."

Chapter 13

Arworthal and Sheviock

Elizabeth, apart from a sore hand sustained from hammering on the locked door of her cell, was unharmed in physical terms but bruised and battered in mind and spirit.

She had been transported, bound, and closely guarded over a long day and night ride from St Germans, to the property at Arworthal hidden away at the end of the Fal estuary.

Although the manor had come to her family as a part of her mother's dowry, she had never stayed there before. Now she was a captive on her own property.

When they had approached it in the early morning, it had looked romantic and picturesque. As they drew closer, however, it became apparent that many years of neglect had taken their toll. Plaster was crumbling from the walls and the stonework was covered in mosses and creeper.

Inside, the majority of the house was barely usable, but one end of the great hall had been roughly repaired to provide some protection from the elements, together with the kitchen and storerooms. One of these, with a small barred window overlooking the overgrown courtyard, was now Elizabeth's prison. It contained a rough bed of rushes and goat skins, two plain wooden stools and a large oak chest. The door, which opened into the kitchen, was solid oak with a small, iron lattice grill.

Alicia's face suddenly appeared at the grill. She looked pale and tired. "Rest, Elizabeth," she said. "I am sorry that you are brought to such discomfort but it should not be for long; when matters are settled you can return to Hall. I am sure my father will let you stay there for as long as you wish."

Elizabeth looked aghast. "Since when is your father able to decide if I can live in my own home?"

"Never mind," was Alicia's weary reply. "We will talk about it on the morrow." She disappeared from the grill.

Elizabeth finally gave way to despair. Her mind was in total confusion. She had vague recollections of some sort of service at the cold cathedral in St Germans and then the long journey to Arworthal, but what it all meant was beyond her. How would Richard ever find her here? It was her last coherent thought before she fell asleep.

Sir Robert Daunay arrived back in Sheviock tired and travel worn. He had completed the long journey from London in four and a half days of hard riding with only brief stops to change horses and snatch some food.

Following his audience with Queen Isabella, Sir Robert had immediately departed London. He reflected that he had achieved the aims of his hurried visit. He had put his version of events to The Queen before the Mohuns got to see her. He had also reaffirmed that his standing at Court was still sound, despite the disapproval of Charles' past relationship with Edward and his acolytes, and had tacit acceptance of his actions in pursuing the illegality of the Fitzwilliam-Mohun alliance with the Bishop of Exeter.

Fortunately, The Queen had chosen not to ask any awkward questions about Elizabeth's marriage to Denyss or the death of the Mohun's falconer. Although events were moving faster than he had planned or anticipated, he felt confident that he was still in control of his grand plan.

Charles was there to greet them, having returned the previous day, following his abortive attempt to prevent Ralph Purves from reaching London.

After a brief rest and change of clothing, Sir Robert, gaunt with fatigue, summoned Charles to sit and eat with him while they discussed the situation and their next actions.

"Obviously you failed to stop Purves," he said. "He arrived in London. What happened?"

Charles gave an exaggerated account of events in Andover. He claimed that Ralph Purves had been accompanied by several armed men, and despite a brave and determined attack by Charles and the two Sheviock men he had conscripted, they had been outnumbered. During the ferocious fight that followed, his companions had been killed, and while Charles battled and put at least three other Mohun men to flight, Purves had slipped away; Sir Robert looked sceptical and cut him off mid flow.

"What is done is done. We have to prepare for the next step. The Mohuns will be on their way here by now. They will be angry and will want explanations. I had wanted more time but now we have to act strongly and decisively.

"You must leave tomorrow for Arworthal, to safeguard Alicia and Elizabeth and ensure that they stay hidden. You must remain there until I join or send for you."

Charles grimaced but nodded. "What will you do when the Mohuns come here? You will be in mortal danger."

"I will treat them with great civility," said Sir Robert. "I will open the doors of Sheviock and Boconnoc to them, show them the copies of the divorce papers and the marriage documents, and invite them to visit the Bishop in Exeter to determine their legality. I will remind them that I have also had audience with Queen Isabella and obtained her approval.

"No doubt the Mohuns will be angry and dangerous, but Sir John at least is a man of honour and will ascertain the legality of the matter before they resort to violence against us.

"With God's will, a little luck and the passing of time, the heat will die down and with the Fitzwilliam lands in our hands, our fortunes will be restored. No thanks to you, Charles."

Charles looked sullen. "So what becomes of me?" he asked, plaintively.

"You, Charles, will lie low. You are not welcome at court anymore; your former cronies are scattered or dead. We need to work quietly but diligently now to arrange an appropriate marriage that will further advance our fortunes. You will then settle down I hope, ready to take on your responsibility for the furtherance of the Daunay family reputation and prosperity that you have so nearly brought to ruin.

"Now, enough talking. I am weary and I have much to do tomorrow. On your way to Arworthal, I want you to go see Denyss and make sure he knows that he may be questioned by the Mohuns. He is to say nothing, other than to confirm that he is married to Elizabeth. If they persist in further questioning, he must feign a collapse." He paused and looked directly at Charles. "Of course, it would be easier if he were already dead..." He trailed off pointedly. "I need to get a message to Bishop Berkeley in Exeter, to warn him that the Mohuns will soon be here. Armand will deal with Wideslade and Bloyou and ensure that they do not give anything away."

He patted Charles on the shoulder and spoke to him in a softer tone. "Let us close the book on the chapter of your recent past, Charles. It has not been a happy time for the family, but we have a chance now to put things back in order. There is risk and danger involved, but be guided by me, do what I tell you without demur, and we can look forward to a brighter future." Charles muttered his assent and moved toward the door.

"One last thing, Charles," said Sir Robert. "Elizabeth is not to be touched by you or harmed in any way. Indeed, you are to ensure that no harm befalls her. God speed your journey."

The door to Henry Denyss' modest house was unbarred and Charles was able to enter easily and silently. He had seen no one on the short ride to Polbathic. Even as he went through the door he was still undecided about what he would do, although he had thought about it many times during the night while mulling over his father's words.

The fact that Denyss was sleeping made his decision easy. Denyss was so weak that he put up little resistance when Charles put the straw filled bolster over his face. The little air that he had in his lungs was soon exhausted and he died very quickly.

Charles re-arranged the bolster under his head, closed the door quietly behind him and proceeded on his way to Arworthal.

Elizabeth awoke to the sound of horses in the yard and then a man's voice, strident and demanding. She knew at once that it was Charles Daunay. She scrambled out of her makeshift bed and put on her robe. Feeling nauseous and fearful, she went to the locked door and looked through the grill.

Alicia, looking flustered and anxious, was running through the kitchen. As she reached the entrance to the ruined main hall, the door burst open and Charles appeared, dirty and dishevelled but grinning from ear to ear.

He saw Alicia but ignored her. He looked around wildly. "Where is the bitch?" he shouted. "She is mine, now." Then he saw Elizabeth's face framed in the barred window of the storeroom. His eyes widened and he beckoned to her. "Come here, woman," he shouted. "I'll show you what you have been missing."

Elizabeth could not speak. Her nausea had intensified and she felt on the point of collapse. Alicia moved quickly to put herself between Charles and the door. Charles looked at her briefly, pushed her aside and strode over to Elizabeth. He rattled the door to test the lock. She shrank back but kept her gaze fixed upon him.

"Mohun may have spoiled you," he hissed, "but you will reap the consequences of jilting me."

He turned away and Elizabeth sank to the floor, quietly weeping with fear and hopelessness. Alicia caught hold of Charles' hand.

"Charles, no," she said, shakily but firmly. "Father has entrusted her to my care until he gets here; our fortunes depend upon her well being."

"Only till Denyss dies," whispered Charles, "and I …" He tailed off. Alicia seemed not to notice his discomfiture.

"Calm down, Charles; you need rest and a change of clothing and then you must tell me what has been going on back at home and in London. There is a room for you in the barn building."

Charles acknowledged her with a wave of his hand and went out into the great hall to retrieve his saddle bag.

Alicia unlocked the cell door and went in to tend Elizabeth, who was still sitting on the floor, weeping.

133

"Don't worry, I will keep you safe," said Alicia soothingly.

Elizabeth looked at her contemptuously. "You and your father and brother have eloigned me, assaulted me, drugged me, and imprisoned me against my will. Why do I doubt you will keep me safe?" She retched dryly. "I am feeling so ill."

Alicia was torn. Her instinct was to comfort and soothe Elizabeth. Her emotions were also overlaid with guilt, knowing the calumny that she was a party to, and the devastating consequences that lay in store for her charge. At the same time, the love and loyalty that she held for her father made her determined to see things through, for his sake.

She had confronted Elizabeth with the details of her marriage to Denyss, hoping that the recognition of what that meant to her future would be so devastating that she might, at last, be vulnerable to pressure and persuasion, and reveal what evidence there might be of Charles' involvement in the murder of the falconer at Hall.

Elizabeth knew that she was carrying Richard's child. Her morning nausea had lasted now for seven days, since she had first arrived at Arworthal. Contrary to Alicia's expectations, the news that she was supposedly divorced from Richard and was now married to Henry Denyss had strengthened her resolve to wait out her captors and seize any chance of escape that arose.

She recognised that Alicia was a reluctant gaoler and also that she acted as a shield against the unwanted and unpredictable attentions of Charles. She decided to use her innate guile to get closer to Alicia, first by revealing her pregnancy and then by giving her what she wanted, albeit with feigned reluctance, the 'evidence' that Alicia had continually requested.

Later that day she made her move and confided to Alicia some of the information that Richard had brought back from his visit to Boconnoc.

"The thing is, Alicia, it is not really evidence," she said. "Just the burned, bloodstained sleeve of a jerkin and a goshawk feather that Richard said he found at Boconnoc. But it was enough to convince my father and Richard that it was Charles who had slaughtered poor Leofric."

Alicia's response was predictable. "You are right. That's

not evidence. Richard could have found the sleeve and the feather anywhere or burned them himself and then presented them to you, to cover his own guilt and encourage you to trust him."

Elizabeth nodded as if in agreement. "Yes, of course that might be possible," she said. "But Alicia, I love him; I married him and I am carrying his child, so what can I do?" She began to cry and Alicia could not help but try to console and comfort her.

"At least you are safe here," she said. "We will tend you until my father comes and then he will help you settle to a new life."

She hugged Elizabeth who continued to sob, although underneath she was confident that she had shifted her relationship with Alicia to her own advantage.

Moonshadow

Chapter 14

Exeter, Cornwood, Sheviock and Hall

The Mohuns had a brief family conference at Tavistock and decided on a plan of action. Baldwin, Lawrence, and Ralph were to go to Hall and scour the locality for any news of Elizabeth. Sir John and Richard would visit the Bishop of Exeter and then Sir Robert Daunay at Sheviock. They agreed to meet up again in three days time at Hall.

The meeting with John Berkeley, the Bishop of Exeter, was brief and unsatisfactory. He rejected their protestations outright, saying that he had made his decisions on the annulment of the marriage based on evidence put before him, backed up by documents signed by Sir Robert and witnessed by priests from his See.

As for the subsequent marriage of Elizabeth Fitzwilliam and her present whereabouts, he denied all knowledge.

"My Lord Mohun," he concluded. "I understand your concern and anger, but you must reconcile yourself to the fact that your son has no grounds for complaint. I urge you to make your peace with Sir Robert Daunay and with the Lord. May his blessings be upon you." He ushered them toward the door.

Sir John stood his ground. "My Lord Bishop," he said, "of course we accept that you will have acted in good faith and based your decisions on the evidence presented. Our concern is that the evidence may be flawed. If we may see the documents and the signatures thereon, then we may ourselves be convinced or perhaps be able to identify any falsehood or calumny."

The Bishop's sharp and immediate response was that the documents concerned had been presented by and handed back to Sir Robert.

"I suggest that you seek your answers from him. And now I have other urgent matters that require my attention."

Sir John tried one last gambit. "My Lord Bishop, can you at least disclose the name of the witnesses, your priests?"

The Bishop hesitated and before he could reply, Richard, with a flash of intuition, interjected. "I believe one of them would be Wideslade," he said. "He has his living from Sir Robert and would be the obvious choice. Am I correct, my Lord Bishop?"

Berkeley was confused and unwilling to tell an outright lie, but his prolonged hesitation answered the question. Leaving the Bishop with his mouth still open to frame a reply, Sir John and Richard took their leave.

They had a brief talk together outside the city gate, and after some objection from Richard they agreed that they should split up. Richard would go to interrogate Wideslade at Cornwood, and Sir John would visit Sir Robert Daunay at Sheviock. They arranged to meet again, in two or three days time, at Boconnoc, before going on to Hall.

Richard, seeing a loaded cart in front of Cornwood Manor, surmised that Wideslade was about to depart. Drawing his dagger, he ran into the house and caught up with the priest as he tried to scramble out of a door at the rear of the hall. Richard grabbed the loose front of the man's habit in his fist and slammed him up against the wall.

"Are you in such a hurry that you cannot spare the time to talk to me?" he hissed.

Wideslade gave a low moan and then screamed as Richard pierced his neck with the tip of his dagger.

"Don't kill me, what do you want with me? You are trespassing. This is Sir Robert's land and manor."

Richard grinned savagely. "Never mind your patronage. I

will kill you painfully and slowly unless you tell me where my wife is held, and why you witnessed the papers used to annul my marriage. Did you attended the false marriage of Lady Elizabeth as well?"

Wideslade looked wildly around him. "I cannot tell you anything. I am called to another parish and need to leave to do God's work."

Richard pressed his dagger further into Wideslade's neck, drawing blood.

"Come, I have no patience. I need answers now or I will despatch you to your maker or more likely to hell. I want the truth and I want it now."

He dragged the now snivelling priest over to a low wall at the edge of the yard and sat him down.

"Now speak, you evil cleric. First, where is my wife?"

"Sire, truly I do not know for certain." As Richard thrust the dagger towards his throat, he shouted. "I will tell you all I know but I swear by all that is holy I do not know where she is, except perhaps with her new husband."

Richard kept the dagger an inch from his neck and said,

"Tell me everything you know."

Wideslade took a deep shuddering breath, but instead of words coming from his mouth, blood sprayed out over Richard's hand and the front of his jerkin. Wideslade slowly toppled forward, bent over as if in prayer, revealing the shaft of an arrow protruding from his back.

Richard glimpsed a flash of something glittering in the sunlight in the archway at the far edge of the courtyard, then heard the sound of hooves moving at a gallop down the track, away from the manor. He turned back to tend to Wideslade but it was clear that he was past any need of earthly help.

Sir John was obviously expected at Sheviock. He recognised Daunay's men stationed on the road at Cremyll and knew that word of his coming had been conveyed to Sir Robert.

Indeed, Sir Robert was waiting on the steps of the manor house as he rode through the gate and into the courtyard. He was alone and unarmed and immediately took the initiative. Serious but courteous, he bowed.

"Sir John," he said. "I know that you must be angered and aggrieved at the apparent injustice suffered by your son and your family. I am sorry that matters could not have been resolved more amicably. I wish you to know that I have acted in good faith and with my own family interests at heart. I could not stand by and see Elizabeth Fitzwilliam married falsely to your son when there was a clear understanding and agreement that she was already promised to my son Charles."

Sir John tried to interject but Sir Robert held up his hand.

"Let me finish Sir John; then I will answer any questions you may have, and show you any documented evidence you may wish to see. I did not bring the matter to the attention of my Lord Bishop at Exeter in order to benefit my son or our family.

"Indeed, the fact that there had been a false but consummated marriage meant that Lady Elizabeth was no longer a suitable bride for my son. I did it because it was the right and honourable thing to do."

This time he paused, awaiting some response from Sir John but none came, and he continued.

"When she was acquainted with the facts, Lady Elizabeth was dismayed, and immediately sought a legitimate union with one John Denyss of Polbathic so that she could overcome the dishonour of the false marriage. As a friend and confidante of her late father, I assisted her in that endeavour and I am assured that her dearest wish is now to tend poor Denyss until his death, then repair to the nunnery at St Germans to do penance and atone for her disgrace.

"That is my side of this sad story. Please, you are welcome to my house; come and partake of refreshment and pose any questions you may have of me."

He turned and went into the manor. Sir John dismounted. Once inside the hall he strode up to Sir Robert and stood face to face with him.

"I have heard you out, sire, now it is my turn. First, is my son's wife, Elizabeth de Mohun, here at Sheviock?"

Sir Robert smiled through his teeth. "No, Elizabeth Fitzwilliam is now Elizabeth Denyss and is not here. You are free to search my house, as I understand your suspicion. But, I repeat, your suspicions are unfounded. I have here," he pointed to the table at his side, "all the documents concerning the annulment of your son's marriage and the subsequent wedding to Denyss. You should peruse them and satisfy yourself that all that I have said is true."

"Before that," said Sir John, "I will accept your offer to search the house."

"Go where you will, take as long as you need, ask any questions of my servants," replied Sir Robert.

It took Sir John over an hour to complete his search of the house, the church, and farm buildings, but there was no sign whatsoever of Elizabeth. Questioning of well rehearsed servants elicited no new information.

When he finally re-entered the great hall, Sir John sat down at the table and started to read the documents.

He read with care and deliberated long over the signatures. When he had finished, he looked across the table at Sir Robert and took a long draught of the ale which had been poured for him.

"Sir Robert," he said slowly, "I am saddened to see an honourable man brought so low. Until now I have assumed that the guilty party in this shabby affair was your son Charles who has, I know, brought shame on your family. Now it appears that you too are prepared to stoop into the mire, to aid and abet his sins. I am not certain of your full evil intent, but believe me, we will uncover the truth and you will suffer the consequences."

Sir Robert flushed and stood up. "Have a care, sir. You are a guest in my house and I have afforded you every facility to acquaint yourself with the truth. Do not abuse my good faith."

Sir John shrugged and gestured to the pile of documents. "These are poor documents," he said. "The fact that they contain Sir John Fitzwilliam's supposed signature and a mark purporting to be that of his deceased falconer give the lie to your story. If my son and Lady Elizabeth are to be believed, then these are false signatures and marks, and I do believe my son and his legal wife.

"How could Sir Fitzwilliam have signed this document and then stood by at his daughter's wedding? You knew him as I did, as the most honourable of men.

"In addition, the so called witnesses to the Denyss marriage documents are those of priests Wideslade and Bloyou, who owe their patronage to you and so, must be suspect. We will need to question them to hear their version of events."

Sir Robert spread his arms. "Of course you must question them but I am certain that they will confirm the facts."

"As there is no trace of Lady Elizabeth here, I propose to search your Boconnoc estate. Do you have any objections?"

"None," said Sir Robert. "Search all you may but I suggest that you would be better employed visiting her new husband Denyss at Polbathic. If she is to be found anywhere she will be there."

Sir John faced up to Sir Robert again, barely restraining his anger and frustration. "Be assured, Sir Robert," he hissed. "We will find her, and for the sake of you and your family, she had better be unharmed."

Sir Robert looked momentarily discomforted but managed a twisted smile. "Do not threaten me, Sir John. You should know that the evidence has been scrutinised and accepted by my Lord Bishop at Exeter and indeed by Queen Isabella herself. You are in danger of sounding treasonable with your refusal to accept the simple truth."

Sir John turned on his heel, remounted in the courtyard, and cantered out of the gate without a backward glance.

Sir Robert breathed a sigh of relief, then called for his steward and left instructions that Armand was to attend him as soon as he returned to Sheviock.

Later that night, Sir Robert and Armand met. Following a brief but intense conversation, Armand and two men at arms left Sheviock, heading towards Exeter.

Sir John did not really need to go into Denyss' house to find him. The sickly, pungent smell enveloped him as soon as he opened the door. It was impossible to tell how poor Denyss had died but dead he was, and no trace of Elizabeth.

Richard was waiting for him at Boconnoc and, there too, there was no trace of Elizabeth. The place was deserted and almost derelict. They even checked the hut where Richard had observed Charles Daunay in hiding. But it was obvious from the untidy state that the hut was in, with bedding and clothing strewn around, and remains of rotting food and drink, that no one had been there since Charles' panic induced flight.

Richard told his father about the murder of Wideslade at Cornwood. "One minute more and I would have got the truth from him. Whoever killed him must have been watching us when we left Exeter. They knew he was a weak link."

Sir John and Richard arrived at Hall late that evening and joined Lawrence and Baldwin, who had travelled together to Hall and Llanteglos and Fowey. They were exhausted after three days of enquiry but had found no trace of Elizabeth and no one had seen her since her departure to Ugborough after the wedding. Hall, they said, was being kept in readiness for her return with Richard.

Godfrey reported to them that Sir Robert Daunay's steward had visited to ask for details of the estate boundaries, as he said they were negotiating to buy some neighbouring land and needed to check the boundary line. Godfrey had declined and told them to ask Sir Richard when he returned to Hall.

Sir John suddenly banged his fist on the table. "Now I see the whole evil plot," he said. "They do not care about Elizabeth; it is the estate they are after. If your marriage is annulled," he said, pointing to Richard, "the estate reverts to Elizabeth and then passes to Denyss when she is married to him. Now he is dead, I will wager my life that it is to be passed to the Daunays. Goddamn the bastards, that's their game." He banged the table again.

Over a meal, they compared notes and opinions and tried to decide on what to do next. Richard and Lawrence were all for direct action and the capture and torture of Sir Robert, and Charles, if they could find him. Sir John and Baldwin urged patience and more thought.

"It comes down to our word against theirs," said Richard, after a great deal of argument and conjecture. "We know that their whole story is built on deceit and lies, and now they are killing off anyone who can tell the truth about what has happened. The other signatory, Canon Bloyou, must be in mortal danger if not already dead. I am fearful now for Elizabeth's life.

As long as the Bishop and Queen Isabella believe the Daunays, we are undone."

He put his head in his hands, overcome with exhaustion and despair. Baldwin patted him on the shoulder. "Come brother, we Mohuns don't give up that easily. We still have two great powers to call upon; God and the Pope, and I have an idea as to how we can recruit them to our cause."

Sir John laughed, the first hint of any mirth since they had started their discussion. "Well said, my knightly priest; what do you suggest?"

"The Golden Rose," said Baldwin. "We must employ its power. Sir John, you know I have it for safekeeping at Luppitt. It has been there since Sir Reginald was re-interred at Newenham. I suggest that our Richard carries it with him to the Pope's court at Avignon, as proof of his standing. If it works and he is granted audience, he should state his cause and ask for his holiness to intercede. If we can subject the Daunays and Bishop Berkeley to a papal inquisition, we may learn the truth and gain some redress. Meanwhile, we will continue the search for Elizabeth. Someone must know where she is."

Richard was sceptical. "Why would the Papal Court take any interest in my personal troubles," he muttered. Baldwin took him by the shoulders and shook him.

"Look at me, brother. The Pope and his Cardinals will listen to you for two very good reasons. First, you will be carrying the Golden Rose with you as testament to your lineage and rank, which alone will ensure you an audience. Second, your grievance involves the Pope's representative, The Bishop of Exeter and his clergy, and that will make it difficult for them to refuse to investigate the matter. On top of that Richard, you must use your eloquence, your passion, your anger, and your desire for justice to stir them and enlist their aid. I think it will work."

Sir John took hold of Richard's arm. "It is worth the effort, Richard, and better use of your time and energy than running round in circles here. Don't worry, we will find Elizabeth, but we will need more than force of arms to defeat the machinations of the Daunays with their royal support."

Richard nodded. "Let me think on it," he said. "I will make my decision in the morning when I have a clear and rested head."

"I will go to Avignon," Richard announced to the group, when they gathered for breakfast.

"Baldwin, will you bring the Golden Rose to Ugborough? I will return there now and prepare for the journey. I shall take Ralph Purves with me to Avignon; he has proved to be tenacious and resourceful and I will welcome his company."

Baldwin slapped him on the back. "I will get to Ugborough as soon as I can, but I need a day or two to attend to affairs at Luppit and the Ottery. You will need letters of commendation from Newenham Abbey and from Buckfast; you can then stay at both Cistercian and Benedictine Priories on the journey across France."

Lawrence and Sir John both started to talk at once, offering advice and suggestions. Richard held up his hand to silence them.

"Just find Elizabeth for me," he said, with a crack in his voice, "and pray God she is unharmed."

Six days later, Baldwin rode into Ugborough Hall, escorted by two of the Newenham monks, bearing with him the Golden Rose, secure in a heavy but beautiful box made of chestnut wood and banded with gold. He handed it over to Richard that evening while they dined.

"Take care of this and guard it with your life," said Baldwin. "It is your laissez-passer to the Papal City and all the monasteries between here and there. And do not forget it is our family's most precious heirloom. Here too is a letter from The Prior at Newenham, commending you to any Cistercian Abbey or house on your route. You will pass Buckfast Abbey on your way to Plymouth and can get the Benedictine blessing and commendation for your journey from Prior Peter. God bless you my brother and keep you safe."

Early the next morning, Richard and Ralph Purves, delighted to be back in action, set out on their journey to Plymouth and to France.

Chapter 15

Exeter and Yartecombe

Armand rejoined his two men at arms in Exeter. He was still conscious that his last minute intervention at Cornwood had been too close for comfort. Had he failed, his own life would have been forfeit. He could barely hold back his pride in the quality of his marksmanship, and the fact that a single arrow fired in haste from some thirty paces had so swiftly and completely silenced Wideslade.

Gregor and Harald had been keeping watch on the Bishop's palace and reported that Bishop Berkeley and Canon Bloyou were both still inside, but it was rumoured that they were about to leave for the Bishop's manor at Yartecombe.

"I'll be at the alehouse by St Thomas's," Armand murmured quietly. "Come and find me as soon as The Bishop leaves; mark well how many men are with him, and if they be churchmen, monks or men at arms."

As he rested with a pot of ale and waited for news of the Bishop's departure, Armand reflected on his orders from Sir Robert. Killing the priest had not troubled him. He had known Wideslade as a grasping and unscrupulous cleric, exploiting the Daunay patronage.

Killing the Bishop and his sycophantic Canon was another matter, altogether. The furore that would follow the killing would be devastating and no stone would be left unturned in seeking out the perpetrators. Armand knew, too, that even if they were successful and made a clean escape from the scene of the crime, his life, and that of his two companions, might well be forfeit to Sir Robert if their silence was to be assured.

On the other hand, the reward promised by Sir Robert for the successful completion of this task was more than tempting. It was impossible to refuse.

To be given his own manor was a prize beyond his dreams. He grinned at the thought and began to make his plans.

Bishop Berkeley and Canon Bloyou set out for Yartecombe early in the morning with just one elderly monk leading a couple of packhorses. They arrived at the Bishop's house in the late afternoon and were welcomed by a small staff of servants who had made preparation for their visit. Fires were lit and a substantial supper was served in the main hall.

After supper and some conversation and prayers, The Bishop and Bloyou retired to their respective and adjoining rooms in the newly refurbished solar. Tired from the journey and replete with good food and wine, they slept soundly.

Armand told Harald and Gregor that they were charged with helping him to carry out a vital but dangerous task involving an attack on Bishop Berkeley's home at Yartecombe. He failed to tell them the real purpose of their mission.

Even so, and in ignorance of the truth, they were uneasy at being involved in an attack on such a prominent churchman.

Armand was, however, prepared for their likely reaction. "Have no fear lads," he said, reassuringly. "This attack is ordered by Sir Robert and has the sanction of higher powers. You will be well protected from any trouble that may follow and the rewards are beyond your imagination. This is vital work, lads. Just follow me, do exactly as I say, and all will be well."

They swallowed the bait without further demur. After trailing the Bishop and his two companions from Exeter at a safe distance, they hid in thick woodland about a mile from the manor.

At around midnight, they rode up to within a hundred paces of the house. Leaving Gregor with the horses, Armand and

Harald crept through the small stable yard to the door of the kitchen.

Armand knocked lightly and waited, sword drawn. He heard the bolts being drawn and the latch click open, and a face peered out, just a white blob in the darkness. Armand thrust his sword savagely into the space below the face. There was no sound other than a sucking noise as he withdrew his blade and the body fell forward at his feet. Motioning for Harald to follow him, Armand moved swiftly and quietly into the kitchen.

The flickering light from the range revealed two sleeping figures lying on either side of the fire. Both were despatched instantly and in silence, with brutal sword thrusts.

Armand again gestured for a now visibly shocked Harald to follow him into the main hall. It was dimly lit by a couple of still glowing torches, and the old monk who had accompanied the Bishop from Exeter was the only occupant. He was lying on a trestle and his eyes were wide open in shock as he saw the two men enter the room.

Making a throat cutting gesture to Harald, Armand moved forward, swiftly and silently, to the steps up to the solar. As he ascended he heard the beginning of a scream from the old monk but it was cut off almost before it started.

Armand reached the solar bedrooms and breathed a sigh of relief that they were apparently unguarded. He sheathed his sword and drew his skinning knife.

The Bishop's life ended mid snore, his throat cut with a single slash and his heart pierced with a single thrust.

Bloyou too perished in a fountain of blood as his throat was cut and his carotid artery punctured.

Armand ran back down the stairs to the main hall. He grabbed one of the torches from the wall and shouted for Harald to do the same. He ran back up the stairs, fanning the torch embers into flame and igniting the bedding, drapes and clothing in both the bedrooms.

As he went back through the solar he overturned chairs and tables, tore down the rich tapestries and touched the flaming torch to anything combustible. Reaching the bottom of the staircase, bloody, wild eyed and wreathed in smoke, he yelled to a transfixed Harald.

"Come on lad, break anything you can break and set fire to anything that will burn. Make it look as if this place was attacked by a crazed mob."

The two of them proceeded to wreck the interior of the hall, overturning the central table, breaking chairs and setting fire to rush matting and tapestries.

Moving into the kitchen, they swept everything off the shelves and tables then raked out the hot ashes and logs from the banked up fire. With smoke and flames now emanating from all around him, Armand gestured toward the door and they both ran out into the yard, jumping over the corpse in the doorway.

Armand pointed to the stables on the other side of the courtyard and led the way to them. As he did so, two figures emerged from one of the stalls, staring in disbelief at the scene in front of them. Smoke was everywhere and flames were now visible through the windows and embrasures of the house. They were unarmed ostlers and had no chance. Armand cut them down before they could even wipe the sleep from their eyes.

"Get the horses out," he shouted to Harald. They both ran through the stables, opening the stalls, cutting the tethers of some six horses and shooing the frightened animals into the courtyard where they made for the open gate and stampeded out into the countryside.

As a final act, Armand torched the straw in the horses' stalls and as he ran out of the building, he hurled the burning torch on to the thatched roof and shouted to Harald to do the same.

Breathless and coughing, as the now dense smoke swirled around them, they rejoined a very anxious looking Gregor who was struggling to control their mounts, panicked by the smoke and the wild flight of the Bishop's horses.

"What in God's name happened?" Gregor yelled. "It looks as if there was a pitched battle in there. I thought you were dead for sure."

"Save your breath for now," said Armand. "We need to get away from here, as far and as fast as we can, or dead we will be."

As they spurred the horses into a gallop there was a crash, and gouts of flame and sparks rose high in the air as the roof of the stables collapsed.

A few miles further down the road, Armand and Harald cleansed themselves and their bloodstained clothing in the fast flowing but shallow water of the river Yarty.

Armand suggested that they should split up and head back separately. "When they discover what has happened there will be a hue and cry across the country but they will be looking for a mob," he said. "It will be safer to travel alone. With luck we will all be home before the news gets out."

"When do we get our reward?" Harald questioned. "Whatever it is, I reckon it should be doubled after that. You didn't tell us what was going to happen. If I had known, I wouldn't have agreed to be part of it."

"Nor I," added Gregor, who was still unsure of what exactly had happened.

"Don't worry, lads," said Armand, soothingly. "I am sure that when Sir Robert hears of our success and your bravery, you will get the reward you deserve; now Harald, you get on your way. We will wait; I'll see you at Sheviock."

As Harald disappeared from view Armand wasted no time. He walked up to Gregor who was looking down into the river.

Armand put his arm around him. "You did well lad but if they catch you, God help you, you will not die easy. This is better." He slid his knife between Gregor's ribs. He quickly dragged the body into the underbrush, stripped it, and threw the clothing into the river. Within minutes he was off down the track, leading Gregor's horse and following in Harald's wake.

Half an hour later he was leading three horses and Harald's surprised and unseeing eyes stared up at the stars from his resting place in the ditch.

Moonshadow

Chapter 16

Arworthal and Truro

The tension at Arworthal was building by the day. Elizabeth, still plagued by her morning sickness, was growing desperate with the discomfort and indignity of her imprisonment in the small, makeshift cell and fear for the safety of Richard and herself.

Alicia too was increasingly concerned at her father's absence and with trying to keep Charles under some sort of control. He was like a caged animal, deprived of his usual status and lifestyle and the adventure and excitement that he had recently experienced.

He blamed Elizabeth for his current exile and took every opportunity to shout obscenities at her when he was anywhere near her cell. He had already struck and injured his groom for some trifling error and had upset most of the female servants with his foul language, suggestive remarks and gestures.

He had twice left Arworthal to seek out an ale house in the small but busy little port of Truro. Alicia had tried to prevail upon him not to go, concerned that he would get drunk and draw attention to himself.

"Don't fret, sister," he chided, "I can take care of myself."

Today he had ridden in again, covering the five country miles in less than an hour. He rode into the stables on the quay, dismounted and tossed the reins to the stable lad.

"Give her some water and a rub down, then keep her saddled and ready, and look lively about it." He threw a coin on the ground and walked toward the ale house.

There were a number of new faces in the noisy, crowded and smoky room. As Charles entered, all went silent. One of the local fishermen who Charles had spoken to on a previous visit quickly came to him.

"Best not be here today, sir," he said quietly. "Not good company for you."

Charles looked around him. Dark, unsmiling, grizzled faces of men long at sea stared back at him. Charles knew immediately who they were. Seaborne outlaws, one of the small number of rogue fisherman crews that plied the Cornish coastline, living off their wits from fishing, plundering wrecks and foreign trading ships, and sometimes raiding coastal villages.

Spoiling for a fight, Charles' first instinct was to demand a drink and dare them to refuse him. At the same time, he knew that it would be a useless gesture and would have an unpleasant conclusion. He tipped his hat, and with a contemptuous glare, he turned and left.

He seethed as his departure occasioned raucous laughter and a hubbub of renewed conversation. As he walked back toward the stables he saw a young woman climbing up stone steps of the quay from a small boat below. She looked pretty enough, with free flowing long dark hair, a pale face with a small stub nose and a loose shift dress that did little to conceal her well formed figure. She was obviously in a hurry and headed straight for the alehouse.

Charles called to her. "Not so fast pretty lady, the company in there is not for you."

She stopped and flashed a brief smile at him. "Thank you for the compliment sir, but on the contrary, after five weeks at sea, the company in there are indeed for me. They need me."

She turned away. Charles ran a few steps after her and caught her arm before she reached the alehouse door.

"Hold up there, whore. I need you more than that rabble in there. Let them wait." Now that he was close to her, he realised she was older than he had first thought but still comely enough.

She pulled away from him. "This is my pay day," she hissed. "Leave me be, sire."

His pent up lust was overwhelming. He grabbed her again and started to pull her toward the stables. She struggled and then let out an ear splitting scream. In an instant the alehouse door crashed open and several of the occupants spilled out.

Charles' reactions were sharp. He let the woman go immediately and ran into the stable. His horse clearly had not been touched but was still saddled. He unhitched the reins, leapt into the saddle and was on the move before any of the mob had time to react.

In truth, they were more concerned with escorting the whore into the alehouse.

Charles fled the scene and only a few of the band ran behind him with some token fist shaking. One of them, however, ran harder and for far longer than the rest, screaming imprecations at Charles' back. Finally he stopped, taking great gulping breaths after his exertions.

"I know you, sire," he shouted after the fast receding figure. "Charles Daunay, you murdering coward." He sobbed then and turned back toward the alehouse.

Geoffrey Morgan, the current leader of the marauders, saw his distress and put an arm round his shoulders.

"What ails thee, Tom? Don't fret over a poxy bastard with designs on our woman."

"I don't care about that," said Tom, still tearful, "but that 'poxy bastard' raped my sister and killed my father, then had our whole family evicted from our home at Sheviock. That's why I joined with you. I had no choice. I thought it was him when he came into the alehouse, but it was dark and I wasn't sure. When I saw him struggling with the whore in the daylight, I knew. I swear I will kill him if he returns."

"And we will help you lad," said Geoffrey. "But be of good cheer; you are better off with us than slaving on the land for that fellow."

Tom grimaced. "You may be right, though it is not worth the death of my father and the ruin of my family. What is he even doing down here? There are no Daunay lands in these parts, as far as I know."

"Old Silas in the ale house seemed to know him," said Geoffrey. "Let's ask him what he knows."

When questioned, Silas' response was guarded.

"I don't know him," he said. "He has quaffed ale here but a couple of times in the past two or three weeks to my knowledge, and has only spoken a few words while here. I think once he made mention of Arworthal, the old manor and village up on the high road."

"How far?" asked Tom, with a tremor of excitement in his voice.

"Oh about five or six mile," said Silas.

"Let's go after him," said Tom. "Let me have my revenge." He started for the door.

"Hold on, boy." Geoffrey held up his hand to stop him. "You forget we sail on the next tide and anyway, there are only two horses in the stables. You'll need more than two of us to bring that bastard down. He probably has men at arms with him at his manor."

Tom looked crestfallen. "Next time," he said. "Next time we are here, I will have him."

Chapter 17

Avignon, The Papal Court

Apart from Ralph suffering from seasickness all the way from Portsmouth to Bayonne, the journey across the Bay of Biscay and then across Aquitaine had been surprisingly uneventful. As Baldwin had predicted, the letters of introduction opened the doors of the monasteries that they visited and ensured that they were treated with extra hospitality.

Richard decided that unless it was really necessary, they would not reveal that they were carrying the Golden Rose with them. News of their treasured possession might get to the wrong ears and invite unnecessary danger.

News of the dramatic events in England was widespread and Richard and Ralph were often questioned about the whereabouts of King Edward following his abdication, and the liaison between Queen Isabella and Roger Mortimer.

The monastic stance was one of approval of the defeat of the Despensers and their evil rule from behind the throne, but disapproval of anything other than a political relationship between Isabella and Mortimer. They cautioned Richard that a number of Despenser followers had fled from England to Aquitaine and were lying low hoping to be forgotten, or for yet another twist of fate that might see them returned to favour.

Richard answered all the questions as best he could and

brought his inquisitors up to date with the latest news of the Scottish threat and the impending battle in the North.

He said little about his own mission, other than he was journeying to seek audience with the Pope. If pressed, he would simply say that it was a private diplomatic matter, the details of which he could not divulge.

On a cool, grey morning, some twenty three days after leaving England, Richard and Ralph left the hospitality of the Benedictine Abbey at St Andre, where they had rested for the night. Crossing the magnificent St Benezet stone bridge across the Rhone, and looking across at the ancient and rather dilapidated walls of Avignon, they were both elated to have reached their destination; at the same time, they were apprehensive about their reception and the outcome of their mission.

They stopped at the little St Nicholas chapel built onto the bridge. Richard bade Ralph stay with the horses while he entered the empty and peaceful chapel, praying quietly for the safety of Elizabeth and for success in seeking audience with The Pope.

As he emerged, a shaft of sunshine broke through the low clouds and illuminated the town with a soft ethereal glow. He felt spiritually and physically uplifted. "Come Ralph; let's go tell our story and ensure that we have right and might on our side."

Ralph laughed, picking up on Richard's mood of optimism. "God favours the brave, sire, so you lead and I'll follow."

Papal guards stopped them at the main gate to the town and checked their papers. They were directed to simply follow the main street in front of them to the top of the hill to reach the Dominican Monastery and the Bishops Palace.

Entering Avignon, they were struck by the contrast between the very old, solid, but somewhat dilapidated facades of the buildings, and the frantic business activity that swirled around them. The town was like one big market, with traders of many different cultures displaying and selling their wares from shop fronts and stalls with a hubbub of noise and a profusion of smells and colours.

Pushing their way through the throng, they made their way toward The Papal residence. They had been told many times en route that Pope John was transforming the Monastery and the adjoining Bishops Palace into a sumptuous residence, worthy of the head of the church in a papal city.

The wooden scaffolding on the outside walls, the piles of stone and marble visible in the outer courtyard, coupled with the quantity of stonemasons and labourers certainly supported that report.

They were stopped by more papal guards at the entrance to the small, inner yard in front of the main door. They handed over the various letters of introduction and Ralph held the box containing the Golden Rose in case it was needed. They waited as one of the guards disappeared into the building. He soon emerged with a young Friar; small, slight, with a halo of fair hair around his tonsure. He introduced himself as Brother Santos, bade them welcome, and took them through cloisters to the refectory.

He motioned for them to be seated. "Please, make yourselves comfortable. I will have some refreshment brought to you and take these letters to the Prior. I will try to arrange for you to see him as soon as he is free."

Before any refreshments appeared, however, Friar Santos was back, looking somewhat agitated and out of breath.

"I am tasked with taking you now to The Bishops Palace for an audience with his Holiness Pope John. The Prior is already there, together with a number of cardinals. It seems that your arrival may be timely."

Richard and Ralph exchanged puzzled glances. "But nobody yet knows the purpose of our visit," said Richard.

"Should I stay here?" queried Ralph. "I am sure that His Holiness does not know of me."

"No." Richard stood up. "Come with me and bring the box with you."

They set off almost at a run behind Friar Santos; back through the cloisters and across the inner courtyard, and into a side door of the Palace. Richard and Ralph gazed open mouthed at the magnificence of the interior. Marble floors, beautifully decorated ceilings, walls draped with fine tapestries and works of art, and sumptuous furnishings to outshine anything that Richard had seen anywhere in England.

They climbed the marble steps of a grand staircase with sweeping carved balustrades and entered a large anteroom, furnished relatively simply with a fine Italianate chestnut table and chairs covered with deep red leather. Two papal guards in full regalia stood at the door of the Pontiff's office. One of them stepped forward and motioned for Ralph to open the box he was carrying. When Ralph displayed the contents he stepped back, smiled, and signalled the little group forward.

Friar Santos stood back. "Go in now," he said in a whisper. "I will stay here with your man, and guide you back when you have finished."

Richard took the box from Ralph and stepped through the door. He quickly took in the atmosphere in the room; it was anticipatory, and many faces turned toward him with an expectation of eagerly awaited news.

Seated at the centre of the room, behind an imposing carved wood desk, was His Holiness Pope John. Surrounding him, five red robed Cardinals, the prior in a grey robe, and a priest in a black surplice edged with scarlet. The room itself was grand beyond compare. Beautifully framed portraits and exquisitely worked tapestries vied for space on the walls. The vaulted ceiling and frescoes were lavishly decorated and embossed with gold leaf in abundance. The floor was constructed from huge slabs of highly polished white marble, strewn with exotic eastern rugs.

Richard, awestruck and nervous, bowed low and was beckoned forward by one of the cardinals until he stood before Pope John's desk. He was scrutinised intently by unusually bright and piercing eyes. "Peace be with you. What news do you bring from England?"

The voice was soft and yet commanding. Richard, still mystified that he seemed to have been expected, hesitated. Before he could reply, the Cardinal who had beckoned him forward interjected sharply.

"What news of our revered Bishop Berkeley of Exeter and his foul murder? Come sire, we wait to hear of your involvement in this evil affair."

Richard gasped and stood open mouthed. Then he collected himself and spoke, hesitantly at first. "Your Holiness, I fear I ... I know nothing of this. We quit England some twenty three days since to travel here, to seek audience with Your Holiness on a personal family matter. To my knowledge Bishop Berkeley was alive and well when we departed. He is—was, however, involved in our situation. It is possible, perhaps, that his murder may be directly connected with our quest."

There was a hubbub among the group of cardinals surrounding Pope John, everyone trying to speak at once. He held up his hand for silence and beckoned to a figure standing close to the door, previously unseen by Richard.

"Come forward, brother and tell us again, Sir Richard as well, your message from England."

As the man stepped forward Richard recognised him as Mark, one of the monks from Newenham who had escorted Baldwin when he delivered the Golden Rose to Ugborough.

"Brother Mark, what are you doing here? And what is this news you bring?" he asked, anxiously. "You must have travelled very swiftly to overtake us."

"Sire," said Mark. "I bring you salutations from your brother. The day after you left from Plymouth, Bishop Berkeley was found cruelly murdered at his manor in Yartecombe, his home desecrated and burned. Canon Bloyou from Exeter and several of the Bishops servants were also killed. Brother Baldwin charged me with getting the news to you here in Avignon with all possible haste, and in the case of your absence, to advise His Holiness of the dreadful news. Your brother says it seems likely that the killing is part of the plot against you, and this news will aid you in obtaining the help and support of His Holiness."

As he finished speaking, all eyes in the room focused on Richard. He took a deep breath. "Thank you, Brother Mark. Your service to our family and to all here is greatly appreciated. You must be sore and weary from your journey." He set the box he was carrying on the desk, opened the lid and produced the Golden Rose, handing it reverentially to Pope John.

"Your Holiness, I have brought with me the Golden Rose, awarded by His Holiness Pope Innocent to my Great

Grandfather, Sir Reginald de Mohun, at Lyon in 1245. It is held by my family and displayed at Newenham Abbey on Laetare Sunday every year."

Pope John leaned forward, tracing the delicate structure of the rose with his fingers, and nodded in approval.

"It was intended to support my credentials in seeking an audience with you. I came to ask for your help and support in resolving an evil plot involving the kidnap of my wife and the sequestration of our manors and our land.

"Bishop Berkeley was, we believe, drawn into this deception and if, as reported, he has now been murdered then the matter has become infinitely more important and something that directly concerns your Holiness."

Pope John gestured for a chair to be brought forward for Richard and bade him to be seated. He replaced the Golden Rose in its open box.

"Your credentials are accepted and we welcome you to our court here in Avignon. The news of the murder of our Brother in Christ, Bishop Berkeley, has shocked us all, especially coming so soon after the dreadful fate of his predecessor, Walter de Stapleton. Let us hear your story, Sire."

Richard, without the time for preparation that he had expected, launched into the story of his meeting and marriage to Elizabeth Fitzwilliam, the kidnap and second marriage to Denyss and her subsequent disappearance, with the apparent involvement of The Daunay family. Then he covered the murder of the priest Wideslade and perhaps Denyss, and now it seemed Bishop Berkeley and Canon Bloyou, all witnesses or signatories to the divorce and second marriage. Finally, he recounted the response from Queen Isabella at the court in London. At one point, Richard asked for Ralph to be allowed into the room, to support him and add his own observations and account of the kidnapping.

There were many questions and it took more than two hours for the whole story to be told.

Finally, Pope John called for silence, then spoke.

"Sir Richard, we thank you for your attendance here and for your lucid expression of the problems you face and the possible connection with the death of Bishop Berkeley. We are moved by your situation and understand your appeal for our help. We will pray for both you and your wife, Elizabeth. Leave us now to discuss the matter among ourselves and to decide on our course of action."

He proffered his hand and Richard bent low to kiss his ring.

"Friar Santos will take you and your bailiff, and Brother Mark to ensure that you are well fed and rested. We will meet again tomorrow after Matins and inform you of our decision on what can be done. God go with you."

Richard picked up the box with the Golden Rose safely restored to it, and led the way out of the room.

Next morning, after an early breakfast, they once again assembled in the anteroom to The Papal Office. The priest who had been present at yesterday's meeting, dressed in scarlet lined black robes, greeted them. He was tall and upright in bearing, with a neatly shaved tonsure of dark hair. His face was gaunt with tiredness, and worry lines creased his brow. He spoke in a low voice, slowly but with authority.

"I am John de Grandisson from England, currently chaplain to his Holiness." He gestured for them to be seated at the table.

"His Holiness is occupied on matters of State and apologises for being unable to see you himself. He bestows his blessings on you."

He took a seat at the head of the table, put down a single roll of parchment, and unrolled it in front of him. "We debated at length yesterday, following your audience. I will outline to you a summary of our deliberations.

"His Holiness will support you, with a full Papal investigation into your allegations concerning the eloignment of your wife, Elizabeth de Mohun, falsification of annulment and marriage documents, and the illegal sequestration of lands and property. The investigation will involve the families of de Mohun and Daunay, and encompass the alleged involvement of the late Bishop Berkeley and other clergy within the Diocese of Exeter.

"As part of the investigation, we will seek to identify the motive for the murder of Bishop Berkeley and if possible, bring the culprit or culprits to justice." He paused, but before Richard could respond, he went on.

"There is more. His Holiness has seen fit to appoint me to succeed Bishop Berkeley, but before my consecration, I am to accompany you to England to lead the investigation. I need three days to settle my affairs here and make preparations."

He looked up and for the first time, he smiled. "So, Sire," he said to Richard. "Your journey has not been in vain."

Chapter 18

Luppit, Tavistock and Bodinnick

A westerly gale made for an uncomfortable but swift return passage from Bayonne to Plymouth. Richard and John de Grandisson decided during their journey to go their separate ways when they reached England, and to meet up again in Exeter, when Richard had news of what might have transpired during his absence.

After lodging overnight in Plymouth, Richard, Ralph, and Brother Mark rode on to Ugborough. Richard harboured the flickering hope that Elizabeth would be there to greet him. She was not, and nobody at Ugborough had any news of her.

The following day, after instructing Ralph to stay and take stock of the estate, Richard and Brother Mark set off for Luppit and Mohun's Ottery, to return the Golden Rose to safe keeping. Richard hoped fervently that Baldwin would be there and would have news of Elizabeth. All the time he nursed the secret fear that Elizabeth might already be dead.

They went first to Luppit church to restore the rose to its secure niche behind the alter screen.

Richard was relieved to see the burly figure of his brother seated in prayer. Baldwin stood up and turned as he heard footsteps in the chancel. A huge smile lit up his face and he enveloped Richard in a bear hug that took his breath away.

"Welcome home, my brother. What news have you? Did the Rose work its holy magic?" Richard took his arm and they sat down together on the alter steps.

"All went well, very well, and soon I will tell you all, but first, brother; what news of my Elizabeth?"

Baldwin's smile faded and Richard's heart began to sink.

"I fear, brother, that so far we have failed to find her. Lawrence, his son and I, Sir William and your father have searched and enquired far and wide but entirely without success.

"Lawrence, Adam and others have had Sir Robert under surveillance day and night around Sheviock, to Exeter and even to London and back. He must know he is being watched but carries on a seemingly normal life, ignoring their presence. At no time has he given any indication that he is harbouring a secret, or has any connection with Elizabeth, Charles or Alicia, both of whom have also vanished.

"On one occasion, Lawrence came face to face with him in the street and asked him directly if he knew the whereabouts of Elizabeth. His reply was, "I do not, and have no wish to know," and he walked away."

Richard put his head in his hands. Baldwin tried to cheer him.

"Do not despair. We must assume that Charles and Alicia are guarding Elizabeth somewhere; God knows where, but at least while all three are missing it seems more likely that Elizabeth is captive but still alive."

"So what do we do next?" Richard whispered, close to tears.

Baldwin stood. "Tomorrow, I am to go to Tavistock and meet again with Lawrence to plan our next search. You must come with us. He will be so pleased to see you safe returned. Never fear, little brother; if we all put our heads together I am sure that with God's will, we will find her."

Even as he said it he knew that he could not convey the conviction that Richard needed. To try and change the atmosphere of gloom, he put his arm round Richard's shoulders.

"Come on then boy," he boomed. "Give me some good news, tell me about Avignon."

The Ferry Inn at Boddinick Steps was jammed to the rafters with damp bodies taking refuge from the storm outside. The usual bunch of local topers were outnumbered this day by the crew of the marauders' hulk that had downed anchor in the creek late that afternoon.

Many of the crew were local men and a good feeling of camaraderie pervaded the room. The buzz of conversation, storytelling and laughter grew louder and more raucous as the evening wore on.

Alric, the local blacksmith, was sitting close to the fire in his usual seat, listening to the general hubbub when he heard, just behind him, a voice raised in anger.

"Charles Daunay, that bastard? Don't talk to me about him. I will have him, yet."

Alric, glanced quickly over his shoulder. Through the gloom and the tallow smoke, he saw the flushed, angry face of a young, fair-headed man, surrounded by a group of fellow seamen.

"Alright Tom; calm down," said one of his companions. "We knows you want him bad and we'll help you string him up when we get back there again."

Alric rose and pushed his way through to the group. One or two of them recognised and acknowledged him.

"Listen, lad," he said to Tom. "If you know the whereabouts of Charles Daunay, there are folk who will pay you handsomely for the knowledge."

Tom, well oiled with the strong local ale, glared at him. "It's not money I want," he hissed. "I want to see him swing for the murder of my father and the ruin of my family." Alric placed him then.

"Ah," he said, "I know you now; you be the lad from Sheviock. Well Tom, listen to me. The people who want to find Charles Daunay have just as much reason or more to see him dead and buried, and if you are willing to tell them where to find him, you might get a handsome reward and their help in bringing him down."

"Don't e turn down the money, Tom," said one of his companions. "You might get enough to get your land back. Worth a try anyways."

Alric interrupted. "How long are you anchored here?"

After a pause, the obvious leader of the group pushed forward. "I am Geoffrey Morgan," he said. "We are making repairs to the hulk and we will lay up in Pont Creek for about three days."

"Alright then Tom; tell me where Charles Daunay hides and I will try to get word to the people who need to know, and who will reward you."

"Not so fast." Geoffrey Morgan put his hand over Tom's mouth. "Don't say a word, Tom. If these people will pay for the knowledge, let them come here with the money. Sorry Blacksmith, but if Tom tells you where he is, what is to stop you collecting for yourself?"

Alric frowned and bristled but realised the logic of the argument and accepted it with good humour.

"Right enough," he said, "although, all here know me as an honest man. Within three days I will endeavour to bring someone here to talk with you."

"Tell them to bring the money," said Morgan, to general laughter.

"And a rope to put around the bastards neck," shouted Tom as Alric made his way to the door.

Over a sumptuous 'welcome home' supper of venison at Lawrence's house in Tavistock, Richard retold the story of his journey to Avignon and back, and the rapid turn of events there with the news of the murder of Bishop Berkeley.

He in turn was told the details of the attack on the Bishop's house at Yartecombe, and of the rumour that a band of outlaws had committed the atrocities.

"We know that Sir Robert was not directly involved." Lawrence drained a pot of ale and continued.

"We were watching him all the time, but we think the Daunays must have had a hand in it. It is just too convenient that The Bishop and Canon Bloyou should be silenced when they were the only people that might still have been able to tell the truth of what happened to Elizabeth. We have lost track of Charles so he may have been responsible; and there was one witness—a farm girl going milking, who swore that she saw three men riding for their lives away from The Bishops Manor toward Plymouth, just after she saw the flames from the fire. She says they were well horsed and did not look like outlaws. We are trying to find out if anyone else might have seen them on the Plymouth road."

There was a general hubbub of questions and speculation until Richard banged his fist on the table. In the following moment of silence, he repeated his question of yesterday.

"So what do we do next? I only have one aim right now and that is to find Elizabeth. Nothing else matters so let us focus our attention on that."

Sir William from Mohun's Ottery, the most senior member of the family present, suggested that they should concentrate on the Monastery and church at St Germans.

"Someone there must have seen something. If your man Ralph Purves is to be believed, that's where Elizabeth was taken, and where, according to the papers Sir Robert showed your father, the so called marriage to Denyss, God rest him, took place. I know that you have already been there, Lawrence but maybe if we all go someone will speak up and—" He paused mid sentence at the sound of someone hammering on the house door and shouting Lawrence's name.

Joan ran to the door, closely followed by her husband. Lawrence held her back and unbarred the door himself. The figure standing in the doorway was dishevelled and breathless. The strong craggy face, framed with close cropped, jet black hair was vaguely familiar, but Lawrence could not remember where he had seen him before.

The man blinked in the glare of the well lit room and took a step forward. "I seek the de Mohun family." His voice was deep and local. "I have news for them."

Richard sprang to his feet. "Alric, Alric the blacksmith, from Fowey? What brings you here? Come in man, sit down; someone give him some ale."

Alric stumbled forward, slumped gratefully onto a chair, and took a long swallow of the proffered ale.

"I be glad to see you, sire." He spoke directly to Richard. "I didn't know you be 'ere but I be told your brother might know where you was. I saw you, sir," he pointed at Lawrence, "and your boy in Fowey market when you was asking folk for news of Lady Elizabeth of Hall." He smiled at Richard. "Pardon, sire. I mean your Lady Elizabeth, and you wanted news too of the Daunays; in particular, Charles Daunay."

"Do you have such news?" Richard asked. Everyone in the room leant forward to better hear the answer.

Alric took another swig of ale and paused, enjoying the tension and being the centre of such concentrated attention.

"I do sire, I ..."

"Do you know where Elizabeth is? Is she alive?" Richard shouted. "Come on man, tell us what you know."

"Some patience brother," said Baldwin. "Let him tell what news he has in his own time."

Alric gave Baldwin a grateful glance. "I am sorry," he said. "I cannot tell you anything of Lady Elizabeth." Richard groaned.

"But I do have news of Charles Daunay. I have found someone who has seen him in recent times."

Revelling in his enthralled, captive audience, Alric related the events of the previous evening at the Ferry Inn and the story he had heard from Tom Weaver's own mouth of his sighting of Charles Daunay, and that Tom, with the help of his fellows, planned to exact revenge on Charles when they returned to wherever it was that they had seen him.

"And that place is where?" said Lawrence. "Come, blacksmith; stop playing with us and tell us all you know."

"Sire, that is all I know. I'm sorry, but they would not tell me more. I said that you would pay handsomely for the knowledge of where Daunay is and they would not trust me with their secret."

Richard took command of the situation. "First I want to know if Elizabeth is alive and still held captive by the Daunays. I do not want this buccaneer crew putting her life at even greater risk. I want to hear the story of his sighting first hand and know what Tom Weaver and his companions are planning. Are they still in Fowey water? Can we get to them before they sail again?"

Alric grinned. "Aye, sire; they have to make repairs to their boat and will be in the creek for another two days, at least. That is why I made such haste to find you. If we leave at first light tomorrow you can have all you need from these buccaneers by nightfall. They will be seeking a handsome reward, mind."

"They shall have it, more handsome than they might believe, so long as their tale is true and they can lead us to Daunay and Elizabeth. We will leave for Fowey before dawn."

They awoke the next morning to hear more bad news. Adam, and Simon, one of Lawrence's stable lads, had returned from their vigil at Sheviock to tell them that Sir Robert had vanished.

"I saw him in the morning at the church," said Adam. "His bailiff rode out toward Pelynt but did not return. Then Sir Robert came out of the Manor about noon, went into his stable and before we could move, he came out at a gallop and headed toward Pelynt. He had the cheek to wave at us as he went past. I took after him but never even caught sight of him again. Simon stayed at Sheviock, in case he returned, but he didn't. We waited till midnight and then we came to tell you. I'm sorry, but he's gone."

Richard comforted him. "Don't worry, Adam; you have done your best and more, and I am grateful beyond words. It may even be for the best because with a bit of luck and God on our side, we may now find all the damn Daunays in one place."

The ride to Fowey was fast and furious. Richard left first with Lawrence and Alric. Baldwin and Sir William stayed for another couple of hours. to organise some fresh horses and despatch one of Sir William's men to Dunster, to inform Sir John de Mohun of the developments.

Richard, Lawrence, and Alric took the shortest route possible. Cutting through the tangle of lanes between Liskeard and Bodinnick, they rode hard and by mid afternoon they were descending the steep hill down to the waterside at Bodinnick.

The two brothers saw to the stabling and care of their horses while Alric engaged one of the many local boatmen to row him around the headland to Pont Creek, where the cog was at anchor.

After a short standoff while Alric was identified, a rope ladder was dropped over the side and he climbed on board. Tom and Geoffrey Morgan were waiting for him.

"Well," said Morgan, "you were quick enough. Did you bring the money?"

Alric smiled. "No, but I have brought the men with the money. I think you will know one of them."

He turned to Tom. "Sir Richard de Mohun is your man and 'e has with him his brother from Tavistock. 'E knows about your family, Tom, and the wrong that you all suffered. Now the Daunay family have kidnapped his wife, Lady Elizabeth, from Hall Manor above you there on the hill. They have 'er hidden somewhere and most likely in the same place as Charles Daunay.

"Sir Richard is desperate to track 'em down and to rescue 'er. 'Ee wants to help you Tom and will reward you well but 'e wants to talk to you face to face and learn from you all that you can tell 'im."

"I do know of him," said Tom. "My father spoke well of him. He has land close to Sheviock and we knew his bailiff."

Alric nodded. "Come this eve around dusk to the Ferry Inn and you can meet and discuss what you know and see what can be agreed. Come alone, they will not negotiate with a mob of you."

Morgan spoke up quickly. "I will be with him to see that he is treated fair. It will need a quick decision. Our repairs are done and we need to sail tomorrow on the tide."

Alric, climbing back to the rowing boat below, shouted, "Sir Richard won't want to delay any longer than is needed, you can be sure of that. 'E is in fear for the life of 'is Lady Elizabeth."

By sundown, Baldwin, Sir William de Mohun and four men at arms with fresh horses had arrived, and all the Mohuns, together with Alric, were gathered in the Ferry Inn.

Tom and Morgan arrived promptly, although only they came into the Inn; half a dozen of the crew made their presence obvious on the quay outside.

Richard got straight down to business. "Tom, I know of the wrong done to your sister and your family by the Daunays and that you are seeking revenge. I too have been wronged by them.

My wife has been kidnapped and her lands and fortune stolen from us.

"We believe that any witnesses to their evil deceptions have been murdered to ensure their silence, and we fear for the life of my Lady Elizabeth, if indeed she still lives.

"The Daunays have gone to ground. We know not where and we are desperate to find them. Alric here tells us that you have seen Charles Daunay in recent times. If you can tell us all you know and can lead us to him, I will put 20 livres in your hand here and now; and, if you wish it, I will provide land for you and your family to farm on my manor at Ugborough. Now come lad, tell us all you know."

Tom glanced swiftly at Morgan, who nodded. Tom launched into an exciting and somewhat rambling story of the incident at Truro, finishing with the description of Charles Daunay's flight and the hearsay from old Silas in the ale house that Daunay had mentioned somewhere called Arworthal during a previous visit.

Lawrence chipped in. "It sounds a bit vague," he said glumly, "and this was how long ago?"

"About forty days or so now," said Tom, "but—"

Before he could go on Richard stood; his face suddenly lit up and he shouted out.

"The clever bastards. Arworthal belongs to Elizabeth! The manor was in her mother's family and came to her when her mother died. Sir John told me about it but he said it was a ruin and Elizabeth had never been there. I had forgotten about it but it makes sense. They gambled that we would never think to find her in her own property, especially a remote ruin. Well, it seems they may have lost the gamble."

He took Tom's hands in his own, pulled him to his feet and embraced him. "Tom, my eternal thanks. You too, Alric, for bringing us together. Now we must make all speed to Arworthal. It will mean some hard riding and we will need to be well prepared. How long will it take us to get there?"

Before anyone could reply, Geoffrey Morgan raised his voice above the hubbub.

"Hold hard. First let's see the colour of your money, sir." He pointed to Richard. "Twenty livres for the information I think you said, sir. On the table if you don't mind." Richard smiled and turned to Baldwin.

"My brother Baldwin holds the purse strings. Come Baldwin, give young Tom here his money, he deserves every penny."

Baldwin delved into his robe and produced a heavy leather purse. He carefully counted out the bright silver coins onto the table. Morgan, rather than Tom, scooped them up.

"We all share in any good fortune that comes our way," he said. "Tom knows that, don't 'ee Tom."

Tom nodded his acquiescence. "Fair enough, Captain Morgan but if we catch these Daunay bastards and the land I'm promised comes to me, I will be leaving you to go back to my family and farming. I will not have to share the land, will I captain?"

Geoffrey Morgan laughed. "No lad, the land will be yours and good luck to you." He turned again to Richard.

"I have an idea, sire, that I believe might suit us all. Our ship sails tomorrow. We are set on going on a little raiding trip to the Scillies. This storm may well have provided a wreck or two. Perhaps though, we might first sail back to Truro, or better still to Devoran, close by to Arworthal. We could take you gentlemen with us and maybe help you find your lady and help Tom to get his hands on the bastard that killed his father, eh Tom. Mind you, sir, if we are to delay getting to the Scillies and maybe miss out on the booty from a wreck, it will cost your banker priest some more of the silver he still has in his purse."

Richard thought for only a moment then reached over and shook Geoffrey's hand. "Done, Captain Morgan. Luck seems to be with us at last. What hour tomorrow do you sail?"

"On the tide at noon," said Morgan. "We will have the ship alongside the quay an hour before, ready to load you onboard. We can take no more than six men with horses and it will be a bit of a press, but given a fair wind and kind sea, we could be close by Arworthal tomorrow evening."

Richard ordered ale for everyone and raised his cup to the success of their mission, finishing with a sentiment that everyone shared.

"Pray God that Lady Elizabeth still lives."

Next morning dawned bright and clear, and prayers were answered with a cold but gentle easterly wind and a calm sea. Horses, weaponry and supplies were assembled on the quay and right on time the large, flat bottomed cog came alongside. Within the hour ropes were cast off and the somewhat overcrowded vessel headed out to sea, low in the water, ungainly but stable.

Chapter 19

Arworthal

After a month spent kicking his heels at Arworthal, Charles was reaching breaking point. Neither he nor Alicia could understand why their father was so long in coming.

Although still respectively gaoler and captive, Alicia and Elizabeth had developed an ever closer relationship, a situation that Elizabeth had quietly fostered. Alicia had managed to protect her from the continual attentions of Charles, who was getting more and more frustrated and violent.

After another of his visits to the ale house in Truro, Charles returned in a foul and violent mood. Alicia heard him ranting at his ostler in the yard. She immediately locked Elizabeth into her makeshift cell and pocketed the key. Just in time.

Charles stormed through the kitchen, intent on molesting Elizabeth. Finding the door locked he became enraged. Kicking the door and rattling the bars, he screamed at Alicia. "Give me the keys or by God I will do you harm." He moved toward her, hand outstretched. Alicia backed away.

"No Charles, I will not. You are supposed to be protecting us not threatening us. What is the matter with you? Do you want to ruin all Father's plans?"

He did not answer her, but drew his hunting knife, put it to her throat and again stretched out his hand for the keys.

Alicia cried out as the knife tip pricked her neck but she kept the keys firmly in her hand.

At that moment, they heard the jingle of harness and raised voices in the courtyard; then, one voice above the rest. Sir Robert, authoritative and commanding, was calling for the horses to be taken care of.

"Thank God," Alicia murmured. Charles, who had sheathed his knife, looked pale and shaken. "This once Charles I will forgive you; but if ever you threaten me again, you had better kill me because I will tell father all that you have said and done."

Charles nodded and with a swift, malevolent glance toward Elizabeth, who was standing at her cell door with her face pressed against the bars, he went out to greet his father.

"My thanks, Alicia," said Elizabeth with feeling. "I think you are brave even if you are misguided. Let us hope, now that your father is here, that he will see reason and let me go back to my rightful home."

Alicia went to her and softly touched her face. "I am sure my father will try his best to see that you are properly cared for. I will tell him that you are with child and need to have more comfortable surroundings than this. Don't worry; Charles will not dare to molest you while father is here."

As she spoke, Sir Robert, looking gaunt and travel worn, strode into the kitchen with Charles in his wake. He embraced Alicia in an enfolding hug.

"Alicia my dear, I need food and some rest. Armand is dealing with the horses, who also need feeding. Can you see to that?" Alicia kissed him and nodded.

"There is a small grazing pasture for the horses just down the track. I will go and tell Armand now. There is a room ready for you in the barn next to Charles. I will bring you food in a moment. We eat here in the kitchen, which is at least dry and warm."

She gestured towards Elizabeth. "She is safe and well and anxious to hear when you will allow her to return to her home."

"Soon, I hope." Sir Robert went to the door of Elizabeth's cell and spoke directly to her.

"You and I will talk later when I am rested and perhaps we can agree upon what happens next. I trust you have been well cared for while staying here. Not the most luxurious lodgings I grant but safe and secure from danger."

Elizabeth looked at him steadily. "I have no complaint with regard to the accommodation sir, given that it is my own property. As to being safe and secure from danger, I fear that any danger I may be in emanates from you and your family. You have no right to keep me here as a prisoner and I demand to be returned to my home at Hall."

Sir Robert sighed and shook his head. "We will talk later. It is time for you to realise that you are in no position to demand anything."

After he had eaten, Sir Robert asked Alicia and Charles to come to his room in the stable block. Despite his weariness, he was animated and paced around the room as he talked.

"I have been watched day and night by the Mohuns. I led them a merry dance around the country for the past five weeks or so. Two nights ago I managed to evade them and have travelled here by circuitous route without rest. We have one more problem to solve and we shall have completed our plan and restored our fortunes.

"Denyss is dead, whether through natural causes or some other intervention." He looked keenly at Charles who was unable to hold his gaze.

"It matters not. He is dead and so, all the Fitzwilliam lands, including this place, are ours. All those party to our deception are also dead. Wideslade, murdered for his goods and chattels as he was leaving Cornwood. Canon Bloyou and Bishop Berkeley …" He crossed himself. "Both dead. God have mercy on their souls. They were slain, along with their household, by a roving gang of cutthroats, who raided the Bishop's house at Yartecombe and razed it to the ground."

Charles grinned. "Lucky for us then; couldn't have managed it better if we'd tried."

Sir Robert glared at him. "Hold your tongue, boy; remarks like that could undo all that we have put in place."

Alicia had gone pale and could barely get her words out. "Father, answer me truthfully; were these deaths of our doing?"

"Of course not, Alicia; do not heed Charles. There is

undeniably a benefit to us from these unfortunate events but that is just the way it is, and perhaps proves the justice of our cause in God's eyes."

But as he spoke the words, his gaze was averted and deep down, Alicia knew.

Charles broke the awkward silence. "So what is the one remaining problem? My guess is the bitch in the kitchen and what to do with her." He rubbed his hands together. "Give her to me and I will solve your problem."

Again, Sir Robert turned on him. "Will you be quiet, sir. Your behaviour does you no honour. No, I have arranged that Elizabeth Denyss, as we must call her, is to be taken in by the abbess Margaret Aunger at Canonsleigh. She will be confined and live the rest of her days in peace and penitence."

"But she is pregnant," Alicia broke in. "She carries de Mohun's child."

Sir Robert looked shocked but quickly recovered. "Then the nunnery is certainly the best place for her. She will be well looked after and safely delivered of her child. I fear, however, that she will be reluctant to accept this solution for her future, so we must stoop to some subterfuge.

"Alicia, you must reassure her that she will be going back to her home in Hall but that first, for her own safety and to atone for her sins, she will spend some thirty days at Canonsleigh."

Alicia tried to interject but her father held up his hand to stop her and went on.

"Once there, she can be restrained and we can leave her in the care of the abbess, who assures me that she will soon submit to God's will. Now, go to her Alicia and tell her the good news which I will personally confirm to her later."

Alicia left to do her father's bidding with a heavy heart. She knew that confinement in a priory would stifle Elizabeth's spirit and condemn her to a life without hope of anything other than a better life in the hereafter.

Charles moved to follow her but Sir Robert bade him stay.

"I assume you were responsible for Denyss dying before his illness took him?" Charles could not evade his father's scrutiny and nodded in agreement.

"Well, as it happens, it was just as well because Sir John de

Mohun visited him a couple of days later and might have learnt more than we wanted him to know. Now it seems your desire to take revenge on Lady Elizabeth may be realised after all."

Charles looked puzzled. "I thought you had decided to confine her to a priory."

"That was for Alicia to hear and believe, but we cannot afford to let Elizabeth live. The chances of her escaping from a nunnery would be too high to risk, and the thought of a de Mohun child growing up, knowing the truth and seeking retribution, is not to be contemplated. Armand is here with me and you and he will take Elizabeth on her journey and ensure that is the last we shall see of her. Now go, make your plans with Armand and leave me to sleep. I am exhausted from travel and carrying the weight of my conscience."

Elizabeth woke with a start and blinked in the light of the candle that lit up Alicia's face as she knelt and leaned over the mattress. She stifled a scream as Alicia put a finger to her lips.

"Shush," she whispered. "Don't say a word; just get up and get dressed as quickly as you can."

"Why?" Elizabeth whispered back, but again Alicia signalled for her to be silent.

"Just do as I say," she mouthed. "We are leaving and when we are safely away, I will explain."

Minutes later, Elizabeth followed her silently through the kitchen, across the courtyard and out of the gate. A pale moon gave a glimmer of light and the path in front of them was just visible. After about a hundred yards Alicia left the track, and taking Elizabeth's arm, led her through some trees and scrub to a small piece of fenced pasture land where several horses were grazing quietly.

"I couldn't manage saddles," Alicia whispered. "We have to ride bareback."

Elizabeth, whose pale face reflected the moonlight, nodded.

"Yes, of course," she murmured, "but where are we going? Do we go to the nunnery now?"

Alicia did not reply but unhitched and mounted her horse, motioning for Elizabeth to do the same. She led the way back to the track, turned away from the manor, and rode toward the junction with the Truro road.

Once on the road, Elizabeth urged her mount forward to ride alongside Alicia.

"I do not know what you plan now Alicia, or where you think you are leading me, but I thank you for giving me my freedom. I can make my own way from here."

Alicia turned toward her, and Elizabeth could see that her face was tearstained; she was shaking with soundless sobs.

"What is it Alicia? What has happened?"

"I heard them," Alicia sobbed, "I heard them, my brother and Armand. I could not believe it to be true; I could not believe that my father would ..." She became incoherent.

Elizabeth caught hold of Alicia's bridle and reigned in both the horses. She dismounted, then helped Alicia down as well. She embraced and comforted her, until the sobbing subsided.

Alicia drew a deep, shuddering breath. "I went to see if my father needed anything more before I slept, and I heard Charles and Armand talking and laughing in the barn store. They did not know I was there.

"They were going to kill you, Elizabeth. Despoil you and kill you and bury you, and all with my father's knowledge and authority. I cannot believe that my father would stoop so low! I heard too that, on my father's orders, Armand and two of our men murdered Bishop Berkeley and Canon Bloyou, then Armand killed the men who had been with him, all to hide the truth about your divorce and marriage." She took another deep breath. "And now I have betrayed my own family ..." She broke down again.

Elizabeth, shocked and yet elated at hearing some truths at last, realised that she had to take charge. She took hold of Alicia's chin and forced her to look at her.

"Come, Alicia; we must move from here. When they find us gone they will hunt us down. We must try to reach Truro before they can find us. Once there, we should be able to find help. Do not feel guilt for helping me. If you had let them kill me and my unborn child you would have been complicit in our murder, and would have had to answer to my family in this world and God in the next. Now, let's move."

She helped the still weeping Alicia onto her horse, re-

mounted her own and together they headed down the starlit road
toward Truro.

Chapter 20

Arworthal, Truro and Devoran

Sir Robert and Charles were awoken well before dawn by loud knocking on the door of their makeshift bedroom in the stables. Before they could rise Armand entered, looking wild and dishevelled in the flickering light of his torch.

"Sire, they are gone, both the ladies have gone. The kitchen maid saw Lady Elizabeth's door ajar when she went to tend the fire and came to tell me. I have searched the buildings and the yard without success but I am told two horses are missing from the field. They are away, Sire."

Sir Robert smashed his hand against the wooden wall of the stable. "God spare us," he seethed. "They must be caught and caught quickly." He paused in thought.

"Alicia would not betray us. She must have been forced to help Elizabeth to escape, but how? Have the Mohuns tracked us down already and stolen them away?" He drew a deep breath and then took command.

"Charles, you and Armand go now and find the women. If they are alone, then rescue Alicia and bring her back here. The fate of Elizabeth will be in your hands as before. I will rouse the household and ensure all the men here are armed and made ready to defend the manor. Now go."

As they saddled the horses, Armand gave words to his thoughts. "I think your father may be wrong. I think that Alicia is complicit in this escape. There was no sign of a struggle or conflict in Lady Elizabeth's cell and the door could only be unlocked by Alicia. I believe the two of them have formed a bond."

Charles looked at him and nodded. "You may be right. I thought they had become too close. If it turns out to be true then my sister will pay. Now, which way would they go, east toward Truro or west? Shall we split up or stay together?"

"I say stay together," he said, answering his own question. "We should go east toward Truro. That's the only road that Alicia knows and for Elizabeth, it is the way towards home. Come on, we could be hours behind them."

Elizabeth sighed with relief as she saw the Truro Quay in front of her. At least they were somewhere that might offer some protection if the Daunays caught up with them.

Alicia had recovered somewhat, and although still tearful, had responded to Elizabeth's gratitude and endorsement of her actions. She had contemplated going back to face the wrath of her father, leaving Elizabeth to fend for herself, but she feared for her own life after her last brush with Charles. She felt too that she was in some way atoning for the dishonour that was being brought upon her family.

The dawning sun tipped its hat over the horizon as they reigned in on the quay. It lit up the front of the ale house and the stables. Two small fishing boats were unloading their catch.

Alicia and Elizabeth were tempted to rest the horses and themselves, but knew that if their flight had been discovered, their pursuers might be hard on their heels and this could be the first place that they would come to.

It was Alicia who had the idea.

"Why don't we try to get one of the fishermen to take us down river towards the sea," she said. "We could trade the horses for the favour. If we could get to somewhere on the coast we might be able to buy our passage to Fowey."

Elizabeth was immediately in agreement. "It's worth trying," she said. "If we carry on along the road I think they will catch up with us sooner or later, but I doubt they will think that we would take to the water. Alicia, you go and charm the fishermen but offer only one of the horses as your bargain bait. I will talk to the ostler at the stables."

Minutes later the deal was done. Mark, one of the young fisherman who understood some English, agreed to take them down the creek and put them off near the chapel at St Just. He was delighted with the generous reward of one of the palfreys.

Meanwhile, in exchange for the remaining horse, Elizabeth persuaded Peter the ostler to tell anyone who might ask that two English women had stopped and taken fresh horses before riding on toward St Austell.

She thought it likely that the ostler, or someone else on the quay, might give them away but it was the best plan she could think of.

Hungry and thirsty after the drama of the night, Alicia bought bread and ale and they sat eating and drinking in the stern of the little boat as Mark rowed them steadily away from the quay.

Within minutes of their departure, Charles and Armand rode into Truro. Charles leapt from his horse and ran first into the ale house. Armand went into the stables and reappeared quickly, grasping the ostler by the arm. He shouted to Charles to join him.

"We are on the right track, sire." There was excitement in his voice. "Their horses are here." He pointed at the ostler. "He says they changed their mounts an hour since and have ridden on. He says their new mounts are strong and safe but slow. If we ride hard we should catch them well before nightfall. Do we go on?"

"We do," said Charles.

Without any further questions they remounted and rode off at a gallop.

Mark could not believe his luck; a fine palfrey in exchange for a few hours rowing was a true bargain.

He was intrigued by his two passengers who were, judging by their manner, high borne ladies although their dress and dishevelled state said otherwise.

His halting attempts at conversation had so far failed to elicit anything other than monosyllabic responses. They were obviously nervous and kept looking back toward Truro, although they were now out of sight of the quay.

After a spell of silence, other than the splash of oars and the crying of gulls, Elizabeth spoke to him using a mix of English, and a few words of Cornish that she had been taught by her father.

"How long will it take us to reach St Just and will we find ships there?" she ventured. "We need to gain safe passage to Fowey."

"About another two hours if the tide stays with us," Mark replied. "It is on the ebb but if it turns before we get there it could take a while longer. There's not much at St Just other than the chapel. If it's ships you want then you be best staying at Truro."

Elizabeth and Alicia looked at each other in some dismay. Mark could see and sense their concern. It had become obvious to him that they were fleeing from something or someone and were seemingly willing to pay for help in gaining their freedom. With the generosity of the current bargain in his mind, he tried his luck.

"My father be a fisherman," he ventured. "He and some in the village have a sea going boat and if you can pay enough, they might agree to take you up the coast. I can't be sure mind," he added, "but it be worth asking."

"But we cannot go back to Truro," said Alicia.

"No need," said Mark, pointing off to his left.

"My home and the boat are up the next creek at Devoran, only an hour from here. Why don't I take you and ask what can be done. It would be a lot safer than trusting to luck at St Just."

Elizabeth nodded, but before she could speak, Alicia cut in.

"Devoran is so close to Arworthal. We shall be going back to where we have just escaped from. They may already be looking for us there. How can we trust that we will not be returned to Arworthal for reward?"

Elizabeth reflected for a moment. "I know there is that risk, Alicia but I think that it would make good sense to go there.

Nobody at Arworthal will expect us to return to somewhere close by if they learn that we have already reached Truro. I think too that I can offer a reward that will ensure the loyalty of the Devoran men." She turned to Mark. "Young man, we put our trust in you. Make for Devoran and let us see what can be done."

After about an hour of hard riding it was apparent to both Charles and Armand that they were on a wild goose chase. Nobody that they met had seen any sign of two women on horseback.

"Either that damned ostler lied to us or they have chosen a different path," said Charles. "They could be anywhere."

They debated their next move. Charles wanted to return to Truro and search again and take out his frustration on the ostler.

Armand reasoned with him that it might be better to return to Arworthal and give Sir Robert the bad news and then re-think what needed to be done before it was too late. Charles compromised.

"God's teeth I fear my father's rage: but you are right. We will return to Arworthal but we should have one more search in Truro on our way, just in case the women are still hiding there."

When they arrived back on the quay there was no one in sight. Another search of the stables and the ale house revealed nothing.

As they paused to water their horses at the stable trough, Charles suggested that they should extend their search to the chapel and the uninhabited castle, or perhaps break into one of the small houses behind the quay and try to force some information from the inhabitants.

"At the point of my sword someone will know something," he snarled.

As they talked, a small fishing boat tied up at the wooden landing stage and an elderly man stepped ashore and walked past them holding a large fish under his arm.

"Good catch old man," Armand called to him. "But hold a moment. We seek two women who were on this quay early this morning. Did you see them?"

The fisherman stopped and turned to look at them.

"Oi did'n see 'em 'ere," he said, "but I seed two women

down river in young Mark's boat. He rowed past me about two hour since."

Charles, who had been sitting on the trough, jumped to his feet. "Where were they heading?"

The fisherman paused. "Home, I would expect," he said. "He be from Devoran. But maybe the ladies want to go somewhere else down river."

Charles was back in the saddle before the fisherman finished speaking. "Back to Arworthal it is." He shouted to Armand. "No point in wasting more time here. If they have been taken to Devoran we have them; if they have gone elsewhere we can wait for this Mark to return to his home and learn from him where they are."

They all but trampled on the old fisherman as they spurred the horses back toward the Arworthal road.

As Mark rounded the long narrow point and turned into Devoran creek, he pointed out a flat bottomed cog coming fast up the main channel from the sea, under the power of both sail and oars.

"We are well to be out of their way. They be a rough crew, wreckers more than fishermen. They will be heading into Truro. Good job that you ladies are not there still."

A few moments later he stopped rowing and looked anxiously down the creek.

"I don't understand it; they are headed this way. They must be Devoran bound. There could be trouble."

He pulled hard out of the stream and into shallow water, close to the muddy bank.

Elizabeth and Alicia looked apprehensive, and at Mark's urgent bidding, they sank down into the bottom of the boat to make themselves as inconspicuous as possible.

"They must have a heavy load or they have shipped a lot of sea," said Mark. "They are very low in the water."

Now they could hear the splash of oars and the rhythmic chant of the oarsmen themselves.

As the cog drew parallel it was only some twenty paces away and they could see clearly that it was indeed carrying a heavy load of men and horses, rather than a catch of fish.

There were several figures standing in the stern of the boat and one stood out from the rest by virtue of his height and bearing; and above all, by the vivid crimson colour of his tunic.

Elizabeth suddenly leapt up, rocking the little boat alarmingly. Heedless of the danger, she screamed out, "Richard!" at the top of her voice and again, "Richard!"

The faces on the platform at the stern of the cog swivelled towards them. The figure in the crimson tunic turned and came to the gunwale, and they could all see the crenulated black cross of the Mohuns on the breast of his tunic, confirming Elizabeth's joyful recognition.

"Oh God in heaven thank you," she wept. "My prayers are answered. He is here and I am safe."

She swayed and buckled at the knees with emotion. At the same time, the wash from the bigger boat rippled underneath them and with a scream of fright, echoed by Alicia, she tumbled over the side into the muddy shallows.

She quickly emerged and stood up, knee deep in the water, streaked with mud, laughing and crying at the same time.

The cog had come to a stop and although it remained in the deeper water channel, it was slowly manoeuvring backward toward them.

Richard's voice rang out, incredulous and excited. "Elizabeth is that you? Who is with you?"

Elizabeth was weeping with shock and joy and could not speak. Alicia responded.

"It is your Elizabeth, sire. She is safe for now. I am Alicia and we have escaped together from Arworthal but we are still in danger."

There was a pause and then Richard's voice again. "Elizabeth, is this true? Are you not a captive of the Daunays?"

Mark had managed to drag Elizabeth back into the boat and sit her down. She summoned the strength to call out.

"Richard, my love, I have been held by the Daunays, but Alicia is now my friend and aided my escape. We go to Devoran but there may be danger there."

There was no reply but there was some discussion and then someone shouted instructions, in Cornish, to Mark. Richard shouted again, his voice firm and reassuring.

"Elizabeth, be calm and have no fear. We too are heading to Devoran. Follow us and we shall be reunited there."

Mark pulled out into the main channel again, just astern of the cog. "We are to follow them into Devoran rather than try to offload you here," he said. "If you fell in out here you might not be so lucky."

The oarsmen on the hulk took up their chant again and both boats headed up the quickly narrowing river.

The last league into Devoran seemed interminable to Elizabeth, who was cold and wet and desperate to be reunited with Richard and to feel the comfort of his embrace.

Alicia was filled with trepidation. She feared the condemnation of the Mohuns for her part in the kidnapping and imprisonment of Elizabeth. At the same time she bore a heavy burden of guilt for the betrayal of her own family.

Mark struggled against the flow of the now receding tide and by the time he had reached the small wooden jetty, the cog was already empty of its load and moving out into deeper water to anchor.

Richard, Lawrence, and Baldwin waited for them while the crew of the cog, led by Geoffrey Morgan, faced up to a hostile gathering of Devoran men.

As Mark and the two women stepped onto the jetty, all eyes were turned on them. The leader of the Devoran men, Mark's father, held up his hand to silence the angry murmurings.

"Mark," he shouted, "What's to do here?"

Mark turned to Elizabeth, who had already embraced Richard and was being hugged by the other Mohun brothers.

"My lady, can you speak to my father please and tell him the reason for this ..." He struggled for the word. "Invasion."

Elizabeth took his hand and Richard's and went forward to stand in front of Mark's father. Wet, mud streaked and dishevelled, she still carried an air of dignity and grace.

She spoke clearly and with feeling. "Sir, if Mark be your son you should be proud of him. He has helped to save our lives today. The reasons for our being here—all of us," she said, gesturing to encompass all the men, women, and horses on the jetty, "will take a lot of explaining and none of us know all the reasons, yet."

She gestured towards Richard. "This sir, is my husband, Sir Richard de Mohun. Until my marriage I was Elizabeth Fitzwilliam of Hall at Bodinnick. Arworthal Manor, close by here, is ours."

There was an appreciative murmur from the crowd.

"We, for reasons we will explain, have been cruelly and forcibly parted and only now met again here on this jetty.

"We come with no harm intended to you, good people of Devoran, but we seek your aid in our quest to recover Arworthal from the present usurpers of our title. For this service, you will be well rewarded."

Richard looked at her with admiration and smiled.

"All that is true," he said. "I also assure you that we mean no harm. We will talk with you, sir and try to explain all. But first, is it possible that my beautiful wife here can gain some dry clothing? I also crave some time and a space for us to exchange the detail of our separate experiences that have led to our arrival here."

The initial hostility of the crowd had evaporated while Elizabeth was talking. Now there was some animated discussion between Mark's father and others and then a flurry of activity.

The result, within a short space of time, was that Elizabeth—attired now in a simple but dry shift— Richard, his brothers and Tom Weaver, who insisted on being present, were seated in the little Devoran chapel.

Elizabeth gave the story of her kidnapping and incarceration, only omitting her being with child. Alicia, despite some hostile glances and comments, tearfully confirmed the detail of the plot hatched by her father. Her revelations in relation to the murder of Bishop Berkeley were greeted with incredulity and anger.

Richard recounted the details of Ralph's brave journey to London, the abortive meetings with Queen Isabella and the Bishop at Exeter, the desperate search for Elizabeth, his journey to Avignon and his return with John de Grandisson.

Finally, he told Elizabeth of the role that young Tom and Alric had played in finding out her probable location.

The subsequent discussion and questions could have gone

on for a long time, but Richard drew things to a conclusion.

"We can add all the flesh to the bones when we have the time. As of now, God be praised, Elizabeth is returned to us, but the Daunays are at Arworthal, still perhaps unaware of our arrival but no doubt hunting for Elizabeth and Alicia. They are still a powerful enemy with friends at court and until their evil acts are exposed and acknowledged, they still lay claim to our home and lands at Hall and here at Arworthal."

He turned to Lawrence. "Brother, will you go out now with Tom and meet with the villagers and our wild seafaring friends? Explain to them the bones of our discussion in here and tell them of our intent to attack and bring the Daunays and their minions to justice. Play on the rightness of our cause and on the potential for substantial reward if they will aid us in our endeavour.

"I need to speak with Elizabeth and Alicia here, and will join you quickly. Assemble those who are willing to aid us and arm them as best you can, and have our horses fed, watered and ready."

As Lawrence and Tom left the chapel, he turned to Alicia.

"My dear, your bravery in helping Elizabeth to escape and admitting your part in her abduction is greatly to your credit. Nevertheless, as a part of your family's conspiracy, you are guilty of a horrendous crime against us."

Alicia's pale, tear stained face crumpled and she began to weep again. Elizabeth immediately went to comfort her and glared at her husband.

"Richard, she is well aware of her guilt but knew nothing of the other evil acts perpetrated by her brother and Armand. As soon as she heard of the plan to kill me she endangered her own life to try to prevent it from happening. Even while imprisoned at Arworthal she protected me from harm. You must not harm her now."

Richard took her hand and kissed it. "Hush, my love. I have no desire to harm her, but I need to know that she will testify, under oath to John de Grandisson in Exeter, everything that she has admitted here. In return for this, she will be pardoned and freed to return to Sheviock."

Elizabeth smiled and squeezed his hand. Alicia, though, still looked troubled.

"What of my father and brother, sire; what of them?"

Richard frowned and his tone hardened. "I am sad to learn that your father, who I once thought to be a man of honour, was so misguided and so driven by greed that he arranged and sanctioned so many evil deeds. As for your brother, I think it is he that brought this burden of dishonour on your family. Both shall pay the price if we find them and bring them to justice.

"Elizabeth, your role is now reversed with Alicia. You must stay here and guard and protect her until we return from Arworthal. She must be restrained from any temptation there may be to warn or assist her father and brother. We need her secure and unharmed and ready to testify in Exeter. Baldwin will stay here with you to ensure the safety of you both."

Elizabeth and Baldwin both hotly protested that they wanted to be with him whatever the danger, but Richard remained firm and understanding his reasoning, they somewhat unwillingly capitulated.

Richard embraced Elizabeth.

"God keep you safe," she murmured. "All four of us await your safe return."

Richard looked puzzled. "Who is the fourth?" he asked, looking around.

Elizabeth patted her stomach. "Your child," she giggled. "It may be hidden but needs you to return."

Richard put his hand on her swelling belly. "I thought you had eaten well for someone in captivity." He laughed out loud with delight. Then, with sudden concern asked, "Are you sure you are alright? Should you have been riding? What about that tumble into the water? You must take more care of my child."

He laughed again and kissed Elizabeth. "This is blessed news, my love. I have business to finish here and then we will take our child back to Hall for his birth day."

He kissed her again and swiftly went out to take charge of the hastily assembled, makeshift little army.

Lawrence had worked wonders. Most of the Devoran men had declared their willingness to support the attack and Morgan and Tom had enthusiastically rallied the crew of the Cob. Weapons ranged from longswords, broadswords and lances to staves and reaping hooks. In all, some thirty men and six horses were assembled and eager for a fight.

Richard, mounted on Grisel Gris and flanked by Lawrence and Morgan, addressed them.

"We have one aim," he shouted. "That is to capture Sir Robert Daunay, his son Charles, and one Armand Gascon, murderers all. I believe this show of force will suffice to deter any opposition to our cause from others who may be at Arworthal. There is no call for unnecessary bloodshed, but if you are attacked and engaged then no quarter is to be given."

He raised his sword above his head.

"Look to me for direction and if I should fall then my brother Lawrence will command. Follow now and God save us all."

They streamed out of the village and turned onto the track leading westwards toward Arworthal.

Chapter 21

Devoran and Arworthal

From a vantage point among the trees on the edge of the village, Charles and Armand watched them go. Luck had been on their side. About to ride full tilt into Devoran after their headlong gallop from Truro, they were alerted by the hubbub from the assembled villagers preparing for battle. They veered off the track, into the trees. Tethering their horses, they crept forward and were in time to witness Richard's rallying call to his makeshift army. They also observed the watching figures of Elizabeth and Alicia in the chapel doorway.

Charles punched Armand on the arm and whispered, "The women are here. We have them."

Armand frowned. "But what do we do, sire; try to take them now or go first to Arworthal? If we cut through the woods behind us, we could perhaps get there in time to warn your father and fight or flee with him."

Charles, shocked by the situation, swallowed hard. "I think maybe we should take them. With Elizabeth in our hands we may have a negotiating position," he said hesitantly, and then, with more conviction, "Come Armand, get the horses. Speed and surprise is what we need. We take Elizabeth alive; I have business to settle with the bitch and I have been kept waiting too long. You take my sister. She will have to answer to her father."

Armand laid a restraining arm on his sleeve. "Sire, men are still in the village and we will be outnumbered if they have the stomach to resist us. Are you sure that—"

Charles turned on him angrily.

"A few old men with women and children, armed with broomsticks? They will not be willing to die to protect those two. Now hear me, Armand. We get the horses and we ride full tilt to the chapel. Cut down anyone who gets in the way. I will take Elizabeth, you Alicia and we ride out on the Truro road."

Armand had one more question. "What if the chapel door is barred?"

Charles hissed in frustration. "Then we break it down or burn them out. I will find a way in. Now move, before it is too late." Armand shrugged resignedly and followed behind Charles to the tethered horses.

At the edge of the village, mounted and swords drawn, they spurred the horses into a gallop, and with scattering villagers, hens and ducks in their wake, arrived at the chapel door in a cloud of dust.

Armand was first to the door but as he reached it, he heard the thump of the crossbar being slammed into place inside the chapel, and the solid oak door did not budge when he pushed against it. Charles added his weight to no effect and he kicked the door in frustration.

"Alicia," he yelled. "Come out now before it is too late. Your father needs you by his side."

There was no reply. He tried again. "Alicia, you are forgiven. Are you and Elizabeth alone in there? Come out now and no harm will come to you." Silence was the response. Charles cursed and hammered on the door with the hilt of his sword. "Alicia, open this door, damn you."

Inside the church, Elizabeth and Alicia sat on the floor in a corner of the chapel, out of sight from any of the narrow embrasures that let in the light.

Baldwin stood just inside the doorway with his broadsword drawn and a finger to his lips, warning them to stay silent. "Stay calm," he whispered. "The door is stout enough, it will hold for now."

While Charles was rampaging at the front of the chapel, Armand circled the building and returned.

"There is no other way out, sire. They must be in there. It seems we will have to smoke them out."

Charles abruptly ceased beating on the door. He sheathed his sword, and in half a dozen rapid paces he crossed the small patch of grass in front of the chapel, into the crowd of local onlookers. Before anyone could guess his intent, he grabbed a small boy of perhaps five or six from his mother's side and put his hunting knife to the throat of the struggling and terrified child.

"Get me straw, kindling, wood and tallow, and bring it here to the chapel door. This lad's life depends on your speed."

There were screams from the mother of the boy and other women in the crowd. A few of the old men moved forward, trying to look menacing.

Armand walked across and faced them. "Do as he says." He spoke quietly and chillingly. "Make no mistake, he will kill the boy, else."

The crowd scattered and in no more than five minutes, all the makings for a blaze were piled up at the chapel door.

Baldwin, with his ear to the door, heard everything and knew what was about to happen. Moving across to where Elizabeth and Alicia sat, he bent down and spoke softly.

"They intend to burn the door and smoke us out. If we just wait they are likely to succeed. We need to take the initiative and I have a plan. The one advantage that we have is surprise. They do not know that I am here and are likely to be over confident." He outlined his plan and both the women, although looking terrified, nodded their agreement, and all three of them took their places.

Armand grabbed a rush light that was proffered to him by the distraught mother of the still captive child. He was about to put it to the pile of combustibles in the doorway when everyone heard a piercing scream from within the chapel. It finished abruptly in a throaty gurgle. There was a shocked silence, then Alicia's voice, weak and trembling.

"Charles, I am coming out. Elizabeth is dead."

Charles, still clutching the boy, nodded to Armand. "When she opens the door, grab her."

As he spoke, they could hear the noise of the bar being lifted and the door slowly opened inwards. Armand could see Alicia retreating from the doorway and as his eyes began to adjust to the gloomy light, he could see the body of Elizabeth lying in front of the alter steps. Alicia, white faced and shaking, seemed rooted to the spot.

Armand kicked the kindling out of his way, took two paces towards her and held out his hand. Suddenly, sensing danger, he half turned his head toward a flicker of movement on his right, but it was too late. The flat of Baldwin's broadsword, wielded with power and accuracy, thudded into Armand's midriff. Totally winded, he fell to his knees with his head bowed low, gasping for any vestige of air. Baldwin's second blow was more deadly. It came down edgewise onto Armand's exposed neck with all of Baldwin's weight behind it, almost severing the head from the shoulders.

Gaping open mouthed in astonishment and shock, Charles involuntarily let go of his captive who dashed screaming to the arms of his mother.

Charles moved very cautiously toward the doorway. He had not yet seen Baldwin and could not understand how Armand had died so violently. The smell of fresh blood that had spattered the chapel entrance was nauseating.

He looked over Armand's body into the chapel and could see both Alicia and Elizabeth, who was now standing, holding Armand's sword and staring back at him.

"God curse you both," he hissed. "You will both die for this."

Sword held ready, he took another pace toward them. Then Baldwin, still out of sight, spoke.

"Take another step, Charles and your death is assured. We are armed and ready for you."

Sensing Charles' confusion, Baldwin decided on his final bluff. He moved out from the shadow of the door and standing astride Armand's corpse, he flexed his bloodstained sword.

"Get ready my lads!" he shouted, looking to his left and right. "He is coming in."

There was silence and Charles took a half step forward, but at that moment, on the breeze, there was the sound of cheering from the direction of Arworthal and the cheers were picked up by the watching Devorans.

Charles knew instantly what it meant and made his decision. Spitting on the ground he glared at Baldwin, turned on his heel, walked slowly to his horse tethered on the green, and to jeers and catcalls from the bystanders, rode out of the village and disappeared down the road toward Arworthal.

Elizabeth and Alicia embraced each other, sobbing in relief.

Baldwin directed the villagers to help remove Armand's remains and fetch buckets of sea water to clean up the bloodstained entrance to the Chapel.

"That was a close run thing," he said. "I thought he was going to call our bluff but it seems that we may have won the day."

They waited then for the news from Arworthal.

At the same time, in Arworthal, a body was being laid out on a trestle table in the shelter of the old barn.

Richard and his little army had entered the grounds of Arworthal manor with no resistance. Three men at arms had been deployed by Sir Robert on the perimeter of the crumbling building. The local servants were told to arm themselves and be ready to fight but all to no avail.

As soon as they saw the strength of the opposition and recognised Devoran men, the locals melted away.

The men at arms attempted some show of resistance but Richard, halting at the gates to the yard, addressed them.

"Lay down your arms and no harm shall come to you. Our business here is with Sir Robert, his son Charles, and with his bailiff Armand; no one else. Resist and you will perish. There is no honour to be gained in defending the thieves and murderers that you serve. Lay down your arms or die."

As he finished speaking he drew his sword and spurred Grisel Gris forward slowly toward the nearest man at arms who stood battleaxe at the ready inside the gateway. As he moved forward, the rest of Richard's men pressed through the gateway behind him, displaying their assorted weaponry.

After a brief moment of indecision, the man at arms threw

down his battleaxe. Making a gesture of surrender and spreading his arms, he gestured towards the Manor House.

"Only Sir Robert is here, sire, and he awaits you."

Richard nodded and rode onwards toward the house. The two remaining men guarding the dilapidated entrance also threw down their weapons and walked away.

Richard stopped about ten paces from the open doorway and dismounted. Behind him, Lawrence and Geoffrey Morgan halted, gave a signal, and the rest of the force fanned out in a semicircle across the width of the yard.

"Sir Robert Daunay." Richard's voice echoed across the yard. "I call upon you to yield. You are to be brought to justice, as my prisoner, on charges of kidnap, deception and murder."

As he spoke, Sir Robert emerged from the doorway. He stood tall but thin and pale. Bareheaded and wearing a chain mail tunic, he carried an emblazoned shield and his longsword rested on his shoulder. His voice was strained but strong.

"I shall not yield to you, sire. You trespass on my lands. You have no rights here."

"Sir Robert, you should know that through God's grace, my wife Elizabeth is returned to me. We know now the extent of your guilt, and that of your son and others under your power. The evil done in your name is so great that even your daughter Alicia will testify against you. So again, sir, I say yield or you will be taken by force."

Sir Robert sighed deeply and his shoulders sagged. He bowed his head for a moment and his lips moved soundlessly as if in prayer. He straightened and took two steps towards Richard. He spoke quietly.

"Sire, I have brought dishonour on my family. What I have done I did with a heavy heart, to try to safeguard my family name and restore our fortune. I have failed and my life will be forfeit. I have made my peace with God and will answer to his judgement, but not to yours or that of any earthly court."

He raised his voice. "I will not yield, so use whatever force you need." He stepped back, discarded his shield, and raised his sword two handed. There was a loud murmur from the line of armed men behind Richard and weapons were readied.

Richard raised a hand and shouted, "My fight; one on one.

Lawrence, a longsword in my hand. If I fall, he is yours."

Lawrence ran forward and handed his longsword to Richard who hefted it from hand to hand, feeling for its weight and balance. He moved backwards several paces, and as Sir Robert followed him, the semicircle of men became a circle enclosing the two combatants.

"I am ready, Sir Robert. No quarter."

With no heavy armour and the weight of the longswords, the fight initially was both cautious and ponderous. Each knew that a single blow landed on a vulnerable spot could be fatal.

After several feints, half hearted lunges and parries, Sir Robert went on the attack, swinging his blade in a flashing arc towards Richard's right side. Just in time, Richard blocked the attempt but was forced to give ground. Sir Robert tried to press home his advantage with three more desperate swings, but the weight of his sword took its toll on his arm muscles and he was slow to recover from the final swing. Richard saw a chance and used just a half swing upwards, under Sir Robert's arm. The honed edge cut deep into muscle and sinew and the point of Sir Robert's sword dropped toward the ground.

Before he could recover, Richard delivered a massive backhand blow to Sir Robert's exposed ribs. It sliced through the chain mail, the blade biting deep into the chest cavity.

Sir Robert staggered and fell heavily onto his knees, then rolled over onto his back. He stared up at Richard through clouding eyes.

He tried to speak and Richard bent to listen. The words came slowly as he tried to use the last remaining breath in his crushed chest. "It is over. I die with honour and ..." His breath and his life left him.

The cheers of Richard's supporters were loud enough to reach Devoran.

The celebrations in Devoran went on late into the night. The only person with a long face was Tom Weaver. He was devastated that Charles seemed to have eluded them and yet, had been here in Devoran.

"I wanted to see the bastard pay," he confided to Elizabeth.

He cheered up however when Richard suggested that he

should become his squire at Hall, charged with serving Richard and accompanying him when he was away.

Mark and his father were feted by the villagers when it was learned that, in gratitude for the safe transfer of Elizabeth and Alicia to Devoran, and the help provided in the attack on Arworthal, the villagers were to be gifted a large tranche of Arworthal land. In addition, there would be work and employment as Richard and Elizabeth wished the Manor to be restored.

Geoffrey Morgan and his band of fisherman marauders were also well rewarded for their part in the success of the mission.

Apart from a generous financial reward, Richard also granted them safe anchorage in Pont Pill Creek when they needed it.

The next day, Armand was buried in an unmarked grave in the woods outside the village.

Alicia pleaded for her father's body to be returned to Sheviock for interment with his ancestors. Richard agreed on the condition that, once it was done, Alicia would return to Hall and then accompany him to Exeter to meet with John de Grandisson.

He insisted that she be accompanied by his brother Lawrence and Tom Weaver so that she would not be tempted to flee from her obligation to testify, and also to safeguard against any attempt by Charles to silence her.

"I hope he does appear," said Tom. "Then I can kill him myself."

Last to leave Devoran that morning were Richard, Elizabeth and Baldwin. With rested horses and light hearts, they set out for the long ride home to Hall.

Chapter 22

Hall and Dunster

The weeks following the return to Hall passed in a blur of activity and excitement.

John de Grandisson carried out his papal assignment with diligence. He heard evidence from all concerned. Alicia's testimony under oath was accepted as proof positive of the Daunay guilt. The naming of Armand as the murderer of Archbishop Berkeley was given extra credence when the bodies of Harald and Gregor were searched for and found.

The documentary evidence relating to the gifts of land at Aylesbere, Cornwood and St Ives from Sir Robert to Bishop Berkeley, Canon Bloyou, and to Parson Wideslade were uncovered amongst Bishop Berkeley's papers at Exeter.

John de Grandisson took with him all the evidence and relayed the full story to Queen Isabella when he presented his credentials at court as the Bishop of Exeter designate.

With Royal assent, the divorce and remarriage of Elizabeth to Henry Denyss were declared unlawful and the marriage of Richard and Elizabeth was reinstated.

It was decided that by way of compensation, Boconnoc Manor and lands should be forfeit to Richard de Mohun, together with the manors at Cornwood and Aylesbere, and the church land at St Ives.

True to their word, Richard and Elizabeth gave a full pardon to Alicia and she returned to her ancestral home at Sheviock.

Weeks turned into months as the chapel at Hall, in memory of Elizabeth's father, was completed and given a papal blessing by John de Grandisson who later returned to Lyon for his formal investiture.

On the 21st January 1328, Elizabeth gave birth to their son John. It seemed that the fortunes of the de Mohun family had emerged from the shadows into sunshine.

The only cloud in the sky concerned the whereabouts of Charles Daunay. A wanted man, he faced certain execution if apprehended, but there had been no trace of him since he rode out of Devoran.

It was assumed that he had met his end, either in a fight or an accident, or had become an outlaw, living in hiding and obscurity. Richard, Elizabeth and Alicia, however, lived with a nagging fear that at some time he might reappear and attempt to gain revenge for his downfall and humiliation.

In April, Dunster Castle was a hive of activity. It had not seen such a gathering of the Mohun family for many years. Surrounding Lord John de Mohun and his wife Ada in the castle were eight of his nine sons and his daughter Eleanora, together with their various spouses, families and retainers.

All were present to celebrate the good fortune of Richard and Elizabeth and to welcome their newborne son, another John.

In the morning, all had attended the christening in the family chapel. The reunions and revelling had carried on throughout the day, culminating in the evening with the grand hall crammed to the doors for the great banquet.

After many toasts and speeches of welcome, Richard rose, hammering on the table for silence before speaking.

"Today we are blessed." He paused, his emotions almost overcoming him. Then, looking across at his wife, he smiled and raised his cup. "Lady Elizabeth is home, our son John is healthy and strong, and our fortunes are restored to us."

The assembled family and all present stamped, shouted,

cheered and clapped. Richard remained standing and again called for silence.

"This happy outcome and deliverance from evil intent has only been possible through the steadfast support and loyalty of this family and some lifelong friends.

"Father, my dear brothers Lawrence and Baldwin, cousin William, and my bailiff, brave and loyal Ralph Purves and many others here; you have the undying gratitude of Elizabeth and myself.

"Above all though, I thank God. He was on our side. Through his holiness Pope John and Bishop John de Grandisson, evil was exposed and rooted out." Again he waited until the ensuing hubbub had died down.

"To give thanks to God, to atone for the bloodshed by comrades and enemies in our pursuit of justice, I have decided, with Elizabeth's blessing, and with Royal assent to my absence, to journey to Santiago. I will carry with me, as a talisman and a testament to our good fortune, our own beloved and sacred Golden Rose."

There was an excited buzz of surprise and excitement before Richard concluded.

"Brave Ralph Purves and my new and trusted squire, Tom Weaver, will accompany me and we plan to leave within the month. God bless all here."

PART III

Transition

Moonshadow

Transition

Research

I came to, with the words still ringing in my ears. "God bless all here," I echoed.

I was back in the sitting room at Hall with anxious faces looking down at me. Elizabeth—my Elizabeth, was holding my hand and gripped it tightly as I opened my eyes.

"Oh, thank God, Richard." She started to cry. "I thought you had gone. You seemed to stop breathing."

Nathan appeared beside her. "The doc is on his way," he said and then he noticed that I was awake.

"Hey, welcome back," he said, with obvious relief. He patted my shoulder. "We were a bit worried about you."

"More than a bit," whispered his wife Margaret as she comforted Elizabeth.

The doctor duly arrived and I was thoroughly checked over. Later, as a precaution, and despite my protests, I was checked again at the local hospital in Truro. They initially suspected that I had suffered a minor stroke, or something called a TGA, but could find no evidence of either.

I was pronounced fit and healthy and discharged with warnings to seek urgent medical help if there any reoccurrence of the problem.

In the short term, I did not divulge the events that I had been made aware of during my brief departure to another time, although the whole experience was still vivid and clear as crystal in my mind.

I was concerned that if I talked about it I would not be believed and people might even question my mental condition.

Only some weeks later, after I had written it all down, did I tell Elizabeth what I believed; both the memories of 'the happenings' in my own life and the story of the distant past that I had experienced.

She was of course incredulous, and although she humoured me, I think she was secretly very worried. It was she who finally voiced the question that had been nagging away at me.

"Alright, Richard," she said one day when, yet again, I had been recalling the experience. "So what was it all about? If your ancestors were really trying to make some contact with you, and show you what had happened, why? What was so important? What did they want from you?"

Much as I wanted to, I could not answer her. I had asked myself the same questions many times and could not give a satisfactory response.

I determined, with Elizabeth's backing, to research as much as we could of the Mohun family history. In particular, all the places that had figured in the story that I lived through; I refused to say that I had dreamt of.

For a period of some seven years, despite many other demands on my time, nearly every holiday was spent 'Moon hunting' as we called it. We spent many hours in libraries, churches, record offices, and The Archives at Kew.

What we found was extraordinary and thrilling. We found that the Mohun family had been very prominent in the West Country for some six hundred years. Some parts of their history were well documented. The deeper we dug the more certain I became that I had indeed been privy to the events that took place in 1327 concerning my namesake Richard de Mohun and his wife, Elizabeth.

Over that period of time we revisited Dunster, Bruton and Hall. Amazingly, we found Boconnoc, Mohun's Ottery,

Arworthal, the site of Newenham Abbey at Axminster, and many other places. Some were in ruins; others, like Newenham Abbey, were completely obliterated.

Some, including Boconnoc and Mohun's Ottery, were still in use or being restored, and often revealed clear evidence of past de Mohun occupation.

Bruton, where I had been to school, ignorant of the historical connections with my family, was a revelation. One discovery there sent shivers up my spine.

Outside the priory building which had been my school boarding house, I found the de Mohun crest; an engrailed black cross on a gold background. When I examined it I realised that it was positioned exactly in front of where my bed had been in the dormitory so many years ago.

I researched old documents and records, and found many references to the de Mohun family, from their origins in Normandy up to the 17th century. They included the same brief description of the meeting between Elizabeth and Richard that I had read in the magazine at Hall. The author had prefaced the reference with the words, 'There is a story of very doubtful origin ...'

Were he alive today, I could tell him that the story was not only true, but even more remarkable than he could have imagined.

With the bit between my teeth, I kept probing and searching. I unearthed a family tree, researched by a distant cousin in Australia. I found ancestral connections with royalty, an original Knight of the Garter, ancestors who had fought in many battles including Hastings, Poitier, Crecy, Agincourt and Trafalgar, and a Mohun who had been tried three times for murder by his peers in Parliament.

But, despite all the research, I found nothing more—not one word—about Richard de Mohun of Hall, other than a brief reference to the eloignment or kidnap of his wife Elizabeth and that he had a son named John. No details about his life or death, no mention of his visits to Lyon to enlist the aid of Pope John, or to Santiago to give thanks. It seemed that I alone knew what had happened, all of seven hundred years ago.

I had reached a dead end! My unique and extraordinary experience of having a curtain lifted on the past seemed to be over. There seemed to be no real reason for all the trouble that had been taken to lead me to it.

With work, family demands and constraints, my research lessened in intensity, and I think to the relief of Elizabeth, ceased to be the all consuming focus of my life.

Moonshadow

Transition

Newenham Abbey and the Golden Rose

In September 2002, events suddenly took another turn. Elizabeth and I were spending a few days in Devon on holiday. Despite Elizabeth's protests, I felt drawn to and could not resist a place that had been on the fringes of the events in 1327; for some reason, it kept nagging away at me. Newenham Abbey.

Standing in the meadows just south of the town of Axminster, I could envisage and indeed feel the spirit of the once proud monastery founded by my ancestors, now returned to the natural beauty of the landscape that had preceded it. The abbey had been destroyed after the dissolution; the stone carted off to be recycled and the land returned to farming. Walking across the fields it was easy to spot fragments of the old Beer stone blocks.

Later in the day, we explored the little town of Axminster. Emerging from the church, where there were many de Mohun reminders, I noticed a small bookshop across the road, with an ancient looking stone arch doorway. I was immediately drawn toward it, and dragged Elizabeth with me. I entered it with an inexplicable feeling of excitement.

I told the owner of my interest in the de Mohun family, and their relationship with the town and the Abbey, asking if he had any books or information that might be relevant. He did not seem particularly interested but directed me to a small section titled 'local history.' At first glance there did not seem to be anything at all that related to the medieval past, but tucked away in a corner of the bottom shelf I noticed a slim, plain brown, cardboard covered booklet. I pulled it out and read the small typed label on the front; 'The History of Newenham Abbey in the County of Devon' by James Davidson.

The content was some 200 rather yellowed, tattered and obviously duplicated pages, each stamped with the Bodlian Library mark.

As I rapidly thumbed through it, I realised I had struck gold. All the familiar feelings of closeness to past events flooded back. Towards the end of the book was a section titled, 'The Family of Mohun.'

To say that I was excited would be a huge understatement. Trying to keep my delight under wraps, I wandered round the shop for a while before presenting the book to the owner saying, "I haven't seen anything of real interest but there is a chance that this might have one or two facts that might be useful, as long as it doesn't cost too much. It doesn't seem to have a price tag on it."

He took it from me and glanced through it with a puzzled expression.

"I've never seen it before," he said. "We did buy a lot of books and documents at a house sale a month or so ago. It must have come from there and my assistant must have put it on the shelf without pricing it. A fiver should cover it."

I paid him and made for the street. Just as I reached the doorway, he called to me.

"If you're interested in the old abbey, look at the entrance as you go out; it's one of the last remaining parts of the abbey. A window arch, salvaged from the ruins."

I stood in the doorway and ran my hand over the smooth stone. The feeling ran like electricity up my arm. I knew that I was reconnected and that I was being moved on.

That night in the hotel, I pored over the booklet. It was a detailed account of the founding of the Abbey in 1245 with funds and land donated by two de Mohun brothers, Reginald and William. It described the arrival of the first abbot, and monks who had been seconded from Beaulieu Abbey.

There was a lot of detail regarding the various transfers and grants of land and the obtaining of royal approval and licenses.

Ploughing through all the detail, written half in French and half in English, I was beginning to feel that, while very interesting background information, it was not moving me any further forward. Then the following few sentences leapt out of the page and brought everything into sharp focus.

'When Sir Reginald saw this done, he went to the court of Rome, which was then at Lyons, for confirmation and ratification of his new abbey, to his great honour for ever; and he was at the court on the Sunday in Lent when they sing the office of the Mass Laetare Jerusalem, on which day the custom of the court is that the Pope gives to the most valiant and honourable man who can be found at the said court a rose or a little flower of fine gold.

They therefore searched the whole court and found this Reginald to be the most worthy of the whole court, and to him Pope Innocent gave this rose or little flower of gold and the Pope asked him what manner of man he was in his own country. He answered, 'a plain knight bachelor.'

'Fair son,' said the Pope. 'This rose has never been given save to kings, or to dukes, or to earls; therefore we will that you be Earl of Est' - That is Somerset.

Reginald answered and said 'Oh Holy Father, I have not wherewithal to maintain the name.' The Pope therefore gave him two hundred marks a year to be received at the altar of St Paul's in London out of his (Peters) Pence of England, to maintain his honour; of which grant he brought back with him Bulls which still have the lead, etc. Together with ten other Bulls of confirmation of his new abbey of Newenham. After this day, he bore the emblem of the rose or little flower in his coat of arms.

Eureka!

Now I had confirmation of the existence of the Golden Rose that had been taken to Lyon by Richard when seeking help from Pope John. The memory flooded back to me: The box being opened and the exquisite and delicate structure of the little flower revealed.

I yelled to Elizabeth, who was lying on the bed immersed in a novel. Excitedly, I dug out my written account of my foray into the past and I got her to find the passage that I had written about the visit to Lyon and the production of the Golden Rose.

"Now," I said triumphantly, when she had read it out. "Look at this." I showed her the document and the description of the Pope giving the Golden Rose to Reginald, just as I had described it.

"Now try telling me it was all a dream."

Elizabeth sighed. "I never said that, Richard. I believe you experienced something stranger than a dream but I still don't know why, or where it is leading you. To be honest, I'm frightened about where it will all end. I thought it had gone away and that we were getting back to normal, but now …" She started to weep. I held her close and tried to comfort her.

"There is no need to be frightened, my love. I don't feel we are threatened or in danger. I just know that somehow, I'm being guided for some purpose that is important but buried deep in the past."

Elizabeth had stopped crying but clung on to me. "You may be right," she said, "but I live in the present and our comfortable world of home and children and grandchildren and love for each other. I am frightened that your obsession with the past will threaten all of that, and it will drive us apart."

I cupped her face and wiped away the vestiges of her tears with my thumbs. Even that act had a sense of *déjà vu*.

We talked and made love well into the early hours and even then I slept fitfully, trying to reconcile the conflicting emotions that were dividing me.

By breakfast time the next morning, I had determined the way forward. I knew I could not give up the quest now that it had received the fresh impetus of yesterday's events. At the same time, I needed to reassure Elizabeth that my pursuit of answers to the questions of what and why would not threaten our long term relationship.

We made an agreement that I should continue the pursuit for one more year, devoting as much time to it as practical. If matters had not been resolved by then I would give it all up, put it behind me, and settle back into a more normal lifestyle.

I am not sure that either of us was convinced that I would stick to the bargain if it was put to the test, but it enabled us to move forward without any immediate conflict.

I knew exactly where to go next. Thinking about everything that had happened, I felt sure that the Golden Rose should now become the focal point for my research.

I went back over all my records and confirmed that the first mention of the rose had come when Brother Baldwin had suggested that Richard should take it to the Pope in Lyon as proof of his standing. It was Baldwin who had been the guardian of the rose and he had collected it from his church at Luppitt, close by Mohun's Ottery.

Several weeks later, in late November, I was down in Devon yet again but I was disappointed when a visit to Luppitt church revealed nothing.

Set in an area of narrow lanes and ancient farms amid beautiful countryside it was a hidden gem, but apart from an exceptionally fine Norman font, little or nothing remained of the Saxon and Norman buildings. Parish records that I had perused on the internet contained nothing of the 14th century history that I was looking for, certainly no mention of the Golden Rose.

Moonshadow

Transition

The Camino de Santiago

I decided to revisit Mohun's Ottery, whose owner had been intrigued by my claim of descendancy from the original inhabitants. After a previous invitation to visit, he had shown me round the newly restored house and outbuildings containing traces of original medieval timbers. I had been thrilled by the fact that on the outside of the impressive, stone arched gateway the Mohun family crest was still visible.

Although on this visit I was uninvited and unexpected, I was made very welcome and enjoyed a pleasant cup of coffee while I talked about my quest. The family had a guest staying at the house, a young university student who joined us. He was introduced as Ian, a family friend and John said, "Ian is here to get some exercise and prepare for his big walk."

"So where are you walking to?" I queried.

"Well, you probably haven't heard of it but I am going to walk the Pilgrim's Way, the Camino de Santiago." He laughed. "Or try to, anyway. At the moment I am struggling to walk to the top of the hill behind the house."

In that instant I was back at Dunster Castle, and listening to Richard in the flickering light of the burning rushes.

"... I have decided, with Royal assent to my absence, to journey to Santiago and to carry with me, as a talisman and

*testament to our good fortune, our own beloved and sacred
Golden Rose ..."*

I was brought back by John gripping my shoulder.

"Are you alright, Richard?" I was aware that he and Ian
were both looking concerned.

"I'm sorry," I said shakily. "I'm fine. I have heard about the
journey to Santiago before, but a long time ago. It triggered
something in my mind." I did not want to go into long
explanations or admit that 'a long time ago' was in fact seven
hundred years back. I quickly moved the conversation on.

"Ian, tell me more about the Camino de Santiago."

"I would love to," he said. "But, I am really sorry, I have to
go. I'm already late for a meeting in Honiton. I will be back this
evening if you are staying?" I shook my head. He stood up to go.

"My suggestion, if you want to know more, would be to
make contact with 'The Confraternity of St James' in London.
They have all the information and advice that you could possibly
need; history, routes, maps, the best guide books available and
very friendly support. Now, sorry again, but I must dash." We
shook hands, I wished him luck on his walk, and he left.

John and I talked for a little longer, then I took my leave
and headed for home.

The next morning I found the website for The Confraternity
of St James. I rang them and made an appointment to visit them
in Blackfriars just before Christmas.

As Ian had intimated, they were charming and friendly
people, and I left with an armful of books and leaflets and an
excellent guide.

On the train home to Cheshire, I read avidly and learned a
great deal about the Camino. I was intrigued with its long
history and the crucial role that it had played in the development
of Northern Spain.

That night, I backtracked through all my notes and research
documents. I did yet another trawl through the internet on the
subject of the Golden Rose. Somewhere in the early hours, I
came to a conclusion and made a decision.

When I broached it with Elizabeth over breakfast, I got the
reaction that I half expected.

"You must be mad Richard," she stormed. "How can you think of hiking through Spain on some wild goose chase? You are not fit enough, you can't speak Spanish, you have no idea where you will be going and you don't even know what you are looking for and ..." She ran out of breath.

I put my arms round her. "You may be right, my love, but I can get fit; or fitter, anyway. I will have a route to follow, I can learn a little Spanish and carry a phrase book, and I do know exactly what I am looking for. I am looking for the Golden Rose. I saw it when I was in Avignon.

"You asked me once what all this was about and what did my ancestors want from me? Well, I know now. The answer lies somewhere on the Camino de Santiago and it involves the Golden Rose. I don't have a choice. I have to go."

There were more tears and more argument. She wanted to come with me but I knew deep down that there could be danger, and if I was ill prepared for such a journey she was even more so. In the end she capitulated. Not with good grace, but she realised that I was not to be dissuaded.

Having decided on my course of action, the next few weeks were frenetic. I was granted three months leave of absence from my consultancy but first had to tidy up and hand over my current assignments. I signed on at the gym and undertook a crash fitness course. I practised walking in our local hills.

With the advice from The Confraternity I purchased suitable boots, socks, rucksack and lightweight clothing, and planned my route based on the guide and records of mediaeval pilgrimages from England.

At last, on the fifteenth of May, I flew from Manchester to Bilbao, took the train to Pamplona and then a bus across the border into the little town of St Jean Pied de Port, one of the starting points of the Camino de Santiago.

Part IV

Camino Real

Moonshadow

Camino Real

Diary entry
Estella - 20 May 2006

I am walking! The first few days have been strenuous and stimulating but uneventful. I crossed the Pyrenees on the first day, re-entering Spain in the steps of Charlemagne at Roncesvalles. I was exhausted but buoyed up with a real sense of achievement. Two days later I was able to explore Pamplona and got a thrill out of staying one night at the La Perla hotel, favoured by Earnest Hemingway.

It overlooks the Plaza del Castillo and the old streets where the famous Bull Run takes place.

I have been walking west each day, getting used to using my legs and to the weight of my rucksack. I have been walking at my own pace, enjoying superb scenery, and the camaraderie of other pilgrims of many nationalities. I usually stay in refugios—hostels specifically for pilgrims—but sometimes, if I want more privacy and perhaps a bath, in small hotels.

To this point, however, nothing has happened to reassure me that I am not on a wild goose chase. I am beginning to feel foolish. Maybe I have read too much into Richard de Mohun's intent to walk this road with the Golden Rose. I have not felt any connection at all.

I know that there are many Camino routes emanating in

France and maybe I picked the wrong one. But I had hoped that, after yesterday, when the two main routes linked up at Puente la Reina, I would make some contact, but nothing.

Diary entry
Los Arcos - 22 May 2006

I am right!! I am right!!!

About two hours walking from Estella, I came to a fresh water spring which was covered over by a graceful stone arched medieval structure that had been carefully restored but retained its ancient ambience. I reflected that, if my assumptions were right, then my namesake would have drunk from this same well nearly seven hundred years before.

Just as the thought came into my head and as I took a sip of the cool water from the cup of my hand, I felt his presence; palpable and all pervasive, I knew he was with me and that substance and shadow had joined forces.

I looked around me, half expecting to see him but only two modern day pilgrims were in sight, walking towards me and still some way down the track.

I walked on in something of a daze. I am elated that my decision to make this journey has been justified, but at the same time, full of trepidation about the unknown outcome that I am moving towards.

I am staying in the town of Los Arcos this evening. I think I need an early night as it's a thirty kilometre walk tomorrow if I am to make Logrono.

Diary entry
Burgos - 26 May 2006

Not sure if I can go on but I know that somehow I have to.

It started as I walked into Logrono. I felt the first twinges in my right leg and the next morning I could hardly move. I went to a local pharmacist who diagnosed Tendonitis. He shook his head when I said I was heading for Santiago but gave me some pills, which he said would help. He cautioned me that I should rest for at least three days.

I rested for two frustrating days and then impatience got the better of me. I sensed that time was pressing.

Four days of hard walking followed. I am not sure if it was me or my shadow that was pushing so hard. We covered about one hundred and thirty kilometres in that time and I am crippled.

I had to get a taxi for the last few miles into Burgos and asked to be taken directly to the hospital. I had the necessary E11 papers and was seen without much delay by a very friendly and efficient doctor.

He bandaged my leg from ankle to knee and gave me pills to reduce the swelling and ease the pain. He told me that I must rest my leg for at least four days and he strongly advised me to abandon the walk.

Now I am here in my hotel room and do not know what to do. I still feel that Richard is with me. He is as desperate as I am to move on. I think too we are both afraid of what is to come.

My common sense tells me to abandon all this and just go home. I will make a decision in the morning.

Diary entry
Burgos - 27 May 2006

Breakfast time

I woke this morning knowing that I have to try and continue if I possibly can. I know Richard needs me. I must give myself a chance to recover and I need to rest my leg for at least another day. I am going to walk the short distance into town and buy a second stick to help take the weight off my leg and make walking a bit easier.

Evening

I am back in the hotel now and in shock.

I bought my new stick and it certainly helps to keep some of the weight off my leg. After my purchase, I sat in the Plaza de Santa Maria enjoying the sunshine. I rested with a glass of Rioja in my hand, enjoying the fantastic architecture of the Gothic Cathedral.

People were preparing for a medieval pageant that is opening this evening with a grand parade. Stands were being erected and flags and bunting hung across the streets. Many people were dressed in period costumes and I could hear the sounds of a Gregorian chant filtering out from the Cathedral to mingle with the general hubbub.

As I relaxed and drank in the sights and sounds, I saw a woman in costume standing at the top of the steps, leading down from the church of St Nicholas. She was looking directly at me. For a moment my brain did not comprehend what my eyes had seen.

Then, blindingly, the picture registered and I cried out, "Alicia."

A man at the table next to me jumped in surprise, spilled his glass of wine and glared at me. There was a moment of confusion. Attentive waiters rushed to mop up, I made an over the shoulder apology, fumbled for money to pay my bill and when I looked again, she had disappeared. I limped across the corner of the plaza and climbed the steps.

In front of me was another, smaller plaza. It was quiet and almost empty of people. Already my mind was telling me that I must have imagined it. A combination of the wine and medication, coupled with the medieval ambience and my relaxed state ... I felt a sense of disappointment. Then as I prepared to descend the steps I heard her voice, soft and tremulous.

"Richard, I am so sorry; you should not have come. Charles is here and waits for you. He seeks revenge."

I turned quickly and stumbled on the edge of the step. I felt myself falling backwards and was powerless to prevent myself from crashing down to the plaza below, but the crash never came...

Moonshadow

Camino Real

Burgos – 1328

Richard de Mohun gazed at Alicia in shock and disbelief.

"Alicia. What in heaven's name are you doing here? What is this about Charles? Have you seen him?"

Alicia nodded. "Yes, Richard. I am so sorry. I had to come. He sent word that he was dying here and needed me. I know that he has committed evil deeds, but he is my brother. Then, before I left home, I heard that you were coming to Santiago without Elizabeth, and I wanted to see you and tell you, tell you ..." she stammered to a halt.

"Tell me what?" Richard put his hands on her shoulders and looked into her eyes. "Tell me what, Alicia?"

"You should have married me," Alicia whispered. "If you had let things be with Charles and Elizabeth and married me instead, none of the terrible things would have happened.

"I loved you the first time I saw you out riding at Cornwood and now, because of me, Charles will hunt you down and kill you." She was sobbing now. "Then he will kill me and seek out Elizabeth and your son." She shook with fear and grief.

Richard took a step away from her. "So he was not dying?"

"No, it was a trick. He wanted to find out what had happened after he fled from Cornwall and he wanted to have me in his power. Richard, I'm sorry; I told him about you, but he threatened me. He is the leader of a band of mercenaries, some of them Moors, living off the land and preying on travellers and pilgrims. He threatened to give me over to them, to use me as they wanted. He meant it, Richard. I told him everything, and that you were travelling to Santiago. He has men out looking for you now. He knows you have passed through Punta la Reina with only two companions. He has sent me into Burgos to see if there is any sign of you here. He cannot come into the city himself; there is a price on his head. Oh Richard, what can we do?" Tears streamed down her face.

Richard drew her into the shadow of the church building.

"I do not know yet," he said. "But first, how did you get here? Is anyone with you? do you have a horse?"

"Yes," she replied. "I came into the city alone, but two of Charles' men await me at the gate to escort me back to the camp. I am under close guard there, and my two escorts from Sheviock have been forced to join with Charles' band."

"How many men are with Charles?"

"I have seen about a dozen."

"And where exactly is this camp?"

"It is a one hour ride east of the city, on the edge of the forest at Villalval."

There was a pause in the questioning and Richard paced up and down. He fingered the medallion that hung around his neck. Elizabeth had given it to him before he departed. It was made of copper, with lion rampant on blue and gilt enamel, and his name was inscribed on the back; it was his good luck charm. He made his decision.

"Alright, this is what you must do. Wait a further hour here, then, with your escort, go back to the camp and tell him that I have been seen in Burgos but have already moved on toward Santiago.

"When you return to the camp, we will be following. Ralph Purves and Tom Weaver are my companions. We will lie up close to your camp and hope that when you report your news, Charles and his band will soon leave the camp to try and hunt us down further along the Camino."

"If most of the band leaves with Charles, we, with the element of surprise on our side, will get you away and I will charge Ralph with getting you back to England."

"What if they make me go with them?" asked Alicia.

"You must avoid that any way you can. Feign sickness, collapse, anything that will ensure that you remain in the camp."

"What will you do then, after I have gone?"

"I will complete my journey to Santiago. Thanks to you, forewarned is forearmed. I will seek to meet your brother in fair combat but if I fail in that, then God willing, I will use any means available to me to ensure that he can no longer threaten my family or you.

"When you return to England you must tell Elizabeth what has happened here and that I command her, for her safety, to repair to Dunster with our son and remain there until I return.

"Now, can you go through with this? There are risks, but I believe we can carry the day so long as you play your part."

Alicia moved toward him and standing on tip toe, kissed him. "God bless and keep you, Richard. I will do whatever you ask of me."

Richard returned to his lodgings close by the Puerta St Martins. Ralph and Tom were sprawled out on the straw covered cobbles of the yard, keeping watch on the horses. They were visibly shaken to hear the news of Charles and Alicia. Ralph was downcast when he learned of the plan to rescue Alicia, and that he was to chaperone her back to England.

"Let the silly girl suffer the consequences of her deceit. Why risk everything for her, sire? She is not worthy of your protection. My place is with you if there is danger ahead, as there surely is if Charles Daunay is between here and Santiago."

"Ralph, I wish it could be so," said Richard. He put his arm around Ralph's shoulder.

"There is no one I would rather have with me, but I cannot abandon Alicia. She saved my Elizabeth from certain death. Now she has given me fair warning of Charles' intentions and has again put her own life in danger.

"I need you to take her home Ralph, for two reasons. First, Tom here is too young and inexperienced to undertake such a responsibility alone. Second, I must be doubly certain that Lady Elizabeth goes with you to Dunster, just in case things do not go well for me here."

Ralph nodded his understanding and acquiescence. Tom was almost bursting with excitement.

"Maybe my wish will come true after all and I will at last be able to avenge my father."

Richard smiled at his exuberance but spoke gravely. "Maybe, Tom; but from now on, you heed my every command. Charles is a threat to my family and like you, I want him dead and gone. Remember, though, that we face dangerous odds against us. Charles is not alone and we will need to employ stealth and guile if we are to prevail and reach Santiago alive." He clapped his hands. "First we have to prepare ourselves for action and rescue Lady Alicia."

Ralph tried one last time. "Sire, should we not all return to England, taking Alicia with us? We would avoid all the risks you run in going forward to Santiago. I fear for your safety and ..."

Richard, already in the saddle, wheeled round to face Ralph. "I have made a vow to atone for past sins and to give thanks for deliverance in the presence of St James," he said angrily. "I cannot break that vow without dishonour. In addition, Ralph, if I do not confront and defeat Charles Daunay here, then he will continue to be a threat to my family. I must end it here in Spain. No more prevarication. We have work to do."

They watched carefully from the corner of the Cathedral Plaza as Alicia rejoined her captors outside the Arcos de Santa Maria. She mounted her horse and they set off eastwards on the Camino.

Ten minutes later, before they were completely out of sight, Ralph followed. Richard set off after a similar interval and Tom brought up the rear.

Just east of Villafria, Richard caught up with Ralph who was waiting at a junction on the path. Ralph pointed to the narrower of the two tracks.

"They went that way, sire. It is not the main track to Villalval. If we follow and anyone is watching, we will be very obvious." They waited for Tom to join them.

"We will go forward together," said Richard. "But we must tread carefully. Keep your eyes and ears open, no talking. I will lead."

They picked their way down the track, pausing every hundred paces or so to listen. To their left they could hear the sound of fast flowing water. Suddenly, Richard held up his hand and urgently motioned for Ralph and Tom to move into the sparse growth of trees and shrubs now bordering the path.

They stood stock still and listened. The sound of voices and laughter filtered through to them.

Richard dismounted and crept forward. He was able to see that some fifty paces ahead was another junction with a path coming in from the right.

On the junction, Alicia was now flanked by three men, all talking and gesticulating. As he watched, two of them moved off further down the track with Alicia between them. The third man stayed at the junction.

Richard crept back to the others. "We must be close to the camp," he whispered.

"They have taken Alicia forward but there is a guard on the path just in front of us. If we attack him we risk raising the alarm, so we must try to pass him by.

"We will go back a little way and cut across to the stream that we can hear. We can follow it, out of sight of the guard, and hope that it will follow the path and bring us close to the camp."

With the running stream muffling the noise of the horses' hooves they passed the guard, and after another hundred paces found themselves in thick woodland. Tethering the horses, all three crept forward in the direction of the path.

"Perfect," said Richard softly. They could hear the noise from the camp while still in dense cover and were able to creep forward to a point where they could observe everything that was going on.

Several makeshift shelters were grouped around a clearing that had a well head at its centre. On the opposite side of the clearing from themselves they could see at least a dozen men already mounted and waiting to leave. Dressed in black leather tunics and white turbans, and armed with scimitars and broadswords, they looked a formidable bunch.

Next to the well, Charles, also wearing a white turban, was struggling with Alicia. He had hold of her arm and was urging her to remount her horse.

He had altered since Richard had seen him last. Browned by the sun, and thin to the point of emaciation, he had grown a dark beard that accentuated his facial scar. As they watched, he shouted at Alicia.

"For the last time, get on the damned horse or I will tie you to it and drag you with us."

Alicia wrenched herself free of his grasp, took a step backwards and fell to the ground, motionless.

Ralph made an involuntary move forward but Richard restrained him.

"Wait," he said.

Charles bent down and roughly turned Alicia onto her back. She moaned but remained inert. He prodded her roughly with his foot then cursed and ran over to where his horse had been readied. When mounted, he pointed to two men in the waiting group.

"Garcia and Ahmed, move her into my tent and guard her with your life until we return."

He wheeled his horse, signalled for his men to follow him and set off at a gallop back toward Burgos.

When the sound of their departure had faded, Richard motioned for Ralph and Tom to get ready to attack.

Before they could move, however, they saw Alicia emerge from the tent where she had been carried. She was bent double and clutching her stomach. Her two captors followed her but she angrily waved them away and signalled that she needed to obey the call of nature. They let her go, reluctantly, unsure of how to deal with the situation.

Alicia kept walking slowly, straight toward the spot where they were hidden. She saw them and veered slightly to the side. Still bent double, she put a finger to her lips as she passed them. "When I call out they will come running. Be ready."

Richard grinned and slowly drew his hunting knife, gesturing for Ralph and Tom to do the same.

Alicia moved further into the trees and then screamed. The two unfortunate guards came running. The surprise was total and complete.

As Tom and Ralph concealed the two bodies in the undergrowth, Richard held Alicia.

"How did you know we were here?"

"I didn't know it for sure," she said. "But it seemed likely that if you had followed me, you would be in the woods rather than on the open side of the camp, so I took a chance."

She took Richard's arm. "Come with me, Richard; I want you to take me home. You have seen my mad brother and his cutthroat band; you are outnumbered. It is foolhardy to pit yourself against them. Charles will show no mercy and is hell bent on revenge. You will be in such danger."

"No, Alicia; I have to go on. You know why. Do not fear for me. I have right on my side and with God's grace, I will complete my journey." Richard gently withdrew his arm and turned away. As he did so, the pilgrim medallion that Elizabeth had given him fell to the ground.

Alicia saw it fall and realising that Richard had not noticed its loss, she quickly retrieved it and dropped it into a pocket of her robe. It was something of his that she could treasure.

Minutes later, Ralph and Alicia were ready to leave. While Ralph retrieved his mount from the bank of the stream, Tom and Richard selected a mount for Alicia and a couple of spare horses from those left at the camp. They loaded them up with clothes and basic provisions taken from the storeroom.

Richard was anxious to see them depart. He kissed Alicia and shook Ralph's hand.

"God speed you both,"he murmured, watching them ride away.

As he and Tom walked back to the stream to collect their mounts, a dreadful premonition swept over him; that only sorrow and sadness lay ahead. Reaching to touch his medallion he realised it was gone.

"Tom," he said shakily. "I think you should follow and go with them. I can see this venture through alone. Without you I will have—" Tom cut him off.

"No, sire; you will need me. You cannot deprive me of my chance to avenge my family. If you cut me loose I will still go forward on my own to find him."

At that moment they came to the bank of the stream. Richard, still considering his response, reached out to untie the rope tethering Grisel Gris. As he did so, a figure sprang from concealment under the banking, and scimitar held aloft, charged towards him. Grisel Gris reared in fright, knocking Richard heavily to the ground. Stunned, momentarily winded and unable to move, he closed his eyes and waited for the blow to fall.

He heard the crunch of a sword blade biting into flesh and bone, and wondered why he felt no pain. Slowly opening his eyes, he saw Tom squatting beside him, looking concerned. He drew a cautious breath and eased himself up on to his knees.

Tom laughed out loud. "Now try telling me you don't need me."

Richard looked about him and saw the dead body of a man he recognised as the guard from the junction on the footpath. Still holding his scimitar, he wore an expression of shock on the face of his almost severed head.

Richard stood and flexed his limbs to make sure he was still in one piece. "Thank you, Tom; I think you may be right," he said, smiling.

His dark mood almost forgotten, he checked that the Golden Rose was still secure in his jerkin, mounted the now calm Grisel Gris and motioning for Tom to follow, set off at a canter through the trees and onto the path heading back to Burgos.

Moonshadow

Camino Real

Diary entry
Burgos - 27 May 2006

Evening

When I opened my eyes I saw the face of the same doctor who had attended to my tendonitis yesterday. I was back in the hospital. He wagged a finger.

"I told you not to walk for four days," he scolded. "Falling down a flight of stone steps will not improve your chances of finishing The Camino. You are very lucky; you do not seem to have sustained any other injury in your fall. The people who brought you in said that you seemed to float to the ground." He smiled. "Maybe our local Rioja relaxed you."

They made me stay for four hours to be sure that I had not been concussed. The doctor gave me a final admonishment to rest totally if I wanted to have any chance of continuing my walk.

Diary entry
Burgos - 28 May 2006

Today I have taken the good doctor's advice. I have stayed put in the hotel and used the time to write up the details of my second immersion in the past.

On reflection, this time was somehow different. Although I can describe what happened as an observer, this time I felt part of what was happening. I actually experienced the fear of death and the premonition of disaster; they remain with me like a bad aftertaste.

What next? Do I wait for another sign? Do I just go forward again or do I simply take the doctor's advice and go home?

I will sleep on it.

Diary entry
Burgos - 29 May 2006

Breakfast

I slept soundly, but this morning I know for sure that I have no choice. I have to go on.

It is a fine morning. I have breakfasted well and obtained a simple packed lunch from the hotel kitchen. I feel rested and my leg, apart from the odd twinge, seems alright.

I have checked my Camino guide and decided on a plan for the day. I am going to be cautious and take a bus for the first ten kilometres or so to Hornillas Del Camino. Most of the route is through the Burgos suburbs and the guide book suggests that it is pretty uninteresting walking.

From Hornillas it is about twenty kilometres to Castrojeriz, the next town of any size. This should be walkable and I feel ready to go.

Evening (in Castrojeriz)

By some miracle, and I do mean miracle, I am here in the

Roman hilltop town of Castrojeriz. Built by Julius Caesar according to the guide book, and now nothing would surprise me.

I took the bus from Burgos to Hornillas as planned and set off from there very happy to be on the move again.

Within a couple of kilometres I knew that I had been very foolish. My tendonitis was back and with a vengeance. Every step was agony and I was reduced to using my two sticks as crutches and just swinging my right leg, trying to keep my weight off it entirely. Progress was very slow and I contemplated turning back to Hornillas and then catching the bus to return to Burgos.

I had decided to do just that when I came to a point where a small track to the left led toward what appeared to be a small church or chapel with a diminutive domed roof. As I paused, intending to turn round and limp back to Hornillas, a figure appeared, as if from nowhere, on the main path. He pointed commandingly toward the chapel. Dressed in pilgrim robes of black, his face hidden by his cowl, he was strangely familiar. I found myself following his instruction without a word being spoken.

About a hundred yards down the little track, I arrived at the building. I looked back. There was no sign of the man who had directed me.

A simple notice board in front of the building read 'Arroyo de San Bol.'

I immediately recalled a phrase from one of the guide books that I had read in London, which extolled the supposedly magical and medicinal properties of a *fuente* or spring at San Bol. It was said that medieval pilgrims who washed their aching feet in the spring water there would suffer no further foot problems on the remainder of the Camino. It had stuck in my mind somehow as an odd piece of information.

I limped into the building and found that it was in fact a small pilgrim refugio with about half a dozen beds, a kitchen and a beautiful little chapel.

Only one other person was there; a local girl preparing a meal for pilgrims expected that evening.

She kindly gave me a cold drink. When I showed her my

now very swollen leg, she grimaced and suggested I should rest on one of the beds in the dormitory.

I asked her about the legend of the *fuente* in my broken Spanish. She laughed but pointed to a little rill in front of the chapel with a small but deep pool in its centre. She mimed dipping a foot into it and indicated that it was very cold.

I took my drink outside and sat by the pool, trying to decide what I should do. I felt totally downcast at the thought of having to abandon matters now at the point where everything I had experienced seemed to be reaching a conclusion.

As I pondered, I almost unconsciously took off my boots and socks and unwound the bandage from my swollen leg. Then, filled with a sudden overwhelming confidence, I plunged my right leg into the pool. The icy cold took my breath away and within a minute or less my leg was totally numb.

I lifted it out and let it dry in the strong sun. As the circulation returned it seemed more painful than ever, but the swelling had definitely reduced. Full of hope, I laced up my boots, stood up and took a couple of tentative steps, then a few more. I walked right round the building, twice. Not a twinge!

I shouted to the girl. When she came to the door I jumped up and down and even hopped a few steps on my right leg. I rolled up my trouser leg and she looked at my previously swollen joints which were now quite normal.

She was amazed. She took my hand and led me into the little chapel where we knelt for a few moments in silent prayer.

Now I am here at Castrojeriz with no sign of any return to pain. Miraculous is not an exaggeration. I am sure now that the figure that stood in my way and directed me to San Bol had been deliberately instrumental in ensuring that my leg was healed. It was someone who needs me to go on. It was Richard.

Diary entry
Castrojeriz - 30 May 2006

Breakfast

Still no pain! It was a miracle. I feel alive and ready for whatever is to come. I know I have been prepared, cajoled, persuaded, urged and assisted to this point. I am now, at last, close to learning the 'what and why' of it all.

Today, if the miracle holds, I will walk to Fromista, about twenty six kilometres.

The guide book tells me that much of the route between here and Sahagun is on the original 'Camino Real' of Roman origin and therefore has been walked by hundreds of thousands of pilgrims before me. I will be walking in Richard's footsteps. I am ready.

Evening

I set off from Castrojeriz towards Fromista, walking now on the Camino Real. It stretched out in front of me, a ribbon of brown shale framed by banks of scarlet poppies and white daisies. The day was beautiful; blue sky, bright sunshine and a pleasant cool breeze. Then, after some ten kilometres and without warning, the world changed.

Suddenly, I was alone on the path. Only moments earlier I had seen fellow pilgrims ahead and behind me. The sky darkened, sounds and colours were intensified, the breeze dropped and the road shimmered in the heat. I was filled with a sense of foreboding.

I heard horses approaching fast; looking behind me, I saw two horsemen at full gallop emerging from the haze. As they came closer, I could see that they were dressed in plain pilgrim cloaks that streamed out behind them, underneath scarlet tunics emblazoned with a black cross. The horses, covered in lather and brown dust, were being ridden hard.

Behind them, I saw the reason why. A dozen or so horsemen were in pursuit, armed and wearing black tunics and breeches, their heads and faces concealed by loose white turbans.

I leapt to the side of the path and crouched, transfixed as the first two riders reached me. Just for a moment the world stopped still, and in that moment, the rider nearest to me, his eyes fixed on mine, smiled and pointed forward.

I whispered, *"Richard"* for I knew who it was. They were past. The second group were upon me and then gone with not even a glance in my direction. To them I did not exist.

Then, as though someone had switched on a light, the beautiful day was back, the cool breeze blowing, the pilgrims in front and behind clearly visible. I waited where I was until the walker behind me caught up. It was Paulo, a young Brazilian computer engineer that I had talked to a few days before in Burgos.

"What was all that about, Paulo?" I said. "Pretty scary!" He looked at me blankly. "The horses," I said.

"What horses, amigo?"

"The horses that passed by you just now. You must have seen them."

"No horses passed me," he said. "I think perhaps you dream something. Shall we walk on together? You don't look so good."

I do not clearly remember the rest of the walk. I was not a good companion. I kept replaying the scene that was so vivid in my mind's eye and that had been totally invisible to everyone else.

To Paulo's amusement I asked several other pilgrims if they had seen horses galloping by. All looked at me as if I were mad and shook their heads.

"I think you have sleep very deep while you are walking," said Paulo.

We reached Fromista at about 5.0 p.m. There was a large and popular refugio and it was the chosen stopping place for all the pilgrims around me. Paulo, still convinced that I had been sleepwalking, tried to persuade me to stay. But I knew I had to go on.

I said goodbye and walked on alone in the fading light, toward Poblacion; my excitement tempered with apprehension.

Diary entry
Poblacion - 30 May 2006 (Night)

Now I am here in Poblacion. I am sitting on a chair that is the only piece of furniture in the room. The room itself is some sort of chapel. There is a wooden cross on the wall, the floor is made of stone slabs with two tombstones set into it; no writing on them, just beautifully carved long swords. Maybe they are crusader tombs?

I am here because I have to be. When I walked down the village street I saw and heard no one. I stopped outside this old building and was compelled; there is no other word for it, compelled by an irresistible force to walk down the stone steps and through the door into this room. I know I am in the right place and that he, Richard, is with me. We are waiting for something.

I can hear the sound of horses.

Moonshadow

Camino Real

Poblacion de Campos - 1328

They reigned in at the far end of the village, where the road divided; trying to decide which way to turn, the two men and their horses radiated exhaustion.

"I cannot go much further, sire." Tom spat the dust from his parched mouth. "Do you think we may have shaken them off?"

Richard shook his head. "No, Tom, they are determined to have us but we need fresh horses. Even my brave Grisel is failing fast. There is nothing here. We must try to reach Carrion de las Condes. We may find sanctuary there and fresh horses. Are you ready to ride on?"

Tom nodded wearily. "I am ..." He froze, looking beyond Richard at the road in front of them, his eyes widening in shock. A small but rapidly growing dust cloud could be seen moving towards them which quickly became recognisable as a group of six or more horsemen.

Moments later they could pick out the fact that most of the riders wore white turbans.

Richard wheeled to look back down the road towards Fromista, and his heart sank as he saw the pursuing group entering the far end of the village behind them.

"We are in a trap, Tom," he said. "They have outmanoeuvred us. It looks as though we will have to fight it out here."

He looked around him. On their left was a small but sturdy stone building with its entrance below the level of the road, only accessible via a flight of narrow stone steps. The heavy wooden doorway was set in a stone archway and appeared to be ajar.

"Quick, Tom," he shouted as he dismounted. "Get down those steps. We can fight from the doorway. They can only come down the steps one at a time." He ran down the steps with Tom on his heels.

Through the open doorway they saw only an empty room with stone walls and a paved floor. A Knights Hospitalier banner hung on the far wall above a simple crucifix. There was only one small barred window on the side wall.

"Sorry, Tom. It does not look good for us," Richard said. "No way out of here unless we fight our way out. I will take the door and you take the window. Stand to one side, out of sight. As soon as you see or sense someone looking in, step out and thrust."

Tom, looking around him, acknowledged the instruction with a nod and a nervous laugh. "I hope Charles Daunay is the first to take a look."

As he spoke they could hear the noise of horses' hooves and excited voices above them, and then the distinctive voice of Charles Daunay.

"Where did they go?" he shouted. "They are not far away, their horses are still here. Spread out and search and remember, I want the bastards alive."

Almost immediately they heard cautious footsteps descending the steps. Richard put a finger to his lips and motioned Tom to flatten himself against the right hand wall, just inside the doorway, while he did the same on the left.

The footsteps paused on the threshold of the open door and then the figure stepped forward. Richard was behind him in a flash and before his opponent could utter a sound, he was silenced forever with his throat cut from ear to ear.

"First blood to us," whispered Tom, as they dragged the body out of sight of the doorway.

It was not long before a second marauder came down the steps, calling out his comrade's name. The attempt to repeat the performance failed in that this time, being more alert, he evaded Richard's attempt to get behind him and was able to cry out in alarm before Tom's sword thrust silenced him.

There was an immediate hubbub up above and shouts summoning the other searchers.

Charles Daunay's voice called for calm and then they heard him speak from the top of the steps.

"Rats in a hole where you belong." He shouted. "I have you now, Mohun, and that poxy runt with you. The building is surrounded. Come out now and fight, or by God we will come and cut you out piece by piece."

Richard went to the door. He spoke calmly and with an authority that belied his feeling of hopelessness.

"Charles, I will come out and fight on two conditions. First, I will fight you, one to one, in honourable combat as I did with your father. Second, your word that Tom Weaver is released unharmed."

There was silence, followed by murmuring and laughter, then Charles' voice again.

"You are in no position to demand conditions, Mohun, but I agree. One to one combat and Weaver goes free. Come out now and let us have done with it."

"Don't go, sire," Tom whispered. "It will be a trick. That man does not know the meaning of honour."

"I know, Tom, but I would rather die in the open than trapped down here. If they cannot flush us out they will starve us out." He called out again.

"Daunay, give me a moment to prepare myself and we will come out." He turned swiftly, fumbled in his jerkin and produced a small package of cloth tied with twine.

"Somehow, Tom, I have to protect the Golden Rose. I cannot let it fall into Daunay's hands. Quickly, where can I hide it?"

They looked around desperately. Tom pointed to a small gap behind one of the two large blocks of stone that formed a bench under the window. Using his dagger, he quickly scraped out some loose dust and mortar and created a narrow fissure just big enough to take the rose.

In a few seconds, Richard slipped the package down into

the space behind the right hand stone. They re-packed loose mortar and dust from the floor into the remaining space until the gap itself was totally concealed.

Richard turned to Tom and clasped his shoulder.

"Tom, it is me that Charles wants and there is a chance—a small chance—that he will let you go free, and you will be able to ride away with at least a head start. If I should fall and you can escape, I want you to swear now, on oath, to tell my family all that has passed and where the rose is hidden. Will you do that?"

"On my honour, sire, I swear it, but what if I do not escape?"

"Then the rose will stay hidden and my family will lose its sacred protection until it is returned to them. God willing, you will live and Alicia and Ralph will tell their story and the truth of all that has happened here will come to light.

"Someone will come and retrieve the rose. I swear that I will not rest in peace until that day dawns."

Richard, followed by Tom, knelt in front of the crucifix and murmured a prayer; then, springing to his feet, he clapped Tom on the shoulder.

"Come, brave lad, and let us close this chapter. God speed and do exactly as I tell you."

As the two of them climbed the steps and emerged onto the street there was a low and threatening murmur from the group of half a dozen or so marauders. Most looked of Moorish origin and were probably descendents of deserters from the Moorish army that had now been driven inexorably southwards during the Christian re-conquest.

Whoever they were, they looked a force to be reckoned with. They stared with cold, hard eyes at the two men standing in front of them with swords drawn.

The local villagers had clearly decided to keep out of sight and there was no immediate sign of Charles Daunay.

"What now?" Tom said quietly. "Where is the evil bastard?"

In answer to his question they heard the soft whinny of a horse, and they both stared in surprise as Charles appeared from the rear of the building mounted on Grisel Gris.

"A fine horse, Mohun," he sneered. "Pity you will not ride him again." He dismounted and proffered the reins to Tom.

"He is yours now, Weaver, in exchange for your sword if you please." Tom held fast onto his weapon but at a word from Richard, he reluctantly threw it to the ground. Charles let it lie.

"You had better go quickly before I change my mind. My men want your blood."

Tom looked at Richard who stepped forward and embraced him. As they hugged each other, Richard whispered in his ear.

"Ride for your life, Tom. Once out of sight, get off the road. Try to find a way across country. Only half of his men are here, the rest will be waiting for you somewhere down the road." He stepped back and Tom swung himself astride Grisel Gris.

"God go with you," said Richard softly. Tom nodded.

"Kill the bastard for me, sire. I will see you in Santiago." He dug his heels into the horse's flanks and quickly vanished from view down the dusty road.

Charles laughed. "See you in hell, more likely. Now, you wanted one to one combat, Mohun and you shall have it; but only after my companions have taken their revenge. I can wait."

He signalled to the waiting group, poised like dogs on a leash, and stepped away as they rushed at Richard with swords and scimitars drawn.

The melee was short and bloody. Richard fought for his life with all the skill and experience that he could muster. Two of the combatants were quickly despatched by his swinging blade that whistled with the speed and ferocity of his attack. The remaining four drew back slightly from the onslaught but encircled him, using speed and guile to inflict cuts to his arms and torso. It became impossible to defend himself on all sides and as he spun, swinging his sword high, his legs were cut from under him with slicing scimitar slashes into the backs of both his knees.

Unable to stand and losing blood fast he sank down, his sword point buried in the ground, his head bowed.

For a moment the attack ceased and the attackers stood back, gathering their breath before moving in for the kill.

"Enough," Charles yelled, his voice shrill with excitement. He stepped forward to stand in front of Richard. "Time now for our one to one combat, Mohun," he jeered.

251

Richard, slowly and with intense effort, raised his head and looked steadily into Charles eyes. He spoke slowly, his voice growing weaker with each word.

"Your father died with some honour. You, Daunay, are a coward and a murderer. God damn your soul, may you rot in hell." He struggled vainly to raise himself but pitched forward on his face.

Charles, with a snarl of pent up hatred, gripped his sword like a dagger and drove it deep into Richard's exposed back.

Richard twitched once convulsively and lay still.

There was no acclamation of Richard's death. The small group of men stood silent. Charles himself was momentarily discomforted. He knew that even in the eyes of his lawless companions he had shown himself to be without any sense of honour.

In the silence, the sound of approaching horses concentrated their attention. In a few moments the other half of Charles' group cantered into the village. Charles realised immediately that Tom Weaver was not amongst them.

"Where is the boy?" he yelled. "I told you to bring him back here alive and that you were not to kill him."

The leader of the returning group, a tall emaciated Moor known simply as Yusuf, replied curtly.

"We did not kill him, Ingles. We did not see him. He never came."

Charles looked shocked then swore. "God's teeth, he must have suspected you were waiting and turned off the road before he reached you. He cannot have got far." He called to Yusuf.

"Leave two men here to dispose of the bodies. Take the rest and search for the boy. Spread out and sweep to the west each side of the road. He cannot have got far. His horse is weary and will be noticed. Now go."

Yusuf had dismounted and was in a huddle with his companions, who had gathered around him and were talking excitedly, gesticulating toward Richard's body.

"Did you hear me?" Charles screeched at them. "Go now and find the boy. I will wait until you bring him to me. Alive, remember."

Yusuf turned and stared at Charles. "Ingles, we are

returning to our camp. We see no profit in pursuing the boy. We have ridden with you too long. You have used us to pursue your own ends and shown yourself today as a weak man with no honour. Four of our companions are dead, and for what? We will take their bodies with us."

While he spoke others had gathered up their dead and slung them over the backs of their horses.

As Charles watched, speechless, the whole group remounted and at a signal from Yusuf they rode off through the village back toward Burgos.

Charles yelled obscenities at their retreating backs and kicked out in rage at Richard's body. He looked around him and swore again as he realised that they had taken his horse with them.

Walking across from the chapel to the house opposite, he hammered on the barred wooden door. There was no response. Hammering again, the sound seemed to echo down the street but when he stopped, the echo carried on and soon became distinct as the soft, rhythmic beat of a horse walking down the street behind him.

Charles whirled round to find Tom Weaver astride Grisel Gris, reining in next to Richard's corpse.

Swiftly taking in the situation, Tom leapt to the ground and grabbed Richard's sword, still embedded tip down in the ground beside his body.

"So, my turn at last," said Tom. "No one to hide behind now Daunay, it is just me and you." Charles took a deep breath but made no move to draw his sword.

"Come, Tom." He tried to smile but only succeeded in a lopsided grimace. "I kept my word and let you go. Mohun gave me a hard fight but he fell to a better swordsman."

Tom spat. He glanced down at Richard's body, noting the massive stab wound in his back.

"I didn't see him fall but I heard your band of thugs disown you as a coward and I can see how he died. If you are such a brilliant swordsman use your weapon now or I will kill you as you stand." He took a step forward.

Panic stricken, Charles tried to run. He dodged round Tom while struggling to draw his own weapon and stumbled toward the chapel. He tripped and fell in a sprawling heap beside Richard's body as his sword slid from his grasp and clattered down the steps, landing at the entrance to the crypt.

Tom advanced toward him, sword held high but paused before delivering the coup de grace. Charles, with an effort fuelled by fear, managed to propel himself forward and tumbled down the steps. He regained his sword and scrambled his way through the bloodstained doorway with Tom at his heels.

"No way out, Daunay." Tom spoke from the doorway. "It is time to die."

Charles, face distorted with fear and rage, ran towards Tom, swinging wildly. As Tom retreated, the tip of Charles' sword snagged against the stone wall and Tom, seeing his chance, lunged forward with a thrust that pierced Charles chest and with their combined momentum, ran him clean through.

Charles staggered backwards into the far wall and slowly slid to the floor, sitting upright, still holding his own sword.

Tom stood over him. "That was for my father and my sister and this ..." He put his sword to Charles' throat. "This is for Richard de Mohun." He thrust again.

In an involuntary death spasm, the tip of his Charles' weapon jerked upwards, deep into Tom's thigh.

Tom felt no pain and thought at first that the sudden fountain of blood had come from Charles' throat, but as he moved back from the corpse, he realised that the blood was his own, and that he was badly hurt.

Tearing off his shirt, he tried to staunch the wound as best he could, to little avail. He crawled up the steps calling for help but the villagers were still keeping off the street and none came to his aid. Weakening fast, Tom collapsed alongside Richard's body. Reaching out, he grasped Richard's hand and clasped it tightly as his life blood ebbed away into the dust.

When all was quiet, the villagers emerged cautiously from their homes and examined the aftermath of the bloody events that had been played out in their usually peaceful village. The chapel and the crypt at the centre of things were already embedded in their history. The building had served for the last century as a Knights Templar hostel and staging post between

Burgos and the castle at Ponferrada. Since the Templar massacre some twenty years earlier the building had been used spasmodically by the Knights Hospitalers but had, in recent times, fallen into disuse.

Some of the villagers had observed everything that had passed and when it came to the disposal of the bodies, Richard and Tom were interred under the floor of the crypt, alongside the crusaders laid to rest there in years gone by. The villagers perceived that the crosses on their tunics earned them that right whereas Charles Daunay, dressed as an infidel, was buried in an unmarked grave on the outskirts of the village.

The spoils of the skirmish, in the form of horses and weaponry, were quickly gathered in and apportioned within the community. Within a few hours, all visible signs of the bloodshed had been erased.

Moonshadow

Camino Real

Diary entry
Poblacion – 31 May 2006

I awoke to the sound of footsteps descending from the street. It was daylight and I was totally confused. I didn't even know what century I was in, let alone what day it was. I was both relieved and disappointed when an old lady with a mop and bucket came through the door. When she saw me she screamed, dropped the bucket and turned to run.

I called to her, trying to reassure her. "Senora ..." but my voice only served to make her scream again and to run, shouting up the steps.

I followed, and by the time I reached the top of the stairs several villagers, responding to the old lady's cries, were hastening towards me. I stood still and raised my arms in a show of non aggression. As they stared at me I said, "Pelegrino Ingles," gestured toward the chapel and mimed that I had been sleeping. One of them stepped forward and spoke to me in good English.

"Senor, I am Miguel. The chapel is not a pilgrim refugio. That is in the schoolhouse." He gestured toward the main street.

"This is the Hermitage of Nuestra Senora del Socorro, Our Lady of Help. It is a tourist attraction and a very old building."

"I am sorry," I said. "I did book into the refugio last night but I came for a walk, found my way into the chapel and I must have fallen asleep. I am very sorry if I scared the senora who came to clean."

He turned to the little crowd of villagers and translated my explanation and apology. There was a lot of laughter and even the old lady raised a smile.

As the crowd began to disperse, Miguel asked me if I would like to have a coffee with him.

"I was making my breakfast when I heard Maria scream," he said, as he ushered me into his house just across the street from the chapel.

I suddenly had the picture of Charles Daunay hammering on the same doorway that I was going through.

We sat with a pot of very strong coffee and chatted about England. He had been a waiter in Manchester for many years. Miguel, it turned out, was custodian of the refugio and he wanted to talk about my Camino experiences. I obliged, but all the while I was recalling the events that I had witnessed or dreamed during the night. The conversation petered out and Miguel looked at me curiously.

"Did you experience anything unusual in the Hermitage, senor?"

I was not sure what to say. "I had some strange dreams," I volunteered. "Why do you ask?"

"Well senor, many people feel that it is an unhappy place and that bad things have happened there in the past."

"You mean it is haunted."

"That is what some people say, senor but it depends if you believe such things."

I did not know how to respond. Part of me wanted to tell him the whole story but I knew that it would test his credulity to the limit and take too long. At the top of my mind and closing out all other thoughts was the now clear picture of the Golden Rose, lying in its cold stone hiding place, waiting for the light of day to reveal its radiant, red tinged beauty.

I took my leave of Miguel with thanks for the coffee and the chat, and for smoothing out the unfortunate incident with poor Maria who was, according to Miguel, someone who did believe that the hermitage was haunted.

I returned to the refugio to write up this diary and plan my next step. I have to get back into the chapel crypt and examine the stonework under the window.

Is the hiding place still intact? Is the rose still there?

Diary entry
Poblacion - 1 June 2006

When I re-entered the crypt later that day, I could feel the weight of expectation and longing that pervaded the room. I was fearful that at this last hurdle I might fail and the patience and waiting of some seven centuries could all have been in vain.

I went immediately to the window and examined the two massive blocks of stone that formed a seat under the casement frame.

At first glance my heart sank. They looked immovable without the employment of hammers, chisels and a crowbar, none of which were in my possession. I knew that if I sought such tools and tried to use them I would draw unwelcome attention to myself and my task, and that the consequences would be very unpredictable.

As I examined the blocks more closely my spirits lifted a little. Although the little gap between the blocks and the wall had obviously been filled in comparatively recently, dampness from the window frame had seeped in, and when I prodded it with my finger, the filler felt slightly soft and crumbly.

I had no idea how deeply it was filled but I felt a glimmer of hope. I needed some small tools, a knife or a chisel, and something to scrape out and lift any debris behind the block and, God willing, the rose itself.

I resolved to return to the crypt that night. I found a couple of old but strong kitchen knives at the refugio and some wire coat hangers. I thought they might serve to hook out loose plaster and other debris, and anything else that might be there.

Later in the morning I visited the single village shop, to buy some tortilla and water. To my surprise and delight, in the recesses of the shop I found a shelf of children's toys and among them a packet of Plasticine that I thought would serve admirably to cover up the damage that I might cause.

I waited in the refugio until all seemed quiet in the village. I emptied my rucksack of most of its usual contents and filled it with the makeshift tools, a blanket from the bed and my torch, and walked down to the Hermitage.

I stood for a while at the top of the steps, and when there was no sign of anyone stirring I went down into the crypt. As I entered I could feel the hairs on the back of my neck standing up. Richard's presence was almost overpowering and so real that I spoke to him.

"Not long now, Richard," I said. "Let's get to work."

I hung the blanket up at the window and switched on my torch. Using one of the borrowed knives I started to dig into the filler. As I had hoped, it had softened with the damp and quickly disintegrated. I was able to simply pick pieces out with my fingers, although quite a lot just fell down the ever widening gap at the back of the stone. Soon there was an open gap nearly an inch deep running the length of the right hand stone block.

"So far so good," I muttered to myself and to Richard. "Now for the tricky bit."

I straightened out one of the wire coat hangers, leaving the hook at one end and pushed it down the gap, feeling it reach the debris at the bottom of the stone. I tried fishing with it for several minutes, hoping to feel it catch on something, but I couldn't feel anything substantial; only dust and plaster and gravel. Either I was not reaching deep enough or there was nothing there.

In my heart, though, I knew that Richard would not be so close to me now unless I was doing what he expected of me.

I had an idea. I pulled the coat hanger out, got the second one from my rucksack, and twisted the two together to make a longer probe that would more than reach the bottom of the fissure. I moulded a large piece of the Plasticine until it was soft and sticky, and wrapped it round the hook of the coat hanger probe.

This time, instead of fishing, I just pushed the probe down and withdrew it with bits of debris stuck to the Plasticine. I repeated this dozens and dozens of times, gradually building up a sizeable pile of stones, dust and plaster. My knees were sore from kneeling on the stone block, my arm ached from the continuous pushing and lifting, and I was beginning to lose faith, when suddenly, the debris stuck onto the Plasticine included a scrap of loosely woven cloth. My heart leapt.

I carefully cleaned the Plasticine, remoulded it, and pushed down again in the same spot. Six more probes all produced more cloth, a lot of it, dry and brittle.

The seventh probe felt different. It was heavier as I lifted it. My heart raced and sweat poured down my face.

As I drew the probe very carefully to the rim of the gap, I could see in the torchlight a dull gleam. My hand was shaking and I could see that the gap was not quite wide enough to pull the object and the probe out without the risk of it falling back down.

I held the probe with my right hand and carefully manoeuvred the fingers of my left hand into the gap. Holding my breath, I managed to grasp part of the object between my index and middle fingers and gently eased it away. Then, dropping the probe and using the fingers of my right hand as well, I was able to ease it through the gap.

It lay in the palm of my hand; exquisite in shape, colour and design, exactly as I remembered it. The reddish gold of the flower, leaf and stem, and the bud with the glowing ruby set in the lid of the miniature cup. The Golden Rose was back in Mohun hands.

"We have it, Richard," I whispered softly. As I said the words I felt a soft, cool breeze swirl round the room and envelop me, and then the shadow that had been with me for so long was gone, leaving behind an atmosphere of calm and peace that was truly indescribable.

PART V

Tresco Abbey

Moonshadow

Tresco Abbey, Isles of Scilly

I continued my personal pilgrimage to Santiago de Compostella, to complete the journey that Richard had started some seven centuries before. In the magnificent cathedral I paid my respects to the relics of St James and offered up a prayer of thanks on behalf of Richard de Mohun.

I resolved to keep the secret of the recovery of the Golden Rose to myself for the time being. I did not want to go through the complications of Spanish or English treasure trove law or the publicity that might be generated if I told the story.

I thought hard about what should be done with the rose and where it should now be lodged. After centuries of being concealed in dark and dusty surroundings, I thought it should enjoy the benefits of warmth and light, and yet be safe, secure, and accessible to the family in times of need. I think I found the ideal place but that is for me to know and others to conjecture.

I knew that there were gaps in the story that I needed to try to fill. The biggest of these was the question of what had happened to Alicia and Ralph, and why there had been no apparent attempt by Elizabeth de Mohun or the family to try to discover what had happened to Richard and Tom Weaver when they failed to return from Spain. Surely if someone had followed their trail on the Camino at the time, the story of their death would have been uncovered. But it appears that they didn't and it wasn't.

I carried out yet more research and uncovered many more fascinating insights into the family history. Elizabeth and her son John lived on at Hall and the family line flourished. It was another four generations before it happened, but the family finally took up residence in a totally rebuilt Boconnoc in 1556.

Despite all the searching, however, I found nothing more written about Richard, and no mention of his fate or the loss of the Golden Rose. I could not understand why.

Then, unexpectedly, I think I found the answer.

Two years ago, I happened to visit the Royal Cornwall museum in Truro, and found there an exhibit which gave me that old familiar feeling of *déjà vu*.

It was a small medallion made of copper with a lion rampant in relief, traces of blue and an edge of gilt. I was transported back to the woods in Villalval, and my recollection of Alicia pocketing Richard's medallion when it fell unnoticed from his neck. I read the museum note, indicating that the item had been recovered from The Isles of Scilly and was thought to have come from an early medieval shipwreck. Could it be Richard's medallion?

I dismissed the idea as fanciful conjecture but it never quite left my mind.

A year later I was on holiday on the island of Tresco in the Scillies and exploring the famous Abbey gardens. I came across some ancient ruins and there, on a plaque, was written:

ST. NICHOLAS PRIORY
THESE RUINS ARE ALL THAT REMAINS OF A
BENEDICTINE PRIORY, WHICH WAS
PROBABLY BUILT DURING THE 12TH
CENTURY. KING HENRY I GRANTED A
CHARTER IN 1114 THROUGH THE BISHOP OF
EXETER TO THE ABBOT AND MONKS OF
TAVISTOCK, CHARGING THEM WITH TAKING
OVER THE EXISTING SIMPLE RELIGIOUS
FOUNDATIONS IN SCILLY AND ESTABLISHING
A PRIORY ON TRESCO.

Tavistock!

Lawrence Mohun's home at the heart of de Mohun country, coupled with the Benedictine order so favoured by the de Mohuns.

I was astonished to find the link between my ancestors and the Isles of Scilly, perhaps my favourite location in the world. I needed to find out more.

I learned, from various sources, that in medieval times the abbot and monks of Tavistock had been given all the rights to wrecks on the islands of Scilly. They were in continuous conflict with pirates and with the secular owners of Ennor, now St Mary's, but jealously guarded their Royal Grant of Benefit from the salvage of the wrecks.

Towards the end of the summer I returned to Tresco, just for a day, to revisit the old priory and enjoy the extraordinarily beautiful gardens that sheltered the picturesque ruins. I sat on one of the thoughtfully placed seats just outside the priory entrance and basked in the warm sun and the tranquil, heavily scented air of the garden.

I reflected on all the happenings and coincidences that had so influenced my life and given me such insights into a past that seemed so real. Drowsily, I pondered the possible fate of Alicia and Ralph.

I like to think I was given the answer in one last glimpse of the past.

Tresco - 1328

The wind howled over the top of the rocky hill behind the priory. Literally howled, like some wild beast desperate with hunger. Every now and then it drew breath and then above it you could hear the deep surging rumble of the waves from beyond the hill and beyond Sampson and Bryher as they reached the end of their journey from the edge of the world and thundered into the bay.

At Lauds, in the safety of the small but sturdily built chapel, Prior Robert prayed out loud for the souls of those at sea. He prayed inwardly that if there were any wrecks as a result of the storm that he and his monks would be first on the scene to salvage the spoils. It had been nearly five months since the last salvageable wreck, and on that occasion the Blanchminster men at arms from Ennor had been first to the scene; by the time the monks arrived, nothing of value remained.

This time he hoped for a better result and when the storm first struck in the early hours, he sent four of the fittest monks out into the night, to watch and listen for any signs of stricken vessels.

As dawn approached, the wind began to abate. While the monks sat in silence at their first prayers of the day, they heard the recognisable bellow of Brother Sebastian who had been on Gweek Hill on Bryher. "Wreck! Wreck!" he boomed as he entered the chapel, windblown and sodden. "Souls to save and rewards for the brave."

There was a mad scramble to surround him, everyone wanting to know where they were to go.

"Less haste, Brothers." Prior Robert called them to order.

"We have a good start on the Ennor men. Remember, the first task is to save lives, the second to recover any valuables. All are to be brought here. Now, Brother Sebastian, where is the wreck? And what sort of vessel?"

Brother Sebastian, still recovering his breath, stood on a bench to address them all.

"It is a cog, I think. It hit a rock just outside the Great Porth. I heard the sound of it striking even above the wind and sea.

It broke apart and the waves have carried the flotsam onto the beach and the rocks around the Porth. There are bodies, but from the hill I could not see if there were signs of life. We need to hurry if any are still living."

The Monks were well rehearsed in attending wrecks. Within a few minutes, twenty or so brothers and six mules were streaming across the sand bar from Tresco to Bryher, sometimes thigh deep in water. They stumbled against the wind, along the coastal track to Great Porth.

It was quickly clear that it was unlikely anyone had survived the wreck. There were seven bodies on the shore; four men, one woman, and two horses.

Prior Robert sent five of the brothers to comb the slippery rocks around the edges of the cove, where waves were still breaking. The rest gathered up the broken bodies and laid them on some wooden planks from the wreck that were scattered around the beach. Then they began the task of salvaging anything that could be of use, placing them in piles for transporting back to the priory. Wood, nails, sodden clothing, saddles and harness, one or two unbroken barrels of sweet water and wine, ropes and sailcloth, all of great value to the little community.

As the sun rose feebly in the still heavy skies, nothing remained except for the carcasses of the horses. Even those would be butchered, the meat salted and the fat rendered for candle tallow.

By midday, everything had been conveyed back to the priory. The Ennor crew had arrived via Sampson but too late, and had departed again without trouble.

The five bodies lay overnight in the chapel. They had been

stripped of their clothing and wrapped in remnants of sailcloth. Prayers were said for them at Lauds and they were laid to rest in the peace of the priory garden.

Later that day, weary from the day's exertions, Prior Robert was roused from an involuntary nap by Brother Jerome, the monk who had responsibility for the laundry. He held in one hand a dripping tunic and in the other, a small shiny object.

"Prior, I was preparing to wash the garments of the poor souls that we buried today and I found these. I thought you should see them."

He laid the dripping and torn tunic down on the stone floor, displaying the gold cross emblazoned on the front of it, and held out his hand to reveal the object that lay in his palm.

Prior Robert took it from him. It was a medallion made of copper with a lion rampant on an azure enamel background, framed with a gilded rim.

"A pretty object," said the prior. "I have seen others like this, a pilgrim medallion I would think, and made for someone of high birth. It is quite valuable, Brother Jerome. You are to be commended for bringing it to me and resisting temptation."

"Look on the back, prior," said Jerome, "it is there that the real interest lies."

Turning the object over, the prior stared in amazement at the inscription on the back. "Richard de Mohun," he read out.

"You are right, Jerome. This and the tunic would seem to confirm that we have buried one of Lord de Mohun's sons. We must send news of the shipwreck and his death back to our Brothers in Tavistock. The family must be informed."

The mournful cry of a seagull carried over the centuries and I jerked awake. Looking around me, I expected to see the priory walls and the wet tunic on the floor, with Prior Robert holding the medallion. Instead, I was restored to the tranquillity of the priory ruins and the gardens.

I knew now why no one had tried to find Richard when he disappeared on the Camino. The family must have been told that he and his companions had drowned in the Isles of Scilly, and had received a Christian burial by the monks of the priory there. The medallion secretly garnered by Alicia and the tunic worn by

Ralph Purves would have been evidence enough. No one would have tried to follow their trail and it would have been assumed that the Golden Rose had been lost in the wreck.

Only I and my shadow know the truth.

End

Postscript

Moonshadow

Postscript

This book was conceived after I undertook the pilgrimage known as the Camino de Santiago.

In 2006, I wrote a journal about the long walk and it was published under the title of 'My Camino, a Personal Pilgrimage.'*

The pilgrimage, and events that preceded it, provided the source material for 'Moonshadow.' I have to call it a novel because I cannot state that *everything* in the book is true. To me, however, the truth and the fiction have become inseparable and I believe that I have been instrumental in recording a story that needed to be told.

Part I, 'Contact' describes a number of strange but true happenings and events that occurred at various times in my life, convincing me that I was being contacted by my ancient ancestors. Some experiences that I had on The Camino sharpened that sense of closeness with past events.

The output of the research that followed, described in the book, and my intuitive writing of the events in the story itself, have proved to me that I have been given extraordinary insight into the past history of my family.

The castle, abbeys, and houses at some time or another have belonged to the Mohun family. Moyon, Dunster, Hall, Boconnoc, Newenham, Mohun's Ottery, Arworthal and many other places all seemed familiar to me. Their present owners or tenants—sometimes aware of the connection, sometimes not—were all welcoming and intrigued with the history that was being unearthed.

Perhaps the most remarkable phenomenon has been the intuitive writing of fictional events and people, only to discover through research at a later date, that they were actually true.

My research has uncovered enough material for many more novels, spanning the centuries. I hope that my shadow will remain with me as an inspiration and guide.

My essential research materials:

A History of Dunster and the families of Mohun and
Luttrell, By Sir H.C. Maxwell Lyte, KCB
The History of Newenham Abbey, By James Davidson
Lakes, Parochial History of Cornwall
The Devon Record Office
The National Archives at Kew
The Internet/Wikipedia
The Confraternity of St James
My own memory
Richard de Mohun?

* A limited number of copies of 'My Camino, a Personal Pilgrimage' are still available through Amazon, The Confraternity of St James in London, some book shops or direct from the writer. (mgmoon1@aol.com)

Printed in Great Britain
by Amazon